THE GIFT OF PATIENCE

ELIZABETH JOHNS

CHAPTER 1

*I*f only she'd been born a man, Patience bemoaned as she sat, legs curled up in the window seat staring at the blurred park through the stream of water running down the window.

Then she would not be stuck inside dratted houses all the time with little to do but embroider or write letters as the dowagers and the aunts did most of the day between their naps. How she loathed both pastimes! Reading was not half-bad, but one could only read a book so many times before every word was memorized and the story was no longer new. In London, there had been Hatchards for as many books as a person could read in a year, but there had also been endless diversions. Promenades in Hyde Park at the fashionable hour, walks and rides other times in the park—she could at least do that here when the second great flood was not occurring, the theatre, shopping, picnics, museums…she sighed with futility. If she were a man, she could pursue any of those at her leisure.

Patience ought to be grateful. Had it not been for their guardian, she would now be a governess or companion. Now her appointed task in life was to be a lady and find a suitable husband. How that was supposed to happen while stuck in the country with no Society was beyond her. She twisted a long, black curl that had come loose around her finger then let it unfurl as she pondered.

She had earned a bit of a reputation for being partial to the military officers. It was to some extent well deserved, but everyone thought she only cared for a man in Regimentals for his looks. But it was much more than that. She wanted to be one of them.

When she was with soldiers, there was an endless supply of entertaining stories. Most of them had fought in the Peninsular War under Wellington.

They did not seem to mind a girl who knew about Corunna or Badajoz, or could differentiate a member of the Guards versus the Rifles.

But none of them wanted more than a brief flirtation and to dance with a pretty girl.

All of the other gentlemen? Their stories were confined to inanities and treated her like an empty-headed chit.

Patience had to find something to do or she would go mad. She stood and stretched, then began to circle the room. She'd likely paced from one end of the drawing room to the other hundreds of times since the great deluge began a fortnight ago. Would it ever end?

Surely her boredom and discontent were in large part due to Faith and Hope having married. The five sisters had been orphaned young and had always been together and reliant on each other for so long. It was odd to think that Faith was soon to be a mother, and Hope was now a duchess and a mother.

Patience was in no man's land right in the middle between her two elder sisters, and the two younger. She never complained about it, but often felt it, nevertheless.

Faith had been a mother figure, Hope the beautiful one and destined for a great match, Grace was more studious and an avid reader, while Joy was mad for all four-legged creatures. Patience wanted adventure.

She was no more likely to find it in the country than she would be to fly to the moon.

If only they could go back to the previous Season when they had first gone to London. Not that Patience would ever wish anything dangerous on her sisters, but how grand it had been to be escorted around by all of those gentlemen on endless amusements! Her sisters had married two of them, but now the rest were gone since the danger was over, and they were back to the way things had been before. Perhaps, if she hadn't known such adventure, she would be content now. That was a lie. She had always longed for adventure.

The worst part was, there had been opportunity, but Ashley Stuart had kept her from it. When Sir Julian had been determined to ruin her sister, Faith, he'd done everything to thwart her helping. Her own sister!

Then, when Hope had been in danger, he'd always redirected her to the safer tasks within the house when help was needed, instead of anything that might be minimally construed as dangerous. As if a mere female wasn't capable. Infuriating man! What she wouldn't give to prove him wrong. She could ride as well as any man and throw a knife with deadly accuracy. Not that she actually had the opportunity to throw a knife at a live target, but she could hit the centre of a still one with her eyes closed.

Maybe she would not be allowed to purchase a commission, but surely the Foreign Office had some use for lady spies. But could she convince Westwood to let her? Only he would be able to open that door for her. However, he was sure to be as bad as his brother.

Well, she was not going to find adventure sitting there. She might as well join Grace and Joy in the barn or stables.

After donning her sturdy boots and an oil skin cape to ward off the rain, she hurried to the barn, dodging mud puddles as she went. The edifice was made of the same stone as the house. A large paddock separated the barn from the stables, and several horses could be seen grazing on the lush, green grass.

When she entered through the wooden doors, she was assailed by the odours of hay and dung, and sounds from pigs, roosters, and goats. Large wooden beams crossed at the ceiling, and straw was spread across the floor. A welcome breeze entered through the other end, where the doors led out into a fenced-in yard.

Patience watched her steps carefully, though, despite the fact that one of the stable hands was sweeping the floor clean.

"Patience!" Grace called when she saw her. "Come and see the new doeling."

Grace was sitting cross-legged in the straw, feeding milk to the tiniest goat Patience had ever seen.

"Why are you feeding her? Shouldn't she be with her mother?"

"The mother is rejecting her, so we have to feed her for now," Grace explained.

"That is horribly sad. How could a mother reject her baby?" Patience asked, kneeling down beside Grace to pet the kid between its ears.

"It will be a lot of work to keep her alive. We will take turns feeding her around the clock."

"I could take a turn or two. Heaven knows I need something to do with this infernal weather."

"I do not mind it here so much. I always did prefer the country though."

"And I always need something to do."

Joy's cat, Freddy Tiger, walked by the stall and paused to inspect what they were doing.

"He is growing very fat," Patience observed.

Grace cocked her head and observed as Freddy rubbed against the edge of the stall.

"I suppose you're right. He's keeping the mouse population under control," she mused.

"Where is Joy?" She must not be too far if Freddy was here.

"Last I saw her, she was collecting eggs. She's so thrilled that she no longer has to do lessons since Miss Hillier left. Though she misses her company."

"That will leave you and me to read to her. I still do not understand why she prefers to be read to."

Grace shrugged. "Miss Hillier was a gifted reader."

"I fear that is all I have to look forward to—either being a companion or a governess." Patience knew she sounded pathetically self-pitying.

"Just because you did not make a match last Season does not mean you are destined for servitude."

"I know, but I cannot think I will be content as a wife and mother, either. At least as a companion or governess, I will have some measure of independence."

"I am not convinced of that, either. Miss Hillier used to tell those awful stories of the position she held before she came to us. Not every household is as agreeable as ours," Grace reasoned.

"Perhaps you are correct. We are wards instead of children, so maybe that makes it different. There must be some way to gain independence. Short of becoming a man."

"Do you want to become a man?" Joy asked, now standing at the front of the stall with Freddy in her arms, her skirts dirtied and tied up, with a streak of mud on her face.

"You cannot tell me you have not dreamed of such a thing, Joy." Patience scowled with disbelief.

"I suppose it would be more fun," she agreed. "But I do not think the Dowager or Faith will allow you to go unwed, let alone masquerade as a man. Think of how scandalized they were to see me wear breeches."

"That is an idea," Patience contemplated.

"Thus far, I am happy helping with the animals here. I dread being dragged back to London. I might be able to be spared one more Season, if I am fortunate," Joy groaned.

"At least in London we had more to do, friends to ride with, and go to balls with. Speaking of, have any of you heard news of Carew or Montford or Cunningham?"

"I had a letter from Vivienne just this morning," Joy said. "I was going to share it with you later. She patted her pocket.

Patience waved her hand. "A summary from you will suffice."

"She says that Mr. Cunningham is on his way here with our promised pup now that he is weaned. Oh, and she thinks Lord Montford will propose soon."

"It seems to be contagious," Patience muttered.

"I am happy for them," Grace said in her always agreeable tone. "After her parents' disappointment with Rotham, hopefully they will be pleased by this arrangement."

At least Patience did not really have anyone to disappoint. Not really.

"What of Carew? I thought he would be back from Ireland by now."

"Westwood does not expect him for another month or so when he will bring some weanlings," Joy answered.

There was still very little to look forward to, then, Patience surmised with a heavy sigh.

If you stared at the ceiling long enough, it looked as though it was coming to life. The scene was one of war; horse-drawn chariots were stirring up dust all about them as soldiers brandishing swords and shields clashed in the middle. Angels hovered in the sky, waiting and watching. Flames from the hearth flickered across the ceiling, adding to the mobile illusion, while the crack of a log consumed by fire added to the ambiance of the scene.

Perhaps he had consumed more brandy than he thought. Ashley lifted his head enough to see his companions looking equally contemplative and solemn. There was little to say that had not already been said between them.

It was often thus with their little troop. They had spent years together under Colonel Renforth with the army during the Peninsular War, but now that Napoleon was defeated for good, only six of them remained, and there was scarce little for them to do that utilized their skills. They remained under the guise of the Household Guards, but in actuality, they were an elite troop called upon to perform the odd tasks that no one else could or would do.

No one ever suspected what they were really up to since the Household Guards were nominally referred to as the window dressing of the British Army. They were usually second or third sons of gentlemen—the rich, titled and powerful, and therefore expendable. Those assumptions were what allowed them to move amongst the *ton* with no one the wiser.

They flirted and charmed their way through ballrooms one night, while scaling walls and breaking into vaults the next. However, the last fortnight, there had been not one single commission. Coupled with the fact that Society was at their country houses for the remainder of the summer, there were no social events they were required to make up numbers for. Not that any of them was sorely missing that responsibility, but it was better than absolute boredom.

"Will this devilish weather ever end?" Fielding asked of no one in particular as he set his empty glass down with a thud that seemed to echo through the wood-panelled chambers.

"Where did Renforth get off to, anyway?" Cholmely asked impatiently.

"Hopefully answering a summons for our services," Fielding muttered as he stroked his side whiskers.

Renforth was the second son of a duke but now a peer in his own right. His mother had been a baroness, and upon her death, was granted the request to bestow the barony on him rather than his brother, the duke, who already held more titles than he knew what to do with. In turn, Renforth had inherited this town house, which he deemed a club for this troop. Instead of hiring rooms elsewhere, they all lived here. Most of their families also had homes in Town should they need to make use of them, but no one understood their lives like each other.

Here, there was no need to pretend to be someone they were not. To a war-hardened, battle-scarred soldier, this was a refuge.

O'Malley, Renforth's former batman now butler, entered quietly and made his way around the circle refilling drinks. Ashley was not certain about the wisdom of drinking more when the cherubs on the ceiling already appeared to be flying before his face, but he did not protest the added measure of brandy.

"Did you happen to see the letter that came for you from Taywards today, Major?" O'Malley asked quietly enough as though not to disturb the general tenor of the room.

"I have not yet been to my chambers. Was it urgent?"

"I could not say, Major. I will bring it to you," O'Malley said, and left before Ashley could protest that he could fetch it himself.

"Do you think it is a summons?" Fielding asked. "I would not mind something to do besides this."

Ashley agreed, but the Whitford sisters were still there, and it did not feel like home when they were present. It was an awful thought to have, but it was not peaceful for a variety of reasons. Soon there would be a little one running about—hopefully this was not to do with the baby. It was too soon for news of a birth.

O'Malley returned and handed him the letter. Ashley broke the seal and scanned the missive. "It's from Westwood." He read a bit more. "There's been some unusual activity on the river."

His brother's property was in Greenwich, ten or so miles down-river from London. There were a fair number of ships that preferred to dock there just across the Thames and conduct their business outside of London. There was far less crime, and warehouses could be attained at a fairer price than having to compete with the likes of the East India Company.

The other gentlemen seemed to perk up at the words *unusual activity*. Ashley had to admit he was intrigued. He read on.

"There is nothing concrete, mind you," Westwood wrote. "However, too many small coincidences. Broken glass at one warehouse, stolen goods from another, lost or missing livestock."

"It could be vagrants," Baines pointed out. He had excelled at extracting information from people during the war. With his size and perpetual scowl, he intimidated people before he said a word.

"True. Read on, Ash," Fielding said.

"We've searched for vagrants and squatters, but thus far none have been found. As the magistrate, I can attest that this has been occurring with increasing frequency. Previously, there would be one or two incidents per year, and now it is weekly for the past two months. I suspect it is due to new activity around the docks, but my jurisdiction is limited there, and frankly, I do not have the time to investigate myself. If you and as many of your troop can be spared to look into the matter, I would be grateful. It may be nothing of consequence, but I would be at ease knowing."

Ashley scanned the rest of the missive and it was more personal, so he spared his friends the reading of it and tucked it away for later. "What do you think?"

"It could be one of the London gangs moving east looking for new territory," Baines suggested. "Especially now with the planned expansions."

"We will need a dossier on the companies that ship through Greenwich," Fielding remarked.

"Who can be spared to go with me? Assuming Renforth agrees?" Ashley asked.

"The countryside gives me hives," Cholmely said. "Besides, Fielding knows more about shipping and the docks than any of us."

Fielding's father had amassed a large fortune in shipping, but he wasn't born into the peerage like the rest of them. He'd raised his sons as gentlemen, with the best that money could buy, but Ashley suspected Joshua never really felt he belonged—especially in such elite company as the Guards. Of course, within their elite troop, his belonging was earned with blood.

"I think you credit me with more knowledge than I deserve," he replied to Cholmely. "We were quite sheltered from the trade."

"It's not in the blood, eh?"

"I suppose as much as raking and gambling is," Fielding drawled.

It was common knowledge that Cholmely's father and brother won and lost their fortunes at Watier's and Madame Fortescue's on a regular basis.

Baines whistled. "He has you there, Chum."

"Touché." Cholmely raised his glass to Fielding. Those words would have caused a dual with lesser friends, but neither took offence.

Manners, who had remained quiet, took another sip of brandy and merely raised one brow.

They heard O'Malley open the door for someone, and they paused

9

their conversation to see if Renforth had returned. They heard him greet O'Malley before he entered the room.

"Good evening, gentlemen." He stopped and poured himself a drink before sinking into one of the red leather armchairs that surrounded the hearth. "I've come from dinner with the Duke and Duchess."

Each of them raised their glasses in empathetic silence. They all knew how familial dinners felt. It was much the same with all of them. What would they do with their lives now that the war was over? Why didn't they settle down and begin a family?

Whatever happened to no expectations for second sons? None of them were fit to be husbands or fathers. Not after what they'd seen and done.

"I received a letter from Westwood asking for our help," Ashley said, breaking the silence.

Renforth raised his brows in question, so Ashley repeated what he had read to the others earlier.

The colonel sat quietly drinking his brandy for a few minutes. It was always thus with him. Ashley knew he would speak when he'd made his decision.

"A large shipment of munitions went missing from an East India ship, whose docks are not far from Greenwich. This might be the connection we have been searching for."

Ashley exchanged looks of interest with Fielding and Manners.

"Why do you not go on ahead in the morning? Go and speak with the viscount and make an initial inspection. I will have Fielding and Chum search out the expected activity for the Greenwich docks from here while we await your report. I'd rather not send the whole troop down there and potentially alert anyone that we are on to them. No one will suspect you visiting your family."

"So long as you find something for us to do. I'm like to die of boredom else," Manners uttered what the rest of them had been feeling.

CHAPTER 2

*T*he next day promised to be as bad as the previous. The lawns now looked like lakes, and the river was overflowing its banks.

Patience, Grace, and Joy had been breaking their fast in their shared sitting room, watching Freddy pounce on a little ball Joy had made for him, tied onto the end of a stick. It was a rather genius invention which allowed them to play without moving from her seat.

After just a few minutes, Freddy laid down and began to bat the ball from his back.

"He seemed to tire more quickly than usual," Joy observed with a frown.

"You need to tell Cook to stop feeding him so many scraps. He's positively obese," Patience scolded.

"Perhaps he needs a playmate," Joy remarked thoughtfully.

"As if all of the animals here and the other barn cats are not enough. Besides, Mr. Cunningham will be here any day now with your pup."

"I hope he likes him. He may not." Joy dangled the ball in front of the cat.

"Maybe not at first, but they will grow used to each other," Grace added.

"I wonder if Freddy can even get here in this weather. I wonder if he would think to come by boat," Joy pondered.

Patience and Grace exchanged glances, indicating they thought that very unlikely. "One is always open to pleasant surprises," Patience said dryly, then sighed heavily. "Surely this rain cannot go on forever. A puppy would be a very welcome diversion right now."

"God did promise never to flood the earth again," Grace pointed out.

"He did not promise England, though."

"You must stop being so cynical, Patience."

"I know. I need something to do." She stood and walked over to the window. "Are my eyes deceiving me, or is that a carriage?" A large black blob appeared to be moving slowly towards them.

Grace and Joy ran over to join her at the window.

"Do you think it's Mr. Cunningham?" Joy asked.

"We will know soon," Grace said, looking excited.

"I suppose that answers our question about maritime considerations," Patience murmured.

Grace chuckled.

"Let us go see!" Joy scooped up Freddy and took off down the stairs. Patience did not bother scolding her. At this point, when she was almost seventeen, she doubted it would do any good.

She followed behind Grace at a more leisurely pace, though she was rather excited at the prospect of visitors. Anything to liven the dread boredom of the past few weeks. They were at the door waiting unfashionably as the coach lumbered slowly towards the house, and they held their collective breath a time or two as it looked as though the vehicle might become stuck.

"At least they are close enough to walk from there…or swim."

"I hope it is Mr. Cunningham or we shall look like complete fools."

"Who else could it be?" Joy asked.

Indeed, it was none other than Mr. Cunningham and Joy could not contain herself when she first saw him alight. She handed Freddy to Grace then took off to greet her friend.

Patience could only laugh at the display as Joy greeted him, then looked inside the carriage for the puppy. Not to be left out, Freddy squirmed out of Grace's arms and went to investigate the new creature.

The butler and a footman were doing their best to shelter this display with umbrellas, but Patience feared it was fruitless. The pup squirmed down out of Joy's arms and began to frolic in the puddles.

"He is a cute little thing," Grace remarked, still watching with Patience from the portico.

"I doubt he will smell too cute once he's finished."

"Oh, look! Is that Vivienne and Lord Montford?" Grace asked.

"It appears to be."

The butler must have given up on sheltering Mr. Cunningham and Joy, and was now walking Vivienne towards the house as Montford followed along.

Mr. Cunningham and Joy decided to take the puppy to the barn. "He's been confined to the carriage for so long and Freddy did not wish to bring the pup in the house wet," Montford explained as he removed his wet hat and shook it before stepping inside.

"I am certain that is appreciated," Patience replied. "We are so delighted you have come."

"Freddy could not be convinced to wait until the weather improved. We have been traveling for ages at a snail's pace!" Vivienne described the horror as she handed her wet cape and bonnet to Armstrong, the butler.

"I will not ask how many times the carriage was stuck," Grace said as she took Vivienne's arm.

"At least I was not the one who had to push it from the mud," Vivienne agreed with a laugh.

"Thankfully you made it here safely. I will ask the housekeeper to prepare rooms for you," Patience said as they walked upstairs to the drawing room.

"Freddy said he sent word ahead, so hopefully we are not unexpected." Vivienne paused with worry in her voice.

"It would not matter if you were. We are so thrilled to see other humans," Grace reassured her.

"Monty! Miss Cunningham. You are very welcome," Westwood said as he and a very expectant Faith entered and greeted the new arrivals. Faith called for tea, and they all sat to hear the latest news since they had seen each other last.

It was a half-hour before Freddy and Joy rejoined them, each holding an animal. Little Freddy was hissing at the new arrival, who was bundled in a blanket and whining.

"Oh, dear," Grace murmured.

"Is this the new pup?" Westwood asked. "Does he have a name yet?"

"I have not had long enough to assess his personality," Joy proclaimed. "Thus far, Little Freddy is not fond of him."

Big Freddy gave a look of disapproval to his namesake.

"I think he is jealous. He wants you to hold him," Joy decided.

"I will take the puppy," Patience offered. She had always been more fond of dogs than cats anyway. She liked Freddy Tiger, but he was somewhat indifferent to her unless she had scraps he wanted.

Mr. Cunningham handed her the partially dry dog, who was thankfully still wrapped in the blanket and seemed content to remain so. She looked down at the adorable little fellow, who licked her face, making her laugh. She sat down next to Grace so she could also meet their new pet.

Grace's hand got a lick, and then the pup quickly fell asleep in Patience's arms. She sat him in between them and continued to pet him while he slept. Maybe she needed her own companion. It certainly worked for Joy, who now had two.

After tea, Faith was tired and went upstairs to rest. Westwood, Lord Montford, and Mr. Cunningham went to the stables to see how the breeding was progressing, and Grace, Joy, and Vivienne went to visit the baby animals in the barn.

Patience stayed behind with the pup, who had yet to be named. As

Joy left with Freddy Tiger, she turned and called back, "He will need to go outside when he wakes."

"I think I can manage that," she retorted.

Once there was a slight reprieve in the rain, Patience decided to take a walk. She already wore a serviceable grey muslin, and she quickly changed into her boots that she had been wearing back and forth to the barn through the mud, though the pup was determined to pull the laces loose as soon as she had them tied. She chuckled. "You are not so different from Freddy Tiger, you know. Maybe he will grow accustomed to you and stop hissing and growling."

Patience took the cat's lead and placed it around the pup's neck. He did not seem to care for it and tried to grab it and chew on it. "Something else to become accustomed to," she muttered.

Even though the rain had ceased for the moment, she could see there would be no way to return from an outing clean. Her boots sank into the squishy mud, as did the puppy, all the way up to the fur on his stomach. "I think another bath is in your future," she warned as they set off.

She was always drawn towards the river, and she followed the path along the stream that eventually emptied into the Thames, even though the path was still covered in water much of the way.

The musky, fresh smell just after the rain helped alleviate some of her indoor isolation, as did watching the little pup run to and fro from tree to tree to smell and leave his own scent behind.

The roar of the river testified to the recent rains long before they came upon it. As they approached the stone bridge, the water was overflowing the banks and had diverted around it.

"Drat," she muttered to the dog. He sat and cocked his head to the side at the sound of her voice. "There is no way to go forward right now. I am afraid we will have to turn around."

They stood there watching the water run rapidly for a few moments before turning back. A short walk was better than no walk, she had to remind herself.

The pup—he really needed a name soon—began to pull hard to her right, so she allowed him to sniff. Likely he was chasing an animal's scent. Was it not almost time for fox cubbing?

He pulled her to a small clearing in the tress, where it looked as though someone had set up camp. A stretched-out cloth was strung out, covering the remains of a fire, and a tent was set up just beneath the shelter of the trees.

It appeared to be deserted, but Patience could feel the hair on the back of her neck rise at the same time the pup began to bark. Without hesitating, she picked him up and began to run as fast as she could back to the house.

With no free hand to hold her skirts, she tripped and fell in the mud, barely releasing the dog in time not to fall on him. She stood and looked down at her ruined dress and could have laughed, except she was still spooked by the feeling of being watched near the bridge.

The puppy sat and waited for her, and she picked up his lead and decided they were close enough to the house that a slower pace was acceptable. Still trying to catch her breath, she looked back to make certain they weren't being followed, then ran straight into Ashley Stuart's arms. Of course. She looked like a drowned rat covered in mud.

ASHLEY HAD JUST ARRIVED at Taywards and was drenched and muddy from the ride from London. A nice long soak in a warm bath was calling out to him. He had just handed off his mount, Caesar, to a groom and rounded the stables when Patience Whitford came barrelling into him.

"Oh!" she exclaimed, trembling.

Ashley frowned. Something was wrong. The beauty was dishevelled and covered in mud. She was even more beautiful thus than when she was dressed like a princess.

"Major Stuart! I wasn't expecting you," she exclaimed breathlessly.

A sodden and muddy puppy was yipping at his heels, and he

kneeled down to let him sniff his hand while he waited for her answer. "What is it? What has frightened you so?"

Her bonnet had fallen back, and she wiped a damp strand of hair that had fallen into her eyes. "I assure you it was nothing. I was spooked, is all."

"You are not one to easily spook," he remarked. It didn't look like nothing. He had felt her trembling.

"I saw a squatter camp. I thought someone was watching me, and when the pup began to bark, I took fright and ran back here. Nothing happened."

"He was trying to protect you. One of Cunningham's?" He knelt again and scratched the pup behind the ears, but immediately Ashley was on alert. If whatever the danger was had reached Taywards, it had to be dealt with quickly. "Can you tell me where the camp is? I will go look into it."

"Of course. I took the path along the stream that leads to the river. I was going to cross the bridge and circle back around, but the water was rushing over it. If I hadn't doubled back, I might not have seen it. The pup sniffed it out and led me to it. The camp was nestled between the clearing in the old chestnut trees. There was a tent set up."

Ashley nodded. "I know precisely the place. Let me escort you back to the house, then I will go back with Westwood."

They walked a few steps in silence, the dog smelling his way ahead of them.

"What brings you to Taywards, sir? I did not realize we were to have the pleasure of your visit." She seemed to rethink what she said. "Not that you need a reason to visit your family. It's just surprising you would wish to ride in this wretched weather we've been having. Although Mr. Cunningham and his sister arrived earlier with Lord Montford. They brought the puppy to Joy."

"It was not planned, but as you say, the abysmal weather has kept me inside far too long. I decided a little rain would not hurt me."

She smiled at that. "I am sure your family will be pleased to see you."

"But not you?" Why the devil had he said such a thing? The last thing he should be doing was flirting with the likes of Patience Whitford.

"We are always delighted to see you, sir."

We. Not I, he noticed.

They neared the barn, and Patience stopped. "I dare not take him to the house like this. I will see you later, sir."

"Do you wish for me to accompany you?" he asked.

"Grace and Joy are here. I will not be alone."

"Very good." He snapped his heels and made her a quick bow before turning towards the stables.

He would dearly love to bathe and rid himself of the muck from the ride, but he needed to investigate this camp as quickly as possible. He wanted to inform Westwood of what Patience had found before he set off alone.

Westwood was showing off one of the new colts to Freddy and Monty. Ashley raised a hand in greeting when he saw his brother. Westwood excused himself and came over to Ashley. "Thank you for coming so quickly."

"You saved me from myself," Ashley admitted. "There was little to do in Town."

"I thought you might bring some others with you," Westwood remarked. "You did come alone?"

"For now. Renforth set some of the others to investigating a few leads in London, and they will send word or join me here if they discover anything."

"What kind of leads?"

"He was not completely surprised when I told him of your request. It seems that some reports of other things in Greenwich had reached the Foreign Office. A large shipment of arms went missing, and the leads went cold near here."

Westwood frowned. "That is much more serious than I'd anticipated if there is a connection."

"Indeed. And just now, I literally ran into Miss Whitford as she was running, frightened by something on her walk."

"Is she harmed?"

"She is well, but she was alarmed. She found a squatter camp near the river and sensed someone might be watching her. The puppy led her to the camp, then began barking. I am on my way to investigate, but I wanted to at least inform you of where I was going."

"Shall I accompany you?" his brother asked.

"I think it would be best if I go alone. I might be there for hours waiting for someone to return if they have not already abandoned the camp."

"Very well, I will come to the bridge after dinner if I have not seen you by then. You can signal to me if you need something."

"It will be like old times," Ashley said with a wry smile. "Except I may be out there indefinitely."

"Then I pray the rain stays away a little longer."

Reluctantly, Ashley left the warm, dry stables and made his way down the path that Miss Whitford had described. He could track her boot prints as well as the pup's paw prints, but he kept to the tree line, so if the path was being watched, he would be obscured.

If someone had seen Miss Whitford, then they would likely have already left when they saw her take fright. There was also the possibility that she could be in danger. Westwood would take care of warning the girls from walking alone again. Likely, he had not thought Taywards to be in danger since it was downriver and across from the Greenwich docks. However, the small pier at Taywards was only used when horses were coming and going, which was only a few times per year. Someone could be making free with the dock and it would likely go unnoticed.

As he made his way along the path, he could hear the roar of the river before he reached the bridge. He was grateful Miss Whitford had the wherewithal not to try to cross the bridge, but 'twas likely having the dog with her made her more cautious. She was temperamental and impulsive and who knows what trouble she would have found herself in otherwise.

It mattered not that she set his blood to boiling. He was not looking for a wife, and besides, his brother's ward was as good as his sister in terms of being protected. Although that did not stop

Dominic from marrying Faith, he thought with no small amount of irony.

He was at the camp in no time. The tall old trees and damp earthy smell took him straight back to the days when he and Dominic had played here in their youth. Sometimes it had been Robin Hood, and other times they'd played Nelson battling the French off the Trafalgar Coast.

Ashley found a perch from which to watch the camp for a while, although it appeared their uninvited guest had already departed. The time returning Miss Whitford and speaking to his brother had cost him, but he could not regret being cautious. There were no signs of any life other than the birds and squirrels. After he was certain no one was lying in wait, he stepped out to examine the remains of the camp. To the unpractised eye, signs of inhabitance might have been over-looked. An effort had been made to hide the fire and smudge the foot-prints, but they were there. He removed his gloves and crouched down, turning over the log which had been thrown over the mud-covered ashes. Sifting through the muck, a flash of metal caught his eye, and he uncovered a small knife that must have been dropped in their haste to leave. Covered in mud, it looked like nothing but an ordinary knife, much like the one he carried himself. As he stood to leave, questions remained. Why were they here, and were they related to the missing munitions? It could be a coincidence, but Ashley did not believe in coincidences.

CHAPTER 3

hen Patience entered the barn, her sisters were already gone, but one of the stable hands was there and gladly took the puppy to bathe. She returned to the house, much in need of a bath herself.

After wishing for adventure, she feared she'd had more than she bargained for. Not only had she discovered intruders on Westwood's land, but Stuart had arrived.

He who thought her no more than an annoying little sister had been present for her humiliation. She knew her infatuation with him was nothing but that, but for him to be the one to find her scared and covered in mud was the worst sort of indignity.

Once she had bathed and dressed, she went downstairs to see if any tea or refreshments were being served. Normally, Patience would indulge every afternoon with her sisters, but with guests here she was not certain.

If she were being completely honest with herself, she was anxious to see Major Stuart again to see if he had discovered anything at the campsite.

Likely, it was nothing more than someone living off the land, much like the gypsies did in the late summer, but since this was not a hop farm, it seemed an unlikely choice. The camp was not large enough for a band of gypsies. Besides, Westwood would have known and warned them to avoid that area.

Deliberately, she took the alternate pathway down the servants' stairs from her chambers to the drawing room so she would pass by Westwood's study. Her efforts were rewarded when she overheard the brothers' voices. She perched near the door, praying no servants caught her snooping.

"Back so soon? Was nothing there?" Westwood asked.

"The camp had been quickly abandoned. They did not have time to do more than take their things, I would think. There were smudged footprints and evidence of a fire."

"Could you tell if it was more than one person?"

"Unfortunately, no. They had been in the spot where we built our old treehouse."

"Between the old chestnuts by the bridge?" Westwood asked.

"The very spot," Stuart responded with fondness in his voice.

"Why there, I wonder? It's not near the pier."

"No, but it's well-protected. Even Miss Whitford mentioned she would not have seen the camp had they continued on the path over the bridge. I'd like to investigate further, but the stream to the pier is too dangerous."

"I wonder where they could have got to. If the stream is so high, it is unlikely they left that way," Westwood pondered.

"That would mean they could still be on the estate."

"I have already alerted the gatekeepers to keep an eye out, but they can hardly patrol the entire border."

"Nevertheless, I think we need to alert everyone in the house. I would not wish for any of our guests or staff to come upon them unbeknownst. They could be dangerous."

"Do you think this is related to the other matter?"

Patience frowned. What other matter?

"It is difficult to tell without any other link. I doubt the water will recede enough by tomorrow to take a boat to the pier, but perhaps we could go further on a mount. I'd also like to question the staff as we let them know about our uninvited guest."

"Do you think that will cause undo alarm?" Westwood asked.

"Possibly, but if it is related to our other matter, those sorts could well become violent to protect their interests."

"I have half a mind to remove Faith and the girls from here until we know it is safe, but she will not wish to go to London so close to her confinement."

Nooo! Patience wanted to scream.

"I do not think we are there just yet, but it might come to that."

"Shall we join the others for tea?"

Patience jumped. It would not do to be found blatantly eavesdropping. Major Stuart already found her meddlesome. She had wanted a chance to prove herself, yet she'd gone running. How was she to have known? It would have been stupid to stay there without reconnoitering and she had hardly been inconspicuous. No, she had done the right thing. But now she had more to prove.

She turned and hurried towards the drawing room, and was just sitting down when the gentlemen entered.

Much to her surprise, Major Stuart seemed to seek her out and come immediately to her side. She was sitting on a settee by herself, and he walked up next to her. "May I join you?" He indicated the seat next to her.

"Of course."

He seemed to take up the entirety of the small sofa. His leg brushed against hers, and suddenly she felt claustrophobic. She scooted closer to the arm on her side, but it was not enough.

"Tea?" she asked because she had to do something.

"Yes, please."

She knew without asking how he took it. She had been with him a great deal last Season during Faith's ordeal with Sir Julian. They had been quite close at one time, but now she felt self-conscious around him. She hated the vulnerability.

After handing him his cup, she cleared her throat. "Were you able to find the camp?"

"I found the spot where you indicated it had been."

"You do not believe me?" she asked, the indignity erasing any self-consciousness.

"I did not say that. The camp had been abandoned."

She breathed a sigh of relief. There was nothing worse than having one's word doubted. "So they must have seen me when I discovered it."

"I think that is very likely."

"I could feel that someone was there." She shivered in remembrance.

He must have noticed, for he put a comforting hand on her arm, which sent a rush of heat through her that she could feel in her cheeks. Dash it, she needed to be brave, not be a simpering miss!

"If there is any threat, we will discover it," he reassured her.

She wanted to be the one to discover and conquer any threat, but she refrained from saying so. That would serve no good purpose to her cause.

However, she had to acknowledge her real fear earlier, but that had been because she'd been caught unawares. It would not happen again.

"Do you think there is still danger?" she asked, knowing the real answer. Would he give it to her?

"One can never be too careful, but it is very likely only a vagrant looking for a safe place to shelter. Westwood has alerted the gatekeepers, and will put extra men about the grounds until we are certain the intruder is gone."

"Did you say intruder?" Faith asked.

Patience noted the murderous glare the viscount sent his brother.

"Patience found what appeared to be a squatter camp when she was out walking earlier. Ashley went to investigate, but it was gone. We are searching the estate as we speak to make certain he is gone, but until then, I want no one to go anywhere alone. Servants included."

Faith gasped. "You do not think this is the person responsible for the local problems, do you?"

"What local problems?" Joy asked.

Now Westwood shot Faith a glare.

"There has been some vandalism and theft in the village."

"And the thief has been hiding out on our estate?" Faith asked.

"We do not know that for certain. Pray they have left the estate and the area after being discovered."

But Patience couldn't shake the feeling that if it were tied to something bigger, then she was in danger.

Armstrong opened the door, redirecting Patience's terrifying thoughts. "I beg your pardon, my lord. Peter has returned with the puppy."

Joy sprang up from her seat and ran to the door to take the dog. Freddy Tiger began to growl and hiss.

"That is an ungentlemanly behaviour," Mr. Cunningham scolded.

The dog whimpered and began to pull towards Patience.

Joy laughed. "I think he prefers you, Sister."

"I think I am the lesser of two evils," Patience muttered. "Come here, little fellow." She held out her hands, and the blessedly clean, dry, fluffy animal ran straight to her and gave her a lick. "He really needs a name," she observed.

"Then you had best name him," Joy said.

"But he is yours."

"For now, Little Freddy appears to disagree."

"He will become accustomed to the pup. It just takes time," Mr. Cunningham protested.

"I am not certain. He is quite spoiled and protective of Joy," Westwood argued.

"He cannot go without a name until the cat decides that he likes him," Patience said.

"Poor little one." Major Stuart soothed the puppy and stroked his ears. "He was trying to protect you earlier. Perhaps Alexander would suit. It means protector."

"I like it, though he is not so fierce." She cast a sceptical glance at the puppy, who was rolled over on his back for belly rubs.

"Give him time. He will be a force when he grows into his paws."

She looked down at the paw he had taken into his hand, and it was quite large for the dog's body.

"Alexander seems rather formal."

"They called him Xander or Alex."

"Xander. That is unusual. It suits. Does that meet with your approval, Joy?"

"Oh, yes. I like it very well."

"Then Alexander the Great it is," Mr. Cunningham said to chuckles around the room as the dog settled in between Patience and Major Stuart for a nap.

ASHLEY HAD DISCOVERED little in speaking to the staff the rest of the evening. The groundskeepers had not noticed anything, but to be fair, their efforts had been to shore up other areas around the estate from flooding, and they had not been worried about the stone bridge since it affected little else when the water overflowed there.

The next morning, he was anxious to go out and do more investigating. He needed to send a report to Renforth, but he wanted to have more to tell him first.

Westwood was waiting for him when he came downstairs. No one else appeared to be awake yet.

"I doubt the waters will have receded enough, but we can certainly go see."

The grooms had both Caesar and Maximus saddled and ready for them. They mounted and set off at a slow trot, the path still muddied from the heavy rains.

"At least it has not rained again since yesterday," Westwood remarked.

A few days' reprieve would certainly help the investigation. "Have there been any further reports since you wrote to me in London?"

"Nothing," his brother answered. As they neared the bridge, Westwood pulled to the left. "I want to look at the campsite."

They dismounted and allowed the horses to graze while they

surveyed the abandoned area. Perhaps a fresh set of eyes would catch some things Ashley had missed.

He took the wider path while his brother went back over the remnants of the clearing and fire. There was possibly a slight trail off to the side of the camp where some of the underbrush had been disturbed, but nothing that appeared to lead anywhere. Besides, the intruder would not have returned, knowing he had been spotted.

"I do not see anything other than what you pointed out," Westwood observed. They were not far from the bridge and walked their horses over. The water was still running high, but the diversion was down to a small stream, no more than knee-deep.

"I think we can manage it," he said.

"I agree." They remounted and crossed the bridge with ease. The horses did not even shy at the water.

The other side of the bridge was untamed as Ashley like to think of it. The only structure being the pier.

They rode along the path which was still muddy. "I think any footprints or wheel ruts were washed away by the rain. If there were any," Westwood remarked.

"I see nothing, but let us proceed."

They reached the river, which was high, moving faster than Ashley had ever seen it.

The estate's pier, which normally extended over a portion of marsh, was covered by running water. Normally used to transport horses across from Lord Carew's large ship, it was a wide, robust structure with a small shelter attached, where someone could wait for the ship to arrive.

They both dismounted and looked around, but Ashley did not expect to find anything.

"Is there anywhere a shipment of arms could be stored here?" he asked aloud, though he was asking himself as much as Westwood.

"There are no structures on the side of the bridge, as you well know. If a shipment was delivered and unloaded here, the evidence is already washed away."

"But if they stockpiled it nearby, where would it be?" Ashley turned in a circle and only saw trees and vegetation.

"You think they must be here and the campsite housed the guard?" Westwood asked.

"I think it's a possibility we must consider."

"If that is the case, then they will not leave them here unguarded." He was already walking back to his gelding. "They will want to move the arms as soon as it is safe."

"I agree. I think I need to send for the others to help us search."

"But where?" Westwood paused.

"If I were responsible for precious cargo, I would stay within sight."

"Then that would mean back over the bridge, much too close to the house for my comfort." His brother voiced what he was thinking. "Did Renforth say how much we are looking for?"

"No. But several crates, I imagine."

"Could they have dug graves for them?"

"I cannot think that would go unnoticed, but anything is possible." They both remounted and followed the path back over the bridge, now looking from a different perspective.

"I think it might be worth organizing a search from the bridge forwards. The rain will have made any freshly dug earth less obvious, but we must look. We can discount the stables and barn as they are never unoccupied."

"What of the dovecote, the chapel, the gamekeeper's hut, one of the follies..." Ashley began naming the estate's buildings that would be unused part of the day.

"We will leave no stone unturned," Westwood agreed with a heavy sigh.

"I will send for the others post haste. With luck they can be here this afternoon."

"I will meet with my steward and begin organizing a methodical search."

When they returned to the house, Armstrong informed them that the sisters and guests were breakfasting.

"Please tell them that I will join them shortly. I will have a letter for one of the footmen to ride to London as quickly as possible," Ashley said.

"Very good, sir."

"And please send for the steward. I will need his attention as well after breakfast," Westwood added.

Ashley did not mince words in his missive. He would fill them in later. He simply requested as many hands as possible to assist, because someone had been found camping on the grounds. They were going to begin searching as soon as possible to see if the arms were hidden on the estate.

Whether or not Renforth would deem that necessary to send anyone, Ashley could not say. He folded the letter and gave the direction to Armstrong, then joined the others for breakfast.

It was rather a more domestic scene than he was used to for breaking his fast. The beauty of all the sisters next to each other never failed to surprise him. He bowed and greeted them, along with Lord Montford and Mr. and Miss Cunningham.

He piled his plate high with kippers, bacon, eggs, and beans. He'd already worked up quite an appetite from the ride this morning. A footman placed a cup of black coffee before him. Just the way he liked it.

"Did you find anything on your ride this morning?" Miss Whitford leaned over and asked quietly, her breath on his ear almost making him jump. He cleared his throat and took a sip of his coffee before answering.

"Unfortunately, nothing. We are going to conduct a thorough search of the grounds."

Why was he telling her this? She was much too nosy for her own good. He did not need her meddling. She had been much the same when they were trying to catch Sir Julian. It had taken all of his wits to divert her from interfering.

"I am glad to hear it. I have already felt like a prisoner within the house from the rain. If I thought I could not wander about freely, I might soon have attics to let."

He refrained from comment and attacked his kippers with devoted intent. He would be much more comfortable if she would move back. Her citrusy scent overwhelmed him. She was still much too close for his own sanity.

"I am glad to hear the water had receded enough for you to cross the bridge."

"On horseback," he corrected, knowing very little deterred her. "I am still not certain it would be wise to do so on foot."

She waved her fork as though she need not be told.

He cursed in his mind. Not only would he have to keep a lookout for the arms smuggler, now he was going to have to watch out for her! Neither Westwood nor Faith seem to understand what trouble she was capable of getting into.

Westwood whispered to his wife, then stood. "Gentlemen, when you have finished, would you mind joining me in my study? There is something we could use your assistance with today."

Ashley could feel Miss Whitford's senses set to attention as she stilled with curiosity. Why could Westwood not have waited until the sisters had left? Now there would be no way to deter her. He waited for her to speak up, then almost groaned when she met his expectations.

"Are you searching for the intruder?" she asked.

"Yes," his brother answered. "We do not expect to find anyone, but it will give me peace of mind."

"May we help? We will go with a group, of course, so as not to be alone, but that's three more pairs of eyes helping. And we are quite familiar with the estate."

Ashley tensed, wanting to object. But he had no good reason that would not make him sound like a pompous arse. She was right, devil take her, and they were all excellent riders. Westwood looked at him in question, and he inclined his head. It was certain to be a decision he would regret.

"Very well. Meet us down here in riding gear in one hour. That will give us time to sort through our plan."

He could feel Miss Whitford's excitement beside him. God help them all. Next, he felt her hand on his arm, and she gave it a small squeeze, which felt like a hot poker branding him.

"Thank you," she said, still much too close to him. She was muddling his good sense.

"For what?" he asked, staring at her hand on his arm. Normally, he detested people touching him, but he was unsure of what to make of it.

"For not dismissing our help. I promise you will not regret it."

"That is an impossible promise to make. "

His eyes flitted from her hand, still on his arm, to her eyes. Another mistake. Those azure blue eyes were bewitching. Mesmerizing.

Her gaze narrowed." I do not know why you insist on finding me meddlesome," she said tartly, thankfully breaking the spell.

"If the shoe fits, as they say," he said, pushing back from his chair and tossing his napkin on the table. "Miss Whitford," he said, with a bow that he feared was a bit too mocking. But he had to get away from there before he said what he really thought, or she put some sort of hex on him.

CHAPTER 4

*P*atience was changed into her riding habit and downstairs in record time. Her body was thrumming with the excitement of having something interesting to do. Granted, she would not be in any danger searching in a group, but nevertheless, they had been included. It had probably galled Major Stuart to allow them, but at least he'd been reasonable.

When they had all gathered, Westwood took them to the muniment room where wooden shelves with ledgers lined three of the walls, and a long oaken table with chairs was the centrepiece of the room. There was a large a map of the estate framed upon the remaining wall, which he was now pointing to. "Some of Ashley's troop may be joining us later to help search, but until then we shall divide into five groups."

Why would Major Stuart's troop be called in for this? Patience frowned. It must be more serious than they'd let on to involve them.

He pointed to an area from the front drive which ended at the barn, and spoke to the steward. "Kerr, you take Miss Joy and Mr. Cunningham and search here."

"From the barn and stables to the chapel will be Monty, Grace, and Chauncy, the head groom."

"Myself, Ashley, and Patience will take the area from the path to the river, the dovecote, and the lane to the boathouse by the lake."

Patience surmised this was the area of highest suspicion, and felt honoured to be included in that group. Though it was likely only so he could keep a close eye on her. She almost snorted aloud.

"The groundskeeper and his crew will search from there back to the other side of the drive to the property. Anything that looks suspicious at all—any newly turned earth, fresh footprints, or wheel tracks, anywhere that would be good for hiding—people or goods—we wish to know about. At no time will you put yourself in danger. If you find something, report back here, and Lady Westwood will send someone to find me."

Patience looked at her sister, very large with child, and could see she was disappointed not to be included in the search.

"There will also be grooms to assist. The faster we can cover every inch of the estate, the better. I suggest spreading out at equal distances and going from edge to edge methodically. The wooded areas will have to be traversed on foot but are more likely hiding areas. We will rendezvous in three hours at the stables. Any questions?"

When no one had anything further, the group headed to the stables, where the grooms were leading mounts out for everyone.

Major Stuart boosted Patience up into her saddle, then mounted on his own magnificent beast, a blond gelding, which suited his own fair colouring perfectly.

He looked to see that she was ready, then turned his horse and urged him forward. She followed along, pulling up beside him as they rode to their designated area. "Is there anything in particular we are looking for? Anything Westwood did not mention?"

He looked at her sideways. "Why would you ask that?"

"It seems as though we are looking for more than an intruder, is all. Your troop is coming to help, and he told us to look for freshly turned earth. Unless you suspect someone of digging graves, why would we be looking for that?"

She could see his jaw clench. She had hit a nerve. But why? What was he keeping from them? Instead of persisting, she decided to hone her energy into the search. If he did not wish to tell her what she was searching for, then she would look for everything!

They took the path she was so fond of walking upon, and she searched diligently, even though they had not yet split up. When they reached the clearing near the bridge, where she had found the campsite, Major Stuart stopped.

"I believe the best course of action is to dismount and go on foot from here. We have not yet searched much beyond this clearing."

Patience slid from her mount and tied her up, where Midnight could still graze. Then she began to untie the skirt she had wrapped over the breeches she'd worn for such an occasion like this. When she turned around, she caught Major Stuart staring as though he were in pain.

She had shocked him. It served him right if he disapproved. Behaving with perfect propriety did not suit him either. "Are you all right?" she asked sweetly.

"Perfectly fine," he growled through gritted teeth.

"Shall we begin?" She turned to ask Westwood, not wanting to deal with Major Stuart's surliness.

"I will take this far edge," he said, pointing. "Patience, if you can stay around twenty paces from me and Ashley, you take another twenty paces, then we will begin walking from here to the boundary of the estate."

Patience was surprised they would be so close, but she did not argue. She stepped off her paces, then Major Stuart did the same and they began to walk, one of them occasionally stopping to lift a log or search inside of a stump. Fox burrows and indentations from sleeping deer were the extent of their finds.

It was tedious, boring work. But she would never give Major Stuart the satisfaction of hearing her complain. She was thankful she had the foresight to rid herself of her skirts as it was, her breeches and boots were scratched by thorns and brush.

Signs of autumn were beginning to show as leaves were tinged with the first hints of crimson and gold, still glistening with raindrops. The sound of their footsteps crunching through the fallen leaves, moss, and ferns were punctuated by the sound of the river in the distance.

By the time they reached the boundary of the estate, the clouds had begun to spit drizzle, and it was not long until her bonnet and hair were soaked.

"Nothing," Westwood said as they stopped at the perimeter of his land. He held out his hand. "Let us move over and return."

Major Stuart stepped off twenty more paces. Patience went twenty beyond him then Westwood, twenty more. They began the tedious, methodical walk back. Halfway to the path, there was a dovecote, which at least broke up the monotony of searching the woods.

Patience had never been inside a dovecote, though the thought of hundreds of birds and their refuse in one place was not her idea of pleasant.

"Shall I search the perimeter?" she offered.

"If you wish," Westwood answered as he pulled out a key to the octagonal-shaped stone building. "But there are no longer birds inside."

"Miss Whitford is not afraid of birds, surely?" Major Stuart taunted.

"A few birds, no. Hundreds of birds in a small space? Fear is not the word I would choose. Nightmarish comes to mind."

Westwood laughed at her as he unlocked the door. "Come and see."

The stone building itself was covered with ledges around the perimeter in varying layers. The iron door was small and she had to duck to enter, and was immediately assailed with a similar odour to the chicken coop. This structure appeared much harder to clean with hundreds of small alcoves for nests from shoulder height up to the ceiling. Light shone down on the dirt floor from high windows around the top.

"Is that how the birds entered?" she asked.

"Yes, and if you notice, the nests do not begin at the bottom. It is to protect them from rodents."

"How…interesting."

"I do not see anything of interest here, Dom," Major Stuart said.

"It would have been an excellent hiding spot," Westwood remarked.

"If you have anosmia, perhaps," she muttered.

Westwood checked his pocket watch. "It is time for our rendezvous. Hopefully, the others have had more luck than us."

"I cannot help but wonder if something is right here but the rain washed the evidence away," Major Stuart said as they exited.

"We will have to remain vigilant until we are satisfied there is no longer a threat." Westwood locked the door behind them.

"I will feel better once the others arrive to help. With luck, they will be here soon."

They continued on back to the clearing, where they'd left the horses, which began to nicker when they saw them.

"Poor Caesar! You thought you were going to have a ride when you were saddled this morning, did you not? You may still be in luck," Major Stuart said to his gelding, who began to lean into his master's hand.

"I'd much rather be riding than walking every inch of the estate," Westwood agreed.

Patience wished they would confide in her what they were looking for. She no longer believed it was a simple vagrant.

As she began to untie Midnight, she noticed her ears were back and she was digging at the ground with her hoof. "What is the matter, old girl?" she asked. "It is not like you to do that."

As she kneeled down to inspect her hooves for stones, she was assailed by the eerie feeling she had felt there before. At least this time she was not alone. She looked around from her vantage point below the horse and saw a pair of black eyes staring back at her. She opened her mouth to scream, but he took his hand and swiped it across his throat, warning her, and her throat seemed to freeze.

She turned to see if Westwood or Major Stuart had noticed, but they were too busy talking to each other. She turned back, and the man was gone.

"There! Over there, he's getting away!" she yelled, finally finding her voice.

Westwood and Stuart rushed to her side. "Who is there?"

"A man with black eyes. He was just there in a brown coat with a brown hat, standing behind that tree!"

"Return to the stables at once and tell the others!" Westwood ordered as they took off after him, but her feet did not want to move. Some adventuress she was turning out to be! She'd waited too late to alert them, and could only hope they caught the man.

She was afraid to stay and afraid to leave. But she had to go for help.

$\sim$

THE FEAR of what could have happened to Miss Whitford thrust him into action. It was the anger that kept him in hot pursuit.

If he'd been close enough for her to describe his clothes and the colour of his eyes…

He knew there had to be more to this than mere vagrancy. No one would risk being caught on a lord's land twice unless there was a very good reason.

This was not Ashley's first pursuit, and when one was in a hurry, they made mistakes. Westwood, while not having Ashley's experience soldiering and spying, instinctively knew to go the other direction, that one of them was bound to cut him off before they reached the river. They had the advantage of spending a great deal of time there in their youth.

Ashley could see where the man had run. When he was not being careful, he left broken branches and footprints in his wake. He was a dead man.

Ashley had a fairly good idea of where the man was headed, and he veered right to cut him off. It was a gamble, but with Dom on the other side, it was a good one. Brushing low branches and wet leaves from his path, it was a challenge to move quickly whilst looking ahead.

He heard him before he saw him. Exertions from the chase caused the man to breathe heavy—much like Ashley himself was doing. He pulled his pistol from his waistband, hoping it would not be needed. The man was of much more use to them alive than dead—but was likely armed himself if he was guarding the cargo they suspected him of doing.

Ashley took a deep breath and pushed harder, knowing that he was close, tasting victory.

He caught a flash of brown and knew he would catch the man. His sides burned and ached, but he would not lose. The man turned to see how far his pursuers were and that was a fatal mistake.

Ashley lunged and caught the man's foot, causing him to go down into the mud. Immediately, Ashley was upon him, knee in his back and forcing his hands behind him. After that chase, he did not relish any hand-to-hand combat or fisticuffs. This man would fight to the death. Dominic was upon them in a matter of seconds. He loosened his neckcloth and took it off, binding the man's hands while he fought and thrashed at his captors.

Ashley paused to catch his breath. From past experience, it would be some time before the deep inhalations did not hurt. Dominic looked over the man's head in question, but Ashley shook his head.

He would not bother to question the man now, anyway. He'd rather leave him wondering when the axe would fall. And fall it would, under the expert interrogation of his troop. He prayed they arrived soon.

Ashley spared no more breath than to order the man up to his feet. Westwood found the man's pistol that had flown a few feet away when he'd gone down. Ashley could sense that he thought about arguing, but one sensation of the pistol shoved into his back made him cooperate quickly enough.

They trudged slowly back through the woods until they reached the clearing. Dominic unhitched their horses and began to lead them back. The mile-long path that had never felt long before seemed to stretch on endlessly, but Ashley did have time to catch his breath.

When they reached the stables, a more welcome sight he could not imagine as he saw Colonel Renforth and the others of his troop speaking with Miss Whitford.

"Major!" his commander called. "We were just about to set forth to search. I assume this is what you were after?"

The prisoner looked down and did not make eye contact. Ashley nodded. "Indeed." He turned to his brother. "Where may we take him?"

"Part of me wants to suggest the dovecote," Westwood returned.

"Not a bad suggestion, but the guards would perhaps not be so comfortable standing watch in the weather. There are plenty of rooms within the stables, and he would be well-guarded there."

"I will take a turn with him," Baines remarked with relish.

"We will join you shortly," Renforth agreed with a nod.

Baines took the prisoner into the stable block, the head groom leading the way.

Ashley could not say that he was sad to be relieved. He noticed that Miss Whitford looked pale and shaken. Perhaps her taste for meddling would lessen after this, though being face-to-face with a criminal was no small matter. She had been brave enough to call out, after all.

The others stood at attention, awaiting directions. "Do you wish us to complete the search?" Montford asked.

"I think it would be best for due diligence, but certainly I know I would not mind some sustenance first," Westwood answered.

The others returned to the house, but Ashley knew Renforth would want to question him more. They waited until the others were out of earshot and his superior turned an enquiring eye upon him. "Do you think this is related to our missing arms?"

"We have not yet found any connection or evidence that would link them, but it is too much of a coincidence for my liking."

"And thus far nothing has been found?"

"We have only just begun searching this morning. I strongly suspect, if anything is to be found, it will be near where we found the man. Why else would he risk capture?"

"Possibly," was all his colonel would concede. "What other likely areas for storage are there along the river? I cannot think anyone would risk transporting such large cargo far from the dock. They will wish to remove it quickly."

"Most of the land between here and Greenwich is owned by Westwood or Sir Horace. I am less familiar with the other side of the river, but Westwood should know."

"After a few words with our captive, I would like to see the area where Miss Whitford first found him, then saw him again."

"They are one and the same. I will take you there when you are ready."

Ashley took the brief reprieve to return to the house for luncheon. He wanted to see how Miss Whitford was doing, but she had not joined the others. Where was she?

Unfortunately, he did not have time to seek her out as he was certain Renforth would require his assistance soon. He quickly ate a sandwich and downed a pint of ale before hurrying back to the stables.

Renforth was conversing outside with Baines and Manners.

"Anything?" he asked as he joined them.

"Nothing, as expected. Just give me a little time. The Baines method has never yet failed." His colleague wore a malicious expression.

"Then, with your permission, I would like to continue searching the estate. Once we are assured that there is no one else here, and that we have looked everywhere for the stored arms, then we can expand our efforts."

"I agree. Baines can stay here and work his charms on our man while the rest of us can assist with the search. I think it's prudent to have Westwood invite your neighbour, Sir Horace, over for a discussion," Renforth said.

"I will inform Westwood. A cold collation has been set out with some good ale, if any of you wish to help yourselves before resuming the search. I must gather the others anyway. I will take you there. If you wish to bring your things, Mrs. Armstrong can also show you to your rooms."

"I will take your things for you," Ashley said to Baines. "I will even have some food sent for you."

"Very gracious of you," Baines retorted.

Ashley could not help but wonder about Miss Whitford as he did not see her still when they returned to the house. He directed the men to Mrs. Armstrong and to the food, then found Westwood to tell him of their plans. If she did not arrive to help with the rest of the search, then he would send for her. Perhaps she was more shaken than she'd let on.

As he was informing Westwood to invite Sir Horace over, he saw her out on the lawn with the puppy, who was sitting and gazing at her in adoration. Ashley could not blame him. He excused himself and joined her.

Xander saw Ashley first and bounded over to greet him. He was jumping about Ashley's knees and wagging his tail. Ashley kneeled down to greet him, and was promptly rewarded by Xander rolling on his back and offering his belly.

"You are already becoming insufferable," he drawled.

"Then you should not encourage him," Miss Whitford scolded. She seemed at ease, which relieved his own fears.

"Will you be joining us to search the remainder of the estate?"

"Of course. Why would you think otherwise?"

"I remember the first time I came face-to-face with a criminal. It would not surprise me if you changed your mind, is all. For what it is worth, I do not expect to encounter any more unexpected persons."

"I will not deny it was a bit unsettling when he dragged his fingers across his throat at me." She demonstrated the motion, and Ashley tried not to react. Suddenly he wanted to strangle the man with his bare hands.

CHAPTER 5

*P*atience could not wait to fall into her bed. They'd finished searching the estate and found nothing. She still wished she knew what they were searching for and what kind of man it was they'd caught and what kind of man would motion to her that he would slit her throat.

It was something she must become accustomed to, as Major Stuart had indicated it happened in his line of work.

So how did she get the vision of the man's evil black eyes out of her thoughts? His face was so vivid in her mind that she could have drawn his portrait.

Shuddering from repulsion, she went to scoop up Xander, who had been waiting for her when she came in the door. There was something deeply comforting about having an animal for companionship. She did not know if she'd be able to relinquish Xander to Joy when Freddy finally accepted him. It was wonderful having him to herself, and she was able to fall asleep with him curled up at her feet.

The next day, Patience awoke early as she often did, and took the puppy out to see to his needs. It felt good to think about something other than herself. Three times during the night she had startled with nightmares of black, menacing eyes. Then Xander had licked her hand reassuringly, and she had been able to go back to sleep.

She stood on the terrace overlooking the lawns as Xander stopped to sniff and mark his territory. It was much chillier that morning, as though autumn had been ushered in fully after the rains.

Xander discovered a stick, brought it to her, and laid it at her feet. Had Mr. Cunningham already trained him to play fetch?

"You wish to play?" She picked up the stick and threw it and chuckled as his fuzzy little body wiggled and bounced towards the object.

As she played with Xander, she could not help but contemplate the situation. It was a relief to know the man had been caught, and that nothing was found, but she could not help but feel as though something had been missed.

A good spy would continue searching, but she knew very well that it wasn't safe for her to go looking alone.

As they walked back to the house, she checked to see if anyone had come down yet who might be willing to go with her, but it seemed as though the guests were still in bed. Normally, Faith was an early riser, but the pregnancy was exhausting her.

Maybe one of the grooms would not mind accompanying her.

Quickly she found Peter, the same boy who had been eager to give Xander a bath the day before. Not that a stable hand would refuse a member of the household, but it was a relief to know they did not mind being taken from their normal duties.

Peter played tug and fetch with Xander while they walked back to the clearing. Patience could not say why, but she felt drawn back to the place.

It looked no different today, but she was not one to ignore her instincts. What were they trying to tell her? She stood there and closed her eyes towards the sky and took a deep breath. She could hear Peter playing with the dog on the path, but she tried to block them out and listen.

Not that she expected the trees to begin speaking to her, but there had to be some reason she felt called to be there.

Opening her eyes, she tried to look at everything from a different angle. The old chestnut trees still encircled the small clearing, which was covered with grass, a few fallen logs, and leaves. After walking back and forth across it, she still was no further along than they had been the two previous times.

"What am I missing?" she asked aloud, looking upward when her eyes caught on a ladder. She walked towards it. Well, not a ladder, precisely, but wooden boards had been nailed into what she and her sisters would have deemed a perfect climbing tree. They looked rather old and she wasn't certain they were steady enough to bear her weight. Had this been the boys climbing tree when they'd been youths? Surely they knew about it. Had they already climbed and dismissed the notion, or were the boards too old to hold an adult, so they'd dismissed the ladder out of hand?

"There's only one way to find out."

Patience put her weight on the bottom one to test it, which was rather difficult as the lowest rung was almost waist high.

"Nothing ventured, nothing gained," she muttered to herself as she heaved herself to the next step.

It held, so she slowly climbed the eight boards until she reached the top, which ended at a saddle-like groove from which the branches originated. It was a glorious lookout, where she could envision many a childhood imagination coming to life.

Being sorely out of climbing practise, she leaned against one of the curved branches to rest, and looked around appreciatively. It must be a high point on the estate, she reflected, as the view was incredible.

To the northwest, she could make out the ball atop the royal observatory, and straight on, she could see the Thames and the docks across the river, with different types of boats moored there, from barges to yachts.

It was lovely and relaxing, and Patience thought she could stay there forever, but knew she should be getting back.

After she climbed down, she walked back to Peter and Xander, and they returned to the house.

A few of the soldiers had come down for breakfast, so she joined them. She was familiar with them from before, some more than others. They stood when she entered. "Good morning, gentlemen." She went to the sideboard to fill her plate.

"Miss Whitford. Your cheeks are rosy. Have you been out for a walk this morning?" Major Stuart asked.

"Indeed. I took Xander out, but do not worry, I took a groom with me."

There were mutual frowns upon all of their faces. Patience bit back a smile.

"I would prefer if one of us were to accompany you until this situation is resolved," Colonel Renforth said.

"I thought it was resolved." She feigned innocence with drawn brows. Would they just tell her what was going on?

"We hope that is the case, but until we are certain, it is best to be safe."

"Oh, of course." Drat. Now she would be a prisoner again herself. "Did the man not give you any clues what he was about?"

She could see Renforth exchange glances with Major Stuart. He was not very talkative, unfortunately.

"If you need a female to have a go at him, I am told I can be very persuasive." She spoke light-heartedly, but the idea was a good one. Unfortunately, that caused all of them to laugh as though she'd uttered the wittiest witticism ever spoken. Her cheeks threatened to blush, but with anger more than embarrassment.

"What is so amusing?" Westwood asked as he entered the room.

"Miss Whitford has been giving us advice."

Dominic raised his brows at her with curiosity.

She waved her hand as though it did not bear repeating.

"Did I see you out with Xander this morning?" he asked.

"Miss Whitford decided it was safe to take a walk." Major Stuart would tattle.

"I was not alone. I took Peter with me. We only walked down the path and back. Not even to the bridge."

"Did you see anything new?"

ELIZABETH JOHNS

"As a matter of fact, I had not noticed the boards on the large chestnut tree. Was that a favourite place for you as a youth?"

"Indeed, it was," Westwood said fondly, then frowned. "Though I cannot think it would be safe to climb those steps any longer. They are quite old."

"I found them to be sturdy enough for me."

"You climbed the tree?" Baines asked with disbelief.

"Of course she did," Stuart drawled.

"I do not see what the harm is. I checked my weight on it before I climbed. I never realized how high that area was above the estate. The view from there was quite spectacular. If only I'd had a looking glass, there is no telling what I might've seen. As it was, I had an excellent view of the river, the docks, and even the ball on the observatory."

Renforth stood suddenly. "I beg your pardon, but Stuart, I think you'd best take me there now."

"Yes, sir." He stood and tossed his napkin on the table. Surprisingly, the others stood and excused themselves to go along.

"You certainly know how to clear a room," Dominic mused.

"What did I say?"

"I believe it is more what you saw that caused their precipitous exit."

She looked at him in confusion.

"None of us thought to climb the tree and look," he explained.

"So you think the man was watching something from there?"

"Very likely. Now we must discover what he was looking at."

THEY ALL TOOK turns climbing up to the vantage point in the tree, and Ashley could only curse himself for not thinking to do so himself—or remembering the view. It had changed over the years, especially with the expansion of the docks to accommodate all of the increased traffic in the Thames.

"The view of the docks is incredible," Renforth remarked as he looked through the glass they had brought along. "It has to be why he remained even after he was discovered. I think one of us will need to keep watch here. There is still a chance they do not know we have taken him captive."

"He still has not spoken?" Ashley asked Baines.

"Not yet, but he will."

"I will stay for now," Manners offered.

"I think it best if we keep two men out here at night. We will rotate the grooms out here to help. You can easily get someone's attention from the stables during the day with a whistle," Ashley suggested. "I will have someone send provisions for you to keep you comfortable."

"And I will come back and check on you often," Renforth added. "I cannot think we will have to wait too long. If only we knew what they were waiting for. Is it a chance to move what they've already stolen? Or do they plan to steal more? I need those dossiers."

"I will enquire of my father to see if there are any more arms shipments expected," Manners offered.

With those plans decided, they returned to the house. Westwood greeted them. "Anything?" he asked Ashley.

"An excellent view of everything going on at the docks. We will take turns keeping watch. If you could have provisions sent, that would be much appreciated."

"Consider it done. I should have thought of the lookout myself. By the by, Sir Horace is expected here within the hour. I received word as soon as you left."

Not only did Sir Horace arrive, but also his lady, his heir, and their three marriageable daughters. Westwood exchanged amused glances with his brother, though he did not think Faith would be amused to entertain in her current condition.

Ashley wanted to hide, but unfortunately, they would have to pass by the cacophony of frills and furbelows who were attached to their pretentious mama. Perhaps Ashley was being harsh, but regardless of how innocuous and countrified Lady Fagge looked, she was a predator, just like all the others he knew. If only he had escaped to the study with the others a few moments before.

The guests were shown into the drawing room, and Ashley could not help but want to murder his brother. "Were you not specific in your wording on the invitation?" he asked quietly before they followed them inside.

"Believe me, I was. I would never deliberately put Faith through a visit. I've half a mind to make her excuses, but I sent up word and will allow her to make the decision. However, I have sent for Patience to entertain them in her stead, and she's likely to murder me in my bed for it. Rupert is overly fond of her."

"The son? What do you mean overly fond?" Ashley bit out a bit too harshly.

"As in he worships the very ground she walks on. It's nauseating to watch."

"I gather she does not appreciate the adoration?"

"Let me say that the man does not understand hints or even overt rebuffs. He attributes her protestations to her maidenly modesty."

"I am beginning to feel sick. I vaguely remember him as a pudgy youth, but have not interacted with him since."

"Consider yourself fortunate. We are forced to interact with them on a daily basis. They have called every single day we've been at Taywards, at least until the flooding began."

Ashley saw Miss Whitford come down the stairs towards the drawing room, and she was most definitely shooting daggers from her azure orbs. He could not help but smile.

"I am only doing this for my sister," she grumbled at Westwood.

"And I appreciate it more than you know."

"You do not intend to feed me to the wolves alone, do you?"

"Where are Grace and Joy and Miss Cunningham? Or Montford and Mr. Cunningham?" Stuart asked.

"I assure you I would have sent for them, but they all conveniently went into the village," she snapped.

Westwood exchanged glances with Ashley. "Would you mind accompanying her?" he asked. "I feel as though I should be there at least for the initial discussions with Sir Horace since he is unknown to the others."

48

"Yes, do come. If you can keep Rupert's clammy paws off me, I will be eternally grateful."

Ashley frowned. Hopefully it was an exaggeration on her part, but he followed her into the drawing room. "I hope you will return the favour. At least you are not outnumbered."

Miss Whitford entered the room and greeted the guests. "What an unexpected surprise. How lovely to see you, Lady Fagge. Unfortunately, my sister is late in her confinement and is not up to receiving guests this morning. I do hope you'll excuse her."

The lady's gloved hands flew to her chest. "I did not realize she was so far along! Pray convey my best wishes to her and tell her to send for me when the time comes. I have a great deal of experience in childbed." Ashley could only pray she did not expound upon that knowledge. Nor did he believe for a moment the woman did not know to the day how far along Faith was. Had Dominic not just said they called every day before the rains began? "Have you met my daughters, Major Stuart?" she asked, knowing full well he had not.

"I have not had the pleasure." He deftly bowed over their hands, and said the appropriate pleasantries, while wondering why the predatorial matchmaking mamas had no taste and raised their daughters to look and act like buffoons.

He glanced at Miss Whitford and could see she was no more enjoying this visit than he.

Rupert was indeed overly taken with Patience. And if Ashley was not mistaken, the man was salivating just looking at Miss Whitford. He was dressed as garishly as any of the London set known as Macaronis. He affected a monocle over one eye, which his Titus-swept hair threatened to cover. His striped stockings with a polka-dotted waistcoat, as well as jewelled buckles on his shoes, were a counterpoint to the high points of his collar. He looked as out of place in the country as a fish in the desert.

Patience was scooted as far away from Rupert on the sofa until she was practically climbing over the edge to get away from him. Poor girl. He almost felt sorry for her, but she could handle herself.

Lady Fagge leaned forward and placed a meaty hand on Ashley's arm. "We are having dinner and dancing at Coventry three nights hence, Major. I do hope you and your friends will be able to join us. We always need more male partners to make up the figures of the dances. My girls need some polish before their first Season." So she was aware of his troop's arrival. He should not be surprised. Like the bloodhounds that picked up scents from miles away, so were mamas with marriageable daughters.

"I am certain they will take quite well, just as they are," he said smoothly, proud that he did not choke on the words. "As for dinner, I am afraid I cannot answer for myself or my colleagues. We are here on a matter of duty, and unfortunately, all of our time and attention is committed to that."

"It sounds very serious," she said disapprovingly.

He spread his arms wide. "I am afraid that is the way these things go."

"I cannot imagine what business the Household Guard can have for you here, unless it pertains to horses," Rupert said a little more acutely than Ashley would have expected.

"Quite," Ashley remarked in a tone that was a perfected mixture of suppression and ennui. It was a necessary part of the position.

Tea was brought in, which at least gave them something to do. Dominic and Renforth had best be acquiring some good information from Sir Horace. Never let it be said that Ashley did not do his part.

His gaze settled on Miss Whitford's efforts to restrain the amorous Rupert. It was humorous, as long as the man did not actually touch her. Then he would be consigned to the devil.

She caught him staring and glared as Rupert leaned in and said something in her ear. It appeared as though she might be physically ill.

How the next scene unfolded, Ashley could not say, but no doubt Miss Whitford was grateful. The dog and cat tore through the drawing room, Freddy Tiger chasing Xander, knocking over one of the small side tables and the tea cups and plates that had been perched upon it. This scene was rapidly followed by a mortified footman, who was no doubt supposed to be keeping them under control.

His cheeks were burning red with embarrassment, and his livery was dishevelled from a probable chase through the house.

Ashley struggled not to burst into laughter. Miss Whitford saw it as her salvation. Quickly, she ran over and scooped the puppy up. He also took the opportunity to gather the cat, who was still hissing and growling his displeasure at the canine intruder.

The footman ground to a halt and stuttered out an apology. "I beg your pardon, miss. I brought him—" he angled his head towards the cat "—back inside, as Miss Joy asked me to do. I did not expect him to set up a chase through the house."

"I understand. They are still growing accustomed to one another. Freddy Tiger is not yet used to sharing the house. If you could take him up to our sitting room, then I will keep Xander with me."

He could hear a disapproving murmur from Lady Fagge, but Ashley understood it was her armour.

The young ladies were immediately taken in by the adorable visage of a fluffy puppy, and surrounded him once Freddy Tiger was gone. Even Rupert was not immune to his charms, though he looked on from a distance. "I've been looking for some retrievers myself. Mr. Cunningham bred them, you say?"

"Yes, indeed. He might even be willing to give you one if they are not already spoken for."

Clever girl.

CHAPTER 6

*P*atience thought the Fagges would never leave. She had never excelled at hiding her feelings, or pretending to like someone—especially encroaching, self-serving busybodies that could not take a hint.

She could not blame Faith for not coming downstairs to greet them. If Patience had the excuse her sister did, she wouldn't have come either.

Even Major Stuart had suffered through the ordeal with her, and been her partner of sorts, though she did not doubt that he enjoyed the way Rupert had discomforted her.

After the door had closed behind them, Major Stuart turned towards Westwood. "Please tell me you found some useful information. I feel soiled after that interlude."

Westwood raised his brows at his brother indicating he was being a touch dramatic. Patience did not think so and gave him a look of sympathy.

"Unfortunately, he was not much help, but I asked him to be on alert for any new people in the area. Renforth was able to explain that he'd been asked to investigate some suspicious activity without completely saying what it was."

"You can never be too careful. In fact, there is always the possibility that one of the neighbours is assisting the criminals," Major Stuart warned.

Westwood looked doubtful.

"I understand your hesitance, but in this instance, it might require more cunning than he appears to possess. But it is not outside the realm of possibility that he could be helping without knowing it."

"That much, I could believe," Westwood agreed.

Patience wondered if they realized they were speaking in front of her. She was not going to alert them to that fact.

"I think it's time we went into the village to investigate. Everyone knows you and me, but they do not know the others. They could take rooms at the inn and see what they overhear."

"Perhaps even across the river would be prudent," Westwood suggested. "Since it seems that might be what our man was watching."

"Good point. Hopefully, Fielding and Cholmely will be here soon to help."

Patience rolled the idea around in her head. Perhaps she and her sisters could investigate the places that the men wouldn't. Of course, she could not tell them her intentions, because they would never agree to it, or to the fact that she could have anything to offer.

Baines entered the front door with a mischievous grin on his face. Patience did not know him well, but he looked the very picture of a rake, roue, and rogue all in one.

"From the look on your face, I can see that the cat caught the mouse. Everyone is in the study. You might as well come in there to only tell it once," Stuart suggested.

Drat! Patience knew she would not be invited, but she fully intended to listen. They still hadn't seemed to notice she was standing there, so hopefully they would not close the door.

They didn't close the door, but she did not push her luck that she'd be invited inside. Instead, she stayed where she was.

"I can see that you've learned something. What did it take this time?" one of the men asked.

"I cannot divulge all of my secrets, but if there happened to be a water trough nearby, then, perhaps someone had an unwilling bath."

"So long as you did not drown him," she thought Renforth muttered.

"Trust me, I did him a favour," Baines offered, smugness evident in his voice.

"Well, who is he, and what is he doing here?"

"He goes by the nickname Devil and belongs to the 666 river gang. He had their symbol tattooed on his arm. You were correct that he was watching the docks. What for, he has yet to divulge."

"Was this the symbol?" Major Stuart's voice asked. She could hear his boots walking across the floor as if to retrieve something and then walking back. "I had completely forgotten about finding this knife the first day, and then it was too covered with mud to discern anything. Armstrong just returned it to me from cleaning it this morning."

"That is the very one."

"At least we can rule out petty crime and squatters. This is definitely an organized crime, but I'll bet Devil and his gang are not the ones who orchestrated it. To know about an arms shipment and hijacking it had to have come from a knowledgeable source."

Patience sucked in her breath. An arms shipment?

"Unless they were extremely lucky, but somehow I cannot believe that is the case."

"Nor I," one of the other men said.

"Perhaps you should consider removing the ladies from the house. I cannot think the gang would retaliate, but one can never be too certain," Renforth advised.

Patience wanted to scream.

"I have already consulted with Lady Westwood, and she does not wish to leave. If the threat becomes more palpable, then of course, everyone will be removed to safety, wishes or no."

"Did you wring anything else out of the prisoner?"

"I only gleaned much of what you surmise. It seems as though he is working for a toff—though he didn't precisely let that slip, but almost," Baines answered.

"Fielding and Cholmely should be arriving today. I have sent for them and hopefully they will bring something useful. Unfortunately, now, we must consider all possibilities."

"I was about to send off a note to my father. I can include our request for anyone with knowledge of that shipment. It should not be a long list."

Patience could not identify that voice, though she thought that was Manners speaking.

"I would make a suggestion if I may, sir," Major Stuart said.

"Of course. I am open to anything at this point," the colonel said.

"I think it prudent to expand our investigation into the village. Since the rest of you are unknown here, it would be easier for you to infiltrate with the locals. Westwood even suggested a couple might go across the river near those docks."

"An excellent notion. Very well then. Manners will request information from his father, Baines will continue to work on our captive, the rest of you will need to gather disguises, and Westwood can tell you which taverns are most likely to yield information, keeping in mind, this began at least two months ago. The gang may not be staying at the tavern, but I would wager they are stopping in for their ale."

"And more," Patience muttered in her most derogatory tone. She knew all about what men went to taverns for.

"I could perhaps go to the other side of the river and not be recognized. I've spent very little time there," Stuart offered.

"Is there a great deal of traffic back and forth across right here, as there is in London?"

"A fair bit," Westwood conceded.

"I am not certain it's worth the risk, but as we do not have Fielding and Cholmely, yet, I could use you."

"I will go and see to rounding up disguises," Stuart offered.

"There should be plenty between the grooms and stable hands. Ask Chauncy," Westwood said to his brother.

Patience realized too late that Major Stuart was leaving the room.

She turned to go, but two warm, large hands grabbed her around the waist.

She gasped at not only the impertinence, but the warmth that flooded through her body at his touch.

He leaned forward and whispered in her ear, "Do not even think about going yourself." She spun about in his arms, having every intention to be indignant, which she quickly realized was a mistake. It took every ounce of fortitude she had to try to mask her reaction, and was quite certain she did not succeed.

She had never been in a man's arms, and the contrasts were striking. She felt overwhelmed by his height, his hardness, and his scent. She dared to look up into his eyes, which were darkened with an intensity she had never seen before. Was it anger? She didn't feel afraid of him. Could it be desire? Or was that only what she wished it were? He seemed to realize their compromising position before she did and stepped away.

"If I had known that was how to make you speechless, I would've done it long ago," he drawled.

Arrogant beast. He knew the effect he had on her, but now she wondered if he was not completely immune to her charms. Oh, she'd no doubt he did not wish to be attracted to her. She reciprocated that sentiment very much.

"I meant what I said, Patience. You are not to interfere. Give me your word."

"Or you will lock me in the stables with your prisoner?"

"Don't give me ideas."

With a swish of her skirts, she flashed him a devilish smile and walked away. If her hips were swinging more than normal, well, he deserved the torture.

ASHLEY WATCHED HER GO, appreciating the show she no doubt was putting on for his benefit, then took a moment to steady his nerves.

Patience Whitford was trouble, and he needed to stay far away from her. She was not for him. But how easy it had been to forget when she was in his arms. Clearing his head of the temporary spell she'd cast on him, he set off to ask Armstrong for extra groom and stable hand attire.

"Devilish, meddling females." If she'd been born a man, she would have made an excellent officer, but it was not his fault God had chosen to make her a girl, so why should she constantly plague him?

When Ashley returned from requesting the clothing, Fielding and Cholmely had arrived. He could hear them briefing Renforth and the others, filling them in on the proceedings so far.

Ashley chuckled when he heard Cholmely's reaction to having to dress like a stable hand and move to the local tavern.

"All for a good cause, my friend," Ashley said as he strode into the room. He held up their new costumes. "We will need to dirty them a bit. Unfortunately, we will have to wear our own boots. There's no having those made in time."

"And we have the dossier on the docks here. It took much longer than expected because there's so much new traffic there," Fielding explained.

Renforth raised his brows as the only acknowledgment as he accepted the satchel of papers. "Is there any method to this? I assume you've combed through it?"

"Yes, sir."

"There was nothing unusual in it that we were able to find, but as you know, sometimes it's in patterns over a long time. This could have been the first time."

"Thank you. I suspect most of this is legitimate and will mainly serve to help us see what is not."

Closer to evening, around the time that most of the workers would be finished with their day and most likely together at the public house, they all dispersed to their chambers to don their disguises and set off to the village taverns to infiltrate themselves with the dock-workers and villagers.

As Ashley pulled on the scratchy linen shirt and buckskins, he thought ruefully about how many hours he'd spent at the local tavern as a young buck. No one would expect him to be costumed like this at least.

Once dressed, they were driven to the edge of the village before they alighted. It would not do to be seen arriving in the Westwood carriage. It was decided that Manners and Cholmely would stay in the Greenwich village, and Ashley and Fielding would head across the river. Baines stayed behind to charm the devil, and Renforth was keeping watch. But first, they all stopped for a pint at The Anchor.

A sense of nostalgia being back in the old familiar place swept over Ashley—the smell of ale mixed with the straw dusting the floor below thick wooden beams running low across the whitewashed ceiling. He stopped and pulled his hat lower. Unfortunately, the publican was still the same.

"You do the talking," he muttered to Cholmely, who did the best East End accent of them all. "They know me well."

While keeping his hat low, he led them to a large, rounded booth flanking one side of an old brick fireplace.

A young, innocent-looking barmaid came over. "What will ye be 'avin'? We've our rabbit pie or mutton stew. I'd 'ave the rabbit pie if I were ye. Once all the workers come in for the evenin', there won't be any left."

"The rabbit pie and ale for all of us then," Cholmely ordered, giving the young girl a wink.

As she left, Ashley could not help but mutter, "I feel distinctly old. I cannot help but think she is probably no older than Joy—"

Cholmely groaned. "Now why did you have to go and say that? You make me feel like a predator, when that was the only promise of alleviating an otherwise boring night."

"She's young enough to be your daughter, Chum," Manners drawled in that quiet, superior manner that he had.

Cholmely was pouting when the girl brought back their food and ale. "Are ye new 'ere? Or just passin' through?"

"We 'eard as there might be better work 'ere with the new docks bein' built. London's gettin' overcrowded, if ye know what I mean."

"Sure do. I can say as we've 'ad some other fellows 'ere with the same thing in mind. They come in about this time every evenin'. Maybe ye could ask 'em."

"Maybe we will."

"I will point 'em out when they arrive, but I suspect ye'll know 'em. They don't exactly blend in 'ere."

"Much obliged," Chum said and tossed her a coin, which earned him a wide grin and a coy look.

"Be careful showing your coin, old fellow. We're supposed to be poor dockworkers," Fielding murmured.

"Maybe she is older than she looks," Cholmely retorted.

When the gang finally came in, Ashley would have described them more as ruffians than labourers. There were five of them, and if Ashley had seen them in the street, he would have crossed it to avoid running into them. They definitely looked out of place in the small, cosy village tavern. But if there were new docks in fact being built, then it might very well change the face of Greenwich and Woolwich.

The group settled in the other round booth flanking the opposite side of the fireplace to them. If they were quiet, they might get lucky and be able to overhear something.

It was hard not to tap his foot with impatience, but they had to wait until the barmaid took orders and served them. There was little discussion happening amongst them as if there was an unspoken agreement not to speak until their bellies were full.

As for their own table, they all knew from experience that patience was the key and they continued to sip their ale and limit their talk to soft mutterings about nothing in particular.

"Any signal today?" one of them spoke at last.

"Nothin' for two days now. I think somethin' 'as 'appened to 'im," a low voice growled.

There was a grunted response. "Well, we 'ave to find Devil. When 'is 'igh and mighty wants 'is shipment taken care of, Devil is the one 'e tells."

Ashley's gaze met Manners', and he deliberately forced himself to take a drink of ale.

"Mebbe 'e was caught," one noticeably younger, higher voice suggested.

"Devil would never let 'isself be caught, Billy," one said with arrogant assurance.

"Then why ain't 'e signalled in two days?"

"Mebbe we should go look for 'im. Search 'is lordship's place."

Ashley barely kept himself from flinching.

"Devil won't like it."

"'E will if 'e's in trouble. It's not like 'im to forget to signal. 'Specially when it's 'is only job."

"Besides, if we do not produce what 'is mightiness wants, then we've got bigger trouble than sneakin' onto that toff's land."

"Let's give it one more day. If 'e doesn't signal tomorrow, then we go in and look for 'im."

Chum pushed back from his seat. He angled his head towards the door. He was going to find the privy. It also meant he was going to get a look at their new friends. Ashley would have to change his plans and go back to Taywards that night to warn Westwood, Renforth, and Baines. Somehow, they would have to force Devil to signal his gang. But how could they guarantee he would signal appropriately? They couldn't.

They had left Renforth on watch that night, but as the gang seemed to gather at The Anchor, he did not know how useful it would be for him to go across the water tonight anyway. As long as someone followed to see where they went.

When Chum returned from the necessary, they all seemed to be thinking the same thing.

"I was able to get a good look at them, but I think two of us should follow when they leave. I think it would be useful to discover where their location is across the river."

"I need to return to warn Westwood and Renforth of their plans. Why do you not return with me, Fielding? You can help Baines with the prisoner and I will help Renforth keep watch."

Plans decided, Manners and Chum remained to follow their gang. Once Fielding and Ashley left the front door of the tavern, he removed his hat and went around back to beg a ride back to Taywards. He did not want to waste precious time walking.

CHAPTER 7

*P*atience hated to admit it, but she was disappointed that all of the men had left her behind to go out and investigate. She still didn't quite understand why cavalry officers of the Household Guard were out doing this kind of work, but that was a question for later.

Sitting in the window seat of her chambers, looking out over the estate in the darkness, it was difficult to think of what she could do to help. Perhaps going into the village and trying to glean information at the shops might offer a little information, but not likely anything useful.

This was definitely a situation where it was best to be a man. The people they were looking for were most likely to be found in seedier places, and if, as a female, she went there, they would only expect that she was a less than virtuous lady.

If only they let her have a go at the prisoner. She had even tried going to the stables to try and had been promptly turned away.

The moon was high in the sky, but it offered her no solutions. She reached over to close the window as the night was growing cold when she heard the sound of a carriage coming up the drive. Who could that be? It was quite late. Had they found some new information?

Patience was filled with excitement as the probability of just such a thing—a new clue—was dangled before her. She had to be in place to hear what had happened. Before waiting to see who it was, she made certain Xander was sleeping soundly, then she quietly rushed down the stairs and positioned herself to hear what she could behind the curtain in the study. There was a small ledge she was able to sit upon and hide herself as long as no one decided to open the window. She thought it more likely for them to open one of the doors overlooking the lawns.

It was not long before Major Stuart and Captain Fielding entered the house, then the study.

"I will just go fetch Westwood. Make yourself comfortable," Stuart said to Fielding.

Whatever it was, it was important enough to rouse Dominic. Her excitement grew. It was not long until she heard two sets of footsteps approaching. Dominic must have still been awake. The door to the study closed behind them. She heard them take their seats and pour drinks.

"I was not anticipating seeing either of you so soon. What news is there?"

"We were fortunate to find our gang at The Anchor. It was a while before they arrived, but it was as if they were rendezvousing to discuss their findings for the day," Stuart explained. "They were indeed signalling each other, and they are wondering why Devil hasn't signalled for the past two days. If they do not receive a signal tomorrow, then they intend to come looking for him tomorrow night."

"I see," Dominic replied in a tone Patience recognized as most displeased.

Silence reigned for what felt like ten minutes before Stuart spoke again.

"We plan to coerce Devil into signalling tomorrow. But of course, we cannot be certain they do not have a mayday signal that would send them all rushing right over."

"I cannot think they would anticipate the situation," Fielding said. "But of course, there are no guarantees."

"I cannot like having the ladies here," Dominic said. "Convincing Faith to leave will be another matter."

"I need to go and report our findings to the colonel, but perhaps if a deal could be made with Devil, then we might secure his cooperation."

"Transportation versus hanging?" Westwood asked.

"We can see how much he values his neck."

Patience found herself rubbing her own at the thought of a thick rope around it.

"Remember, there is no honour amongst thieves," Westwood remarked. "However, if he betrays us, I will shoot him dead on the spot."

"You will have to beat me to it," Stuart said.

"Go inform your commander," Westwood said. "It grows late."

"I believe I will go visit the prisoner," Fielding added. "We have limited time to gain his cooperation, and I intend to make the most of it."

"Baines is still there. He is of a mind with you." Dominic scoffed. "And to think the world sees all of you as window dressing."

"We prefer it that way, Brother," Stuart said, and Patience could hear an affectionate slap on the back. It made her wonder what else these men had done under the guise of secrecy. So they were some special secret unit! I knew it! Now she had to wait for them to leave. The last thing she needed was to be caught at this point.

Once she heard the front door close behind Stuart and Fielding, it was sometime before Westwood took himself back to bed. He was likely trying to decide what to do with all of the ladies in his life. Patience prayed that he did not force them to leave. This was too good to miss.

When she finally crawled into bed, Xander raised his head and then gave her an affectionate lick on her hand as she soothed him back to sleep. She was asleep herself almost as soon as her head hit the pillow.

Patience was awake early the next morning despite the late time she went to bed. Her mind was too full of the thrill of the chase. She dressed and took Xander down to the back lawns as had become their habit. Part of her was wondering if she would run into someone or if the men would be talking where she could hear. Had anything happened overnight? It galled her not to be able to even ask.

After playing with the puppy for a few minutes, she went inside to the breakfast room, hoping someone would be there, but it was empty. Likely, they were all trying to catch some sleep.

One of the footmen, James, came in. "Would you like any food, miss? His lordship sent word to delay a little."

"Do not bother Cook, but if some coffee could be prepared, that would be lovely."

"Yes, miss."

Coffee was a guilty pleasure for Patience. She knew it was frowned upon by most ladies, but she would enjoy it when she could.

That was how Major Stuart found her, eyes closed, savouring the bold, smoky scent. Purists might argue at the amount of cream and sugar she added, but it was heaven in a cup to Patience.

"I will have what she's having," Major Stuart's deeper than usual voice said, causing her eyes to pop open and her cheeks to flush with embarrassment.

"Do not stop on my account." He waved at her drink, though he was looking at her strangely.

"I enjoy coffee," she explained, feeling the need to defend herself. And, she'd thought herself alone.

Xander had gone over to him when he entered the room and he knelt down to pet the pup. "He has become your shadow."

Patience smiled. "I am surprised to see you here. Were you not supposed to be going somewhere else last night?"

"Indeed." He inclined his head. She could tell he was toying with what to say to her. He took a sip of the coffee James set before him. "It is very good."

"Why did you return last night?" she prompted with a wave of her hand.

"I suppose you know too much already. We found the rest of the gang at the local tavern, and overheard them discussing their missing member."

"Devil," she provided.

"Just so. They mentioned he had not signalled to them in two days and have decided to come looking for him if he does not signal today."

Patience gasped, trying to pretend she had not heard any of this before. "So what will you do?"

"Fielding and Baines were going to attempt to convince Devil to cooperate. I am headed to check their progress after I finish my coffee."

Patience took another sip of her own while trying to think how else she could be involved.

"I see your mind working, Patience. If I have my way, Dominic will send you to London until this is over."

She scowled at him.

"This is not a game."

"I never said it was."

"These men would slit your throat as soon as talk to you. If they did not violate you first."

"No need to be vile. I understand what criminals like him do to females like me."

"Good. I do not want to have to worry about your safety."

Joy burst into the room before Patience could deliver the stinging retort on her lips.

"Have you seen Freddy?" Joy asked as she came into the room looking harried. Xander ran to her and she petted him absently.

"The cat or the human?" Stuart teased.

"The cat, of course. He did not come to my room last night. He is always there when I wake!"

"Perhaps he found something to entertain him in the barn last night," Stuart suggested with a wag of his eyebrows, which caused Joy to look heavenward in exasperation.

"He has plenty of time for that during the day. I will go check the barn."

Patience would've thought that Xander might follow Joy, but he came directly back to her. Animals usually followed Joy like a magnet, and with Freddy absent, it was somewhat heart-warming that the dog had chosen her instead.

AFTER FETCHING a basket full of warm—and most importantly fragrant—rolls from the kitchen along with a jug of ale, Ashley walked to the stables. More and more, Patience was on his mind and not in a good way. Being around her was too tempting.

He prayed that they could get what they needed from their prisoner and finish this assignment quickly, then hope she found some worthy fellow next Season. He shook his head to clear it. The thought of her with someone else bothered him at some very deep level, but it was hardly fair for him to not want any other man to have her when he could not have her himself. The fact that he was even thinking such thoughts was disturbing in the extreme.

As he entered the stables, Ashley nodded to the old retainers that had been there since his youth, as well as some of the younger grooms. He strode through the long row of stalls that held many of Westwood's and Carew's prized breeding stock. Many of the horses looked out to greet him and some looked out of curiosity as he passed, likely desirous of the food he carried.

"This is to tempt someone else altogether," he said, holding the basket out of reach.

Naturally, his own horse demanded a personal greeting. After scratching Caesar's favourite spot behind his ears, Ashley kept on. The stable master's office was at the end of the row and held his quarry.

"Any progress?" he asked as he entered to see Fielding and Baines circling their prey. They had to be exhausted, but by the third day, prisoners were usually ready to negotiate. All three turned to eye the basket, which held the delicious smells of warm, yeasty goodness infused with currants.

"We were just convincing Devil here that it's in his best interest to cooperate," Baines explained.

"I ain't afraid of the hangman's noose."

"Be that as it may, transportation to a better clime has its appeals," Ashley said.

"I ain't a snitch."

"Are any of your gang worth dying for?"

He sniffed and looked away.

"All I'm asking you to do is agree to signal them that you are still alive. That does not require snitching." Ashley set his basket down on the dusty desk and pulled out one of the golden buns. He waved it close enough to Devil's face for him to appreciate and salivate before offering one to Baines.

"Don't mind if I do." Baines took the warm bun and took a bite, savouring it loudly.

"Captain?" Ashley offered Fielding one and they all tortured the by now starving Devil.

Ashley finished his roll, then made a great show of licking his fingers. "I don't know, Captain. If he doesn't want to cooperate, then it will draw all of his gang into our laps. Then we would have all of them."

Devil narrowed his eyes a little, but it was the only outward sign he made. He had likely not considered that fact.

"Actually, that might be a better idea. Perhaps we should run it by the colonel."

"Don't. I'll do it," Devil growled.

"Now that I think about it, why would we not want to capture the whole gang? Surely one of them will tell us who they're working for."

"That younger one would be easy to crack. He didn't even have a beard yet," Fielding pointed out.

"I said I'll signal for you."

"I think you're going to have to do one better than that," Ashley said. "I want to know what the signals mean."

The man looked exhausted. He wanted to refuse, but he must know that the game was up. He would never have freedom unless he escaped, and he would never be left alone to try.

"One flash means nothing new."

Ashley nodded.

"Two means the game is spotted."

"Go on," Ashley encouraged with a roll of his hand.

"Three means it's time to move in for the kill."

"Now was that so hard?" Ashley asked, then plucked a roll from the basket and tossed it to him.

He caught it with his mouth and bound hands, then devoured it within seconds. He reminded Ashley of a wild animal that had been starved.

"There is more where that came from when you oblige us with more information," Baines taunted.

"What time do you normally signal?" Fielding asked.

"A drink," Devil demanded.

"It just so happens I have some home-brewed ale." Ashley pulled the cork from the jug and wafted it where Devil would be tempted.

"Eight in the evening," he answered practically chasing the bottle with his hanging tongue.

Ashley held the bottle to his mouth and let Devil drink a good, long swig. He swallowed and hung his head back with relief.

Ashley set the bottle down just out of reach. "The rest is yours when you tell me what you're waiting to signal for."

Now that Devil had had the worst of his hunger pains relieved, he had a little more resistance.

Ashley could see him firm his resolve. Curse it all. It was a fifty-fifty shot whether people gave in to hunger and ran their mouths like a river, or had enough to keep going and the game of torture had to begin all over again.

"Do you receive signals as well or do you get messages elsewhere?" he asked, hoping he wouldn't stop giving information.

Devil's eyes flickered at the latter.

"So somewhere else."

He looked at Fielding and Baines to see if they'd also noticed. A slight incline of their heads acknowledged that they had. He knew from experience it would be a while before he was ready to tell them the rest of the information.

"Where is the cargo you moved?"

Devil's face was frozen in place. He was done cooperating for now.

"I will leave that here in case he decides he'd like to say more. I'll go and give the report and see what the colonel wishes to do." They were careful not to use real names around criminals as such for the slightly protective benefit.

He saddled his horse and he took Caesar out for a brief run towards the clearing. Westwood was taking a turn in the tree and looked down with a grin when Ashley pulled the horse up beneath him.

"Oh, fair maiden! Shall I rescue thee?" Ashley called.

"My brave knight, come to rescue me!" Westwood simpered.

"You might as well come down. Devil finally told us they signal at eight every evening. It rings true with the time the others showed up at the tavern."

"Did he tell you what the signals were?"

"Aye, and they also ring true. I knew Cook's famous rolls and ale would not fail me."

"Like water to a parched man," Westwood agreed.

"Even better, delicious, refreshing ale." Ashley was thinking he wouldn't mind some himself about now. "One point we had not considered was not signalling and drawing them in here. I know you think it a risk to the ladies, but it might be a nice trap to catch all of them."

"Be that as it may, I need to remove everyone that could possibly be harmed if it comes to that," his brother reminded. Ashley was grateful he did not have the weight of all those females on his conscience.

"I will discuss it with Renforth and see. He may wish to keep them operating as is so we can catch the bigger fish."

"That would be my preference. If not this gang, they will always find another willing to do anything for coin. I best continue to keep my eye out. We need to discover where he's receiving his information from to signal them about."

"I'm fairly certain it's not another signal, but how would someone get a message to him here?" Ashley pondered aloud.

"Other than the river?" Westwood asked, thinking. "No one would be able to sneak in the gate, and the only other option is Sir Horace's land."

The look they shared indicated neither one of them thought Sir Horace had the wits to organize a dinner party, let alone a smuggling operation.

"There is also the possibility that one of your servants could be passing messages even unwittingly."

"I find that harder to fathom than someone sneaking onto my estate, but it bears looking into," Westwood agreed with a heavy sigh.

"Who would be the most likely to go into the village or Town frequently?"

"That is a better question for Armstrong, Mrs. Armstrong, and Chauncy. I do know that James has an ailing grandmother in the village and goes home to her at night, but he's been with us for so long it would be hard to fathom him doing such a thing."

"Presented to him as something innocent, the right amount of coin could make a lesser man do much worse things." Ashley had seen it time and time again.

"Sadly true."

"I will go and speak with the servants. It's an avenue we hadn't considered that bears closer scrutiny." Ashley saluted, then turned Caesar around to head back.

"Tell Cook to send any extra rolls she has," Westwood called after, making Ashley smile.

As he rode back, it occurred to him that this might be one instance where the Whitford sisters' observations might come in handy. One Whitford sister in particular, who was always looking for ways to meddle, would be thrilled to be involved. *Don't do it*, his conscience warned, but he already knew he wouldn't listen.

CHAPTER 8

*Y*et again, Patience found herself at *point non plus*. As usual, once Ashley Stuart left her sphere, her spirits were downcast. Even though he made her furious at times, he was exciting.

Once the rest of the guests were done breakfasting, there would be something to do. But for now, since no one else was down yet, she took Xander and wandered to the barn to see if Joy had found Freddy. "Come on, Xander. If anything will bring Freddy out, it's you."

He wagged his tail, delighted that she was speaking to him. They trudged through the still somewhat sodden earth until they reached the barn.

They were greeted by a cacophony of animal sounds, some of which were still not used to the puppy. Looking from stall to stall, she finally found Joy sitting, bent over an animal.

"Did you find Freddy?"

"Patience! Look!"

Xander was already trying to worm his way in, but Patience held him back. She looked over Joy's shoulder and gasped. "I guess that explains why he was looking fat."

Freddy was lying there nursing six kittens.

"Are they not the most precious things you've ever seen?"

"They are adorable," Patience agreed, though at the moment, they looked like drowned rats. "I had best keep Xander out of here so we don't disturb her."

"Would you mind telling Mr. Cunningham? I think he should know. And of course, tell Grace and Vivienne."

Patience smiled to herself. "I will go tell them at once."

Joy returned to adoring the cat and kittens, and Patience took Xander out of the barn and back to the house. "I do not think Joy is going to be your mistress after all, Xander, which suits me just fine."

By the time they reached the house, the other guests were in the breakfast room.

Lord Montford and Mr. Cunningham stood at Patience's entrance. She waved them back into their seats and filled a plate. Her cup of coffee was long gone.

"I have news," she said once she sat at the table.

"Pray tell!" Mr. Cunningham said.

"It seems our little Freddy Tiger is more of a Frederica."

He frowned, trying to decipher her meaning.

Grace understood and gasped. Apparently none of them had ever thought to check or perhaps even knew how.

"Indeed. Frederica has birthed six kittens this morning. Joy is in the barn with them now."

"Well, I'll be..." Mr. Cunningham seemed to think better of what he was about to say. He wiped his mouth and tossed his napkin on the table. "If you'll excuse me?" He was already running out of the door before anyone could answer.

They all laughed at his exuberance.

"You'd think his heir was born," Montford scoffed.

"I think it's very sweet," Grace said.

"Did you get a good look at them?" Vivienne asked. "Are they all orange tabby like Freddy?"

"Right now, they look more like wet rats than anything, but I did not get a good look. I was trying to keep Xander back so as not to disturb Freddy."

"She certainly has not taken to him, but I suppose having kittens explains it," Grace reflected.

"Indeed," Vivienne agreed.

"We will go take a peek when we finish here," Grace suggested.

"Peek at what?" Major Stuart asked as he strolled into the room, looking dapper in buckskin riding breeches and a dark blue coat.

"Freddy Tiger had kittens this morning," Patience answered.

He raised his brows. "I thought Freddy was male?"

"We all did, though I cannot say I would know the difference," Grace remarked with a blush.

Major Stuart grabbed a roll and sat down next to Patience. He was entirely too close. His leg touched hers beneath the table. She scooted over to the edge of her seat, then he put his arm on the back of her chair. He was doing it on purpose! She turned to glare at him. He smiled roguishly and her heart almost stopped.

"May I help you with something?" She remembered to be incredulous, but his deep blue eyes were watching her knowingly as if he knew exactly what he was doing to her insides.

"As a matter of fact, you can."

"I can?" She narrowed her gaze. He was trying to disconcert her.

"Indeed. Is that not what you wanted?"

She looked around at the others finishing breakfast and preparing to go visit the kittens.

"Is this some sort of trick?"

He smiled again, so that the edges of his eyes crinkled in a most attractive fashion.

Grace turned back as the others left the breakfast room. "Are you coming?"

"Perhaps a little later when Xander is napping."

Grace's eyes looked questioningly between her and Major Stuart, but then she nodded and left the room. Leaving her alone with Stuart's arm still draped over the back of her chair.

Nervously, she lifted her coffee cup to take a sip, but found it was empty.

"What may I do to help?"

"I'd like to question the servants, and it will go much faster if you help."

He truly thought for her to assist him? What was the catch?

"We are certain someone was getting messages to our prisoner and we need to see if one of the servants is helping."

Patience frowned. "Most of them have been with your family for years, if not generations."

"I know, but we must be thorough. It could have begun as some-thing innocent, such as being asked to leave a note somewhere."

"I suppose you're right. What am I supposed to ask the servants though?"

"I thought we could begin with the upper servants and see if there are those that leave the estate often and might be in the village where they would be interacting with others. Or any sort of pattern that might be an opportunity for information to be brought onto Taywards lands. Any irregularity might mean something, no matter how small."

"Yes, I see." She began to feel the rush of excitement at the possibil-ities. She did not try to hide her enthusiasm and smiled back at him. "When do we begin?"

"Now, if you are ready. I thought to call them into the study one by one. We can interview Armstrong and Mrs. Armstrong together so you can see how it goes, then we can divide up and talk to the rest of the staff."

Patience was relieved to see that she'd be able to watch him first. She had never interrogated anyone before. Well, besides her sisters.

He stood and pulled out her chair for her. "Shall we?"

Patience left the breakfast room, trying not to shake her head at the change in him as he spoke to Armstrong. Why was he suddenly being nice and including her?

The butler followed them into the room, and Major Stuart closed the door behind him, disconcerting Armstrong. "Please, take a seat."

The upper servant did, sitting on the edge of the chair, his back ramrod straight.

"Armstrong, if you would be so good. We just have a few simple questions. As you know, someone was trespassing on my brother's land, and we have that person restrained in the stables."

"Yes, sir."

Of course the butler knew what was going on. He would know everything. It was his business to know.

"We are trying to ascertain if any of the staff could have unwittingly helped pass information to the man."

Armstrong's posture stiffened, and his face showed offence.

"I know, Armstrong. We do not wish to think ill of any of our retainers, but it could be something very simple."

Patience watched with deepening respect for Major Stuart. Questioning someone was full of nuances and he had set the butler at ease.

"Is there anyone at all that goes into the village often—spends a good deal of time at the tavern, perhaps?"

"Most of the stable and farm hands go to the tavern on their evenings off." He frowned. "I imagine I could procure a list for you of those that go, though Chauncy would know their movements more precisely."

"That would be most helpful. What about anyone that might have connections in the village and go there more often?"

"Well, there is James, who goes every evening to help take care of his grandmother. But I cannot imagine him passing any information on, even unwittingly. He's a very sharp lad."

Major Stuart nodded encouragingly. "What about anyone that has connections with Sir Horace's household?"

Now that was a question Patience most definitely would not have thought to ask.

She saw the butler hesitate for a fraction of a second before answering. "My nephew, Samuel, is walking out with one of the maids, Molly. I know it should be frowned upon, but thus far it has seemed harmless. They often meet at the turnstile near the bridle path at the western gate."

Major Stuart nodded. "I'm sure it is harmless as you say. Anyone else?"

"Not that I can think of, sir. But perhaps Mrs. Armstrong or Chauncy can tell you more."

"You've been most helpful, Armstrong."

"May I ask, sir, what do you think is happening?"

"I am not sure, Armstrong. I think someone was bringing notes to our guest in the clearing."

"I cannot think anyone besides the grooms would be able to do that without causing suspicion, sir. They are the ones who take the horses out all over the estate. Anyone else doing that would cause notice. They also go into the village most frequently."

"I suspect you are correct, Armstrong. Thank you for your frankness."

"I wish for this dastardly business to be resolved as quickly as possible, sir. If I think of anything else, I will let you know at once."

"If you could send Mrs. Armstrong into us next, please?"

"Of course, sir." The butler stood and bowed before retreating.

"I think you may be on to something," Patience remarked. "Other than the river, the easiest way to deliver a message would be through Sir Horace's land. It is not surrounded by walls as Taywards is."

"I believe Westwood has set someone to watch there, but I will double-check."

They split up and interviewed the rest of the servants—he, the men, and her, the women, but unfortunately, she was unable to uncover any clues that would lead anywhere.

Ashley found that he did not mind Patience helping him. She had not interfered with his questioning and even had some helpful insights.

However, he had exhaustively questioned every one of the servants and found nothing more. There had to be some way the information was getting to Devil. His instinct told him it was so, and he learned over the years to always trust it. But how?

He sat in his brother's study, looking out the window, pondering just that when Westwood himself walked in.

"You look done in, Brother," Ashley said as he turned to see who had entered.

Westwood gripped his back and rolled his neck. "Sitting in a tree for hours is not as easy as it used to be."

Ashley chuckled. "That is the least favourite part of surveillance," he agreed. "Any luck?"

"None. It's almost as if they know we are on to them."

"The only way that could be is if someone is passing information. But Miss Whitford and I have spent the morning questioning the servants and there's very little to go on."

"What little is there?" Westwood asked as he slumped in one of the comfortable armchairs.

"I cannot say that it's much of anything, only that one of Sir Horace's maids is walking out with one of your grooms—Samuel. We have already deduced that the bridle path between the two estates is probably the easiest access to Taywards."

Westwood nodded and frowned. "That is the groom that I've had watching that entrance."

"It may be nothing more than innocent meetings, but we need to find out."

His brother inclined his head. "I will change the watch up or set someone to watch him."

Faith waddled in the room, and they both rose to their feet.

Ashley could not miss the look of concern on his brother's face. Faith's time was coming and it was understandably worrisome.

"I saw you come in. Did you learn anything?" she asked.

"Nothing except a better acquaintance with our neighbourhood. There is a surprising amount of traffic at the docks, with a great deal of building going on. How are you feeling?"

"As a whale about to burst."

Ashley struggled not to smile.

"And now, Lady Fagge is insistent we and our guests attend her dinner party." She waved a letter about.

"Can she not see you are in no shape to attend social functions?" Westwood's voice was laced with annoyance.

"I am perfectly capable of attending social functions. I simply hate being pressured into it because she has daughters she cannot rid herself of."

Ashley had a thought, though a reluctant one. "Perhaps we should attend. More insight into our current situation?" he suggested.

Westwood scowled. "This is the best excuse I've had to avoid our neighbours in years and now you say I must? I know, you and your illustrious troop may go. It is the bachelors she wants, after all."

"That is hardly a neighbourly sentiment," Ashley teased.

"No, indeed," he retorted with a heavy sigh. "When is the dinner?"

"Tonight," Faith replied.

"I doubt Renforth will wish to send everyone. We need to remain vigilant in our watch."

"He just relieved me at the clearing. Why do you not find out who he wishes to send and then I will send a reply to Lady Fagge."

"I beg your pardon, my lord," the butler said from the doorway.

"What is it, Armstrong?"

"A missive has just come for Major Manners. His messenger will be in the kitchens resting should you wish to reply."

Ashley stood and walked over to Armstrong. "I will take it. There is only one person who would be sending something to him here." He broke the seal and opened it. "As I suspected, it's from Lord Upton."

THERE IS EXTREMELY limited access to the knowledge of these arms shipments. I've taken the liberty of listing the committee members' names for you. Even those who are shipping the munitions are unaware that they are doing so. This particular shipment that went missing was en route to India. As you would suspect, it was on board one of the East India ships.

There was no known attack. In fact, it was sometime before the arms were discovered to be missing. All further shipments have been halted until this investigation uncovers whether or not this is a continued threat.

. . .

"No one would have thought to check again once the goods were loaded," Westwood remarked.

"But were the arms loaded? Or something else in their place?" Ashley countered.

"An excellent question to investigate."

"Someone knew there would be arms on that ship and likely substituted something in their place."

"And what's the connection to the Greenwich docks and Taywards? Or is there one?"

"It could simply be an excellent place from which to watch."

"But we found nothing on an exhaustive search."

"There has to be a link. We are just missing it."

"I think the key may be discovering who had the knowledge and who is passing messages to Devil. What names are on the list?"

"Lord Marsh, Henry Cavender, and Sir Percival Layton, in addition to Lord Upton," Ashley read.

"None of which he can think of any reason they would have to betray the information. All of them understand the necessity of secrecy with such shipments." Westwood frowned. "Then one of them must have unwittingly revealed the information."

"So we need to investigate connections. Manners is the best man for that. I will speak to Renforth about it. But I've heard of Layton. He has a younger son with quite a reputation as a gamester," Ashley said. "Perhaps he was desperate for funds."

Westwood frowned. "Still, I would not think Layton would leave that sort of information lying around."

"Some parents are blind to their children's faults. Certainly, it's a theory that bears looking into." Ashley stood. "I must report to the colonel."

"Do not forget to mention the dinner," Westwood called after him as he left the room.

Ashley shook his head. He had every intention of fobbing that off on one of his friends. He made his way towards the clearing, deciding to walk this time. He found Renforth sitting in the lookout tree with the spyglass to his eye.

"Report."

Ashley read the missive from Lord Upton, then conveyed his and Westwood's thoughts.

"I know Layton well, he served in the regiment with me when we were both green lieutenants. But his son is a wastrel. Still, it's hard for me to fathom him leaving any information around that his son might compromise." He pursed his lips. "I have a connection that could look into this for me. I cannot spare to send any of you back at this juncture. We need to see if the others have discovered anything by following them. Go and see if they've got anything to report."

"Very good, sir. Also, there is a dinner at Sir Horace's. I think it might be worthwhile for us to see if there are any other local connections that we might've missed, as we suspect someone of high standing is involved."

Renforth angled his head. "I suppose you could be spared, but I cannot afford to lose eyes on the rest of the gang."

Ashley wanted to protest, but he'd had the very same thought himself. He'd hoped that Renforth would not want to spare him either. The thought of that harpy, Lady Fagge, made his skin crawl, and that was without consideration of her insipid daughters. Ashley groaned, then smiled. If he had to suffer through it, then so did Patience.

CHAPTER 9

*P*atience smiled when she heard Colonel Renforth direct Major Stuart to attend the dinner that night. If she had to suffer, then it was only fair that he did as well.

He would have her head if he knew she was out there alone—well, not alone as Xander was by her side—but without a male escort.

However, she was restless and needed to do something so she decided to investigate the pathway between Taywards and the Fagge estate. When she'd seen Major Stuart, she had followed him to the clearing. She'd been afraid Xander would give her away, but he'd remained quiet by her side.

Now, Major Stuart was off to see if his colleagues had discovered anything and she would not be able to go into the village, dash it all. No one would believe her if she said she wanted to shop. Those words would taste like venom on her tongue and would be known for the lie they were.

"Let us go on towards the gate then, Xander."

It was a fair distance and a bit of a climb up a hill. She stopped to catch her breath and rested a moment beneath the shade of a large oak tree whose leaves were beginning to turn a beautiful shade of yellow.

Xander took the opportunity to roam around sniffing when she heard him growl.

"Xander, come," she whispered and crouched down beside him. "What is it, boy?"

They were getting close to the turnstile, so likely it was one of the grooms Westwood had put there to guard, but again she knew she should not have gone out alone. Certainly, she did not wish to be caught. She quieted the puppy by stroking behind his ears and tried to listen for what had made him growl.

She stood trying to see if it, in fact, could have been the posted guard. But even he was not visible. She took a few steps closer, but there was a large gorse bush obscuring her view. She stood on her tiptoes and could just see the top of someone's hat. She could see the groom accepting what looked like a coin, but could not make out the other person. Drat!

She pushed down on the branches and leaned just a little more, then lost her balance and tumbled down the incline right into the path.

"Miss Whitford!" A nasally, familiar voice exclaimed.

Patience wanted to die.

Xander began growling and barking at Rupert.

"I'll say! Call the dog off!" Rupert whined, trying to hide behind the groom that was manning the turnstile.

"Xander, no!" she commanded and the puppy ceased, however much she would've enjoyed watching Xander take a little piece out of the buffoon. He was a very perceptive dog. She patted his head, then stood and brushed the dirt from her gloves and tried to smooth her skirts.

"Whatever are you doing here, Mr. Fagge?" He was dressed quite differently than his normal outré colours and patterns, in subdued black and grey. He wore tasselled Hessians instead of his favoured heels, which Xander was nipping at.

"I was about to ask you the same thing. You should not be wandering about with a vagabond on the loose," he scolded self-right-eously as he tried to shoo the dog away.

Patience narrowed her gaze. He dared scold her? His voice had taken on a slightly different tone than she was unaccustomed to hearing from him.

"I was walking the dog. As you can see, he is an excellent protector. Why are you here?"

"Mama sent me to call to see who was attending our dinner. She said no one has answered yet."

My what a pushy, distasteful woman Lady Fagge was. "My sister was trying to ascertain the precise number of attendees. You must realize not everyone is present as they are on duty, and there is some difficulty with gathering the names." She hoped she sounded civil, because she felt anything but. She also wanted to remind the oaf that her sister was nine months with child, but she did not think Faith would appreciate her saying such. "You may assure your mama that a reply will be coming forthwith."

"Yes, yes, I will do that. May I escort you back to the house?"

Patience wracked her brains for any reasonable objection. "That will not be necessary, kind sir. If I am seen with you, then I will be scolded for wandering too far, indeed. Then I would not be allowed to attend your dinner tonight."

It was hard not to laugh, watching the thoughts run across Rupert's face. But he could see the validity of her argument and would risk his mama's wrath for someone not to attend her dinner party.

"You are certain you know the way?" he asked in one last effort to change her mind.

"Oh, yes. I know precisely where I am now." Never mind that Patience had never been lost a day in her life. "Good day, Mr. Fagge."

She hurried off down the path, praying he did not change his mind and come after her. She would rather take her chances with a vagabond than be alone with Rupert any day.

Now, she would have to endure an entire evening of his fawning and clinging. She shuddered at the thought. He disturbed her as much as Major Stuart, but in an entirely different way. It wasn't disgust she felt when she thought of Ashley Stuart, but she could not quite put a name to it...yet it was still entirely uncomfortable. What was it when someone irritated you, yet you could not stop thinking about them? At least she could say she had not been bored since his arrival. There had also been Lord Montford with Mr. and Miss Cunningham and Xander, of course. She had hardly spent any time with her other guests, but they were more friends with Grace and Joy anyway.

Her mind drifted back to seeing Rupert. Was Lady Fagge actually so pushy as to send Rupert over after she herself had sent a note that very morning? It was very odd, indeed. Something niggled at the back of her mind and she wondered whether she ought to mention it to Major Stuart. Should she tell him about the meeting and possible coin exchange she just witnessed? Then she shook her head. He would not appreciate the fact that she had defied his orders, and would likely tell Westwood. The last thing she needed was to have him on her case. Besides, was that not the groom's job to report any traffic through that part of the estate? What had the groom accepted from Rupert, and where had he gone off to? It was not as though anyone would stop one of the neighbours from visiting. It had to simply be her dislike of the man that made her wish him to be a villain. He was too much of a fool and too much under his mama's thumb to dare try anything nefarious. Patience gurgled a laugh at the thought.

Imagine being shackled to one as he! No doubt there would be three people involved in that marriage and Lady Fagge would direct every movement. Patience made a face of distaste.

How did so many women survive marriage without choosing their mates? Patience would rather die than be shackled to someone like Rupert. She was fortunate to have a choice in the matter, though would they allow her to remain as a spinster forever?

It was not that she hated men or even the idea of marriage if she could be assured of one such as Faith and Westwood had. Her more practical nature was quite certain affection like that did not come along very often. Since Hope also seemed to have found love, Patience felt the odds were even more against her, statistically speaking. There were few gentlemen she'd met that she could imagine such a union with. Dancing with most gentlemen was bad enough.

She would have to dance with Rupert, and the thought made her ill. At this point, she would not even have to feign a megrim. But she had heard Major Stuart and Colonel Renforth discussing the necessity of scouting out the neighbours, and she knew she was good at noticing small details. If there was any chance she could help solve this mystery, then she would suffer through. Now perhaps feigning a sprained ankle might be just the thing…

ASHLEY DONNED his uniform for the dinner because that was what was expected. He never minded formal dinners in London where people knew how to play the game, where the matchmaking mamas went after the bigger prey not the second sons. But there was always more expectation in the country where they were content to marry their daughters to a family name instead.

Not only did he have to suffer through this dinner, he would miss the signalling which he was keen to be a part of. He was certain something was going to happen tonight, and he'd be stuck doing the pretty to simpering upstarts.

When he could no longer delay the fact that he was ready, he made his way downstairs. Fielding was there eyeing him knowingly.

"Do not say a word," he warned.

"That's hardly fair when you would rub it in our noses were the positions reversed."

Ashley glared mockingly.

"Besides, our man could very well be at that dinner."

"I don't know." He picked at an imaginary piece of lint from his jacket. "I do think something will happen tonight, but my money says it will be here."

"Do you think Devil will betray us?"

"It is a possibility. They must know something is afoot. Devil has not signalled and no messages have been received with him in the stables."

"Devil hasn't cracked again?"

"Not since I asked an hour ago."

"I feel like we are missing something obvious." Which was normally how he felt during investigations until they were solved.

"If it was obvious, we would not still be here," Fielding drawled.

"Manners and Cholmely are still following the others?"

"Yes, they tracked them to a warehouse near the East India docks. They seem to be squatting in the area at night." That explained the petty crimes and vandalism that had brought them here in the first place.

"So they are looking for opportunities, it seems."

"Or waiting to be told when to act. None of them strikes me as overly initiative in nature."

"Members of gangs usually aren't. They follow the leader."

"Which is Devil. I must admit he's proven to be quite resistant to Baines' and my charms. He would have made a good soldier."

"We need to think like he does. Why is he resistant to giving up his leader? He must know he will not be able to walk free."

"Unless he thinks he will be able to escape."

"He's more afraid of the leader than us."

"I hope Renforth's contact is able to uncover something. If they are playing that deep, there must be some reason."

Fielding looked at his watch. "It's time to go."

"Perhaps I will join you and be fashionably late to the dinner," Ashley pondered. "I feel like that is too important to miss."

"We are not in Town, Ash."

"Yes, but Lady Fagge will be so grateful to have a bachelor there that she will forgive me."

"Suit yourself." Fielding shrugged.

He told Armstrong to inform Westwood that he would join them late. "I will be but a few minutes behind them."

"As you will, sir," Armstrong replied stoically.

Ashley accepted his hat and was about to follow the others to the stables when he caught a flash of pink out of the corner of his eye. All of his senses warned him to keep going and not turn, but he looked anyway. Patience was standing there, looking like a vision from heaven in a frothy concoction that accentuated her fine figure.

Their eyes met, and disappointment was written all over her face, but she held her tongue for once. He inclined his head and left, trying to catch up to the others.

Why was he feeling guilty for leaving her behind? This was his duty and he would fulfil his other obligation as well.

As they walked, an idea occurred to him. "Do you think perhaps he is related to the other gang members?"

"Devil? I suppose anything as possible," Fielding answered.

"It would explain some of his reluctance."

"Somehow, I have a hunch."

"Worth a try, I suppose."

They entered the stables and found Baines still with Devil.

He narrowed his gaze when he saw Ashley dressed in his uniform.

Ashley ignored the obvious disdain and sauntered over to him and sat on the arm of the chair he occupied, however unwillingly.

"Now is your time to shine," he told Devil with a mischievous grin.

Devil snorted.

"I just want to make clear that any mischief will affect your gang."

Devil's jaw clenched.

"The young one is pretty green."

"Leave him out of it," Devil growled.

Ashley's eyes met Baines' over Devil's head.

"As long as you cooperate, we won't touch a hair on his head. He is too young for a beard. What's he to you? Your son? Your nephew? No matter." Ashley waved his hand in the air and then uncrossed his legs and stood. "As long as we understand each other. Let's make this quick. I have a dinner to attend."

They led Devil with a gun pointed to his back down to the clearing.

Renforth and Fielding climbed different trees to try to get a good view, though it was in the dark with only a gibbous moon.

"There are two pistols pointed at you as there will be on your gang. Yes, indeed, they are being followed."

"Five till eight. Best be getting into place," Renforth ordered.

Baines unbound Devil's hands long enough for him to climb into the tree then he tied a rope around his ankle, linking them together.

"One minute," Renforth called.

Ashley lit the lantern and handed it up, then cocked his pistol and pointed it just to remind Devil of his task.

"Now."

Devil took the lantern and slid back the shield, lifted it, then shut it again and lowered it.

Fielding was watching across the river, but Ashley kept his eyes on Devil.

"They flashed back. What does that mean?"

"Message received."

"Excellent. Let's go."

As they slid down from the tree, Devil thought he had his chance. He thought wrong. As he kicked out, Ashley took his leg and twisted it. He spun and fell down, Ashley landing atop him with a quick blow to the ribs causing Devil to lose his breath. Ashley could feel beneath him as he gasped, trying to catch air through the pain.

"They won't be patient much longer," Devil said as they wrestled the ropes behind him this time.

"Neither will we," Baines growled. "As soon as you tell us what and whom you're waiting for."

"I can't," he spat.

They walked a few feet, Devil no longer fighting.

"It's your boy you're worried about. He's threatened him."

Devil nodded reluctantly. "I need to get to him first."

"What if we agree to take care of him? Transportation does not have to be a death sentence. We could arrange for the both of you to have decent accommodation for the right information."

"I heard they lock you in cells and most don't survive the trip."

Finally, he was showing some interest.

"It depends on the level of prisoner. Arrangements can be made. Not everyone on those ships is a prisoner," Ashley explained. He could tell Devil was contemplating the information. "Why do you not sleep on the idea? Tell us in the morning. I have to get to the dinner."

"I will join you since we are done for the night," Fielding announced.

"Jolly good of you."

"It is rather," the captain agreed.

Their horses were already saddled, so they mounted and took the bridle path towards the Fagge estate. As they rode, Ashley thought about what had happened that night and he had a nagging feeling that the answer was right under his nose. Was it the link between the two estates that was the key?

At least they had made progress that night. He was certain Devil could be persuaded to give up his leader.

As they arrived at the stables and dismounted, he checked his watch. Only half an hour late. Not late enough for his tastes.

CHAPTER 10

*P*atience was annoyed. Not only had Major Stuart neglected to accompany them to the dinner, but he was late. It was clear that Lady Fagge was also irritated by the slight and was holding off dinner as long as possible.

The drawing room, though perhaps once the height of fashion, bore the marks of shabbiness compared to the splendour of Taywards. Faded damask curtains and worn carpets gave evidence to that theory. The elegant furniture, though crafted from fine mahogany, showed signs of wear, with threadbare upholstery and the occasional creak of overuse. Apparently, all of the Fagge funds went to Rupert's toilette.

She'd already endured Rupert's clammy hands and spittle in her face. Why did he not wear gloves? And why must he stand so close?

It would have been much better if all of the soldiers had been able to attend that night so she would not feel cornered by the attentions of one person, but at least when Major Stuart finally arrived, she knew she'd have an ally.

As she tried to discreetly wipe away the latest spray of spittle from Rupert's machinations about something or other, she remembered that they were supposed to be considering any of the neighbours that might have involvement in the scheme and or who might be delivering missives to Devil.

She scanned the party that had gathered thus far. By far the largest group was that of the Fagges with their three daughters and two sons. It was hard to imagine any of them with enough wits to organize such an operation as they behaved as though they all shared one brain together. Perhaps it was harsh, but they had yet to convince her otherwise.

The remainder of the party, besides the one from Taywards, consisted of the other local gentry. A vicar and his wife who were elderly with twenty grandchildren and as sweet as could be. A very unlikely candidate.

The only other possibility was the Honourable Charles Greening, the third son of a viscount, who did not strike her as anything but refined. He was well-mannered and unpretentious—well-dressed but not a dandy who overspent his income. His wife was elegant, but quiet, and spoke of their three young children with love.

No one fit the bill of someone she would call a scheming criminal. For that's what would be necessary to steal a shipment of arms from the government, was it not?

"Why are you frowning, my dear?" Rupert asked with concern. Had he finally noticed she was paying him no mind?

"Just thinking about the criminal at Taywards. It is difficult to understand why he is still there."

"I wish I could understand it myself. Why would Westwood keep all of the ladies there in danger?"

"He is doing no such thing," she argued hotly. "I am certain he has his reasons. Not that he would share them with me." She remembered herself almost too late. Not that she suspected Rupert, but neither should she give anything away in case someone was listening.

"Of course not. Although it is rather strange not to have already sent the man to Newgate."

"I believe they were discussing that very thing," she said evasively.

"I am glad to hear it. The sooner the blackguard is gone from the neighbourhood, the better. You must promise me you will not go traipsing about the grounds alone again."

"With all of the soldiers around to protect me, I am not worried. You yourself were there." The last person she would heed was this man.

"I am capable of defending myself, though." He puffed out his chest, though it was already rather far out to begin with.

Patience clenched her jaw and ground her teeth so she did not pull the dagger she kept hidden on her person out and stab him in the heart with it.

The butler appeared. Apparently, they had grown tired of waiting for Major Stuart. However, instead of announcing dinner, he announced the infuriating man and Captain Fielding. Then, of course, he would outshine every other gentleman in the room looking impeccable in the Guard's Regimentals. "Forgive our tardiness, but duty called." One smile from him, and he charmed Lady Fagge into forgiveness. Patience wouldn't be surprised if she melted into a puddle at his feet.

"We understand, sir," she cooed. "Where would we be without gentlemen like yourselves to protect us?"

Patience looked to the ceiling with disgust.

"Now that all of our guests have arrived, shall we go on in to dinner?" It was clear that Lady Fagge intended to monopolize Major Stuart. When they were seated about the table, she put her two eldest daughters to either side of him. Predictably, Patience was seated next to Rupert, though his conversation surprised her as they received the first course and began to eat.

"Parliament will be in session soon. Will you be removing to London when Lord Westwood does?"

"We have not yet spoken of our plans. Everything at the moment revolves around Lady Westwood and her confinement. I suspect he will choose to go back and forth."

"Oh, yes, of course."

"Will you be removing to London yourself? I know it is only a short ride there when you need entertainment."

"But what I seek is right here," he said pointedly. Surely he didn't mean her?

"And what is there to delight a man of your sophisticated tastes here?" The sarcasm in her question eluded him, and had quite the effect of him again puffing out his chest with pride that she had noticed such a quality in him.

Major Stuart was sitting directly across from her and raised a brow at her question. He was eavesdropping, drat the man.

"Why you, of course."

Patience began to choke on her soup.

"Are you all right, Miss Whitford?" Stuart drawled from across the table. He was enjoying every minute of her discomfort. She glared at him between unladylike coughs.

Rupert put a glass of water to her lips and she took it from his hand. That would be the last straw of her dignity at the moment to have him hold her glass.

Once her coughs settled, and the others had returned to their conversations, Rupert must have decided since she had not rebuffed him thus far, he could continue.

"Indeed, Miss Whitford, if you have not gathered by now, I intend to speak to your brother-in-law about courting you in earnest. My prospects have recently improved such that I can comfortably support a wife in the leisure to which you're accustomed, even before I inherit the baronetcy."

She opened her mouth to give him a set down when she felt a kick under the table. Her eyes looked up swiftly to see Major Stuart give her a slight shake of his head. Did he mean for her to encourage Rupert? What could he mean by that? Did he wish for her to draw Rupert out? She glanced at him, attempting to discern his meaning.

"I-I am very happy for your good fortune," she said carefully. "Have you made some investments? If they are so good, perhaps Westwood would be pleased to know about them."

Stuart gave her an approving nod.

"You could say that," Rupert replied, lowering his voice.

"Oh, I see. You do not wish for others to know about it?"

His eyes darted nervously around the table. "I would rather not have word get out that I have made my fortune, if you know what I mean."

"Indeed, sir. Your secret is safe with me." She mimicked his low voice.

"I also do not think the friend that enlightened me to the scheme would appreciate sharing the wealth, so to speak."

"Oh, I only thought it might be something in which my brother would wish to invest. I can see it is not that sort of scheme." She waved her hand as though the thought had already left her mind. And Rupert was not acting his normal self. She tried to think of how else to draw him out as she turned to give her time to her other dinner partner, Mr. Greening. It was clear Rupert did not wish to tell her more about how he made his fortune as he put it, but what if this friend was the mind behind the theft and he was using Rupert as a puppet in his scheme? Rupert must have friends in London, but she'd never actually run into him there. When it was time and she turned to him again, those questions were burning in her mind. Was he not welcome in Westwood's circles? If he had an unsavoury reputation, then surely Westwood would not associate with them here. He was at least ten years Westwood's junior, so perhaps he ran about with a younger crowd. However, if he was seeking to court her, that was not the behaviour of someone running wild with their set. She frowned, trying to work out the mystery.

ASHLEY SAT across from Patience and amongst the two eldest Fagge daughters. She stood out like a rose amongst the thorns. However, he knew she had her own well-hidden ones, including her prickly tongue.

He could not keep from listening to her conversation. She was doing an admirable job of trying to draw Rupert out. Was his idiocy all an act? Or was he merely the pawn of Layton's son? He would have to be looked into. Ashley had a strong dislike for the plump tulip. It certainly could not be because of his obvious interest in Patience Whitford.

If only he could be the one to interrogate Rupert, but talking across the table simply was not done in polite circles. Not that he thought anyone would mind in such a small gathering in the country. Certainly any host with as many marriageable daughters would forgive anything to a wealthy bachelor with such connections as Ashley had. He would have to wait until the ladies left.

When the ladies withdrew, and the port was poured, Ashley took the opportunity to move close to Rupert. Westwood raised a brow as Rupert was not exactly Ashley's normal sort of acquaintance. He would have to explain the conversation he heard earlier.

"Mr. Fagge," he said, leaning back lazily in his chair and swirling his port. "Do you mind if I call you Rupert? We are neighbours of sorts."

Of course, Rupert looked pleased as Ashley suspected he would.

"And you may call me Ash, like my friends do, if you choose. We never crossed paths much before. I was mostly away at school and then with the army. May I ask what your interests are?"

"M-m-mine?" He sputtered as though no one had ever asked him such a thing.

Ashley shrugged with Gaelic nonchalance. "I don't have much time for amusements hereabouts, but surely you must know what there is. Westwood has become eminently respectable since his marriage." Ashley's mouth formed a moue of distaste.

"To be honest, there is very little here unless you've an interest in the river. All other pursuits, you must unfortunately ride back into Town."

"As I suspected. But the river you say? Do you mean boating?"

Rupert shook his head then leaned forward as though he were going to say something very clever. "Speculation," he enunciated with a great deal of spittle.

"Oh, is this the investment you mentioned to Miss Whitford?" He tried to look abashed. "I could not help but overhear a little."

His eyes held a knowing and self-important gleam. "Indeed. And if you could assist me in the matter of convincing Miss Whitford to accept my suit, I might be inclined to let you in on the secret. We would be family then, after all."

"Ah, I see. Miss Whitford might not appreciate my meddling. She is rather strong-willed."

"Nothing my firm hand could not mould into a dutiful wife."

"Just so." Ashley could only hope that he was a better actor than what he was feeling inside. Because his blood was like a molten pipe about to erupt in a massive explosion, which took Rupert's head with it. Right now, he could not afford to alienate this pompous arse.

But he did have an empty glass, and the decanter was sitting right in front of Ashley. Perhaps just a little more port to loosen the man's tongue? Ashley couldn't think of any better alternative at the moment. It might even be worth trying on Devil, though he imagined it would take a great quantity before Devil spilled his secrets. He was protecting that young boy.

They listened to the conversation around them while Ashley kept refilling Rupert's glass. His cheeks were now ruddy, his eyes glossy, and his speech was well slurred.

In a break in the conversation, Ashley swirled the red liquid in his glass watching it as it spun into a nice little vortex. "So how can I be sure the speculation will be worth my while?"

Rupert giggled. Yes, giggled. There was something disturbing about a grown, rotund man giggling like a small child. Ashley had to turn away from the sight of his multiple chins jiggling with mirth.

"I don't know about you, but as the second son, I would think thousands of pounds would be very worth your while."

Ashley raised his brows, showing appropriate intrigue.

"Now I have your 'tenshion.'"

"Indeed, you do."

"So you'll help me?"

Ashley pretended to think. He swirled his port back into another nice vortex. "How do you suggest I help?" he asked.

"Help me meet with her alone. Maybe draw her to the western gate so we can walk."

Ashley frowned. "I'll not be party to compromising her," he said. "That is quite a different matter than helping your courtship. Besides, Westwood has forbidden her from going out alone."

Rupert scoffed, which drunk, produced an inordinate amount of spray.

Ashley was compelled to take his handkerchief and dab at the unfortunate remains that had hit his face. "Why scoff, sir?" Ashley asked in a tone that was difficult to disguise as other than irritation.

"Because I met her out alone only thish morning."

"I see." Ashley took a fortifying sip of his own port. "And where did you meet her?"

"She was near the turnstile between the estates." He spluttered more as though he realized what he'd confessed.

Ashley's suspicion grew more and more by the moment.

"I was coming to speak with Lady Westwood about the dinner."

So he says. "I tell you what, I will put some favourable words into Miss Whitford's ear about you, though I am certain your own charms will do more than any of my words could."

"You really think sho?" he slurred pitifully.

No, nothing short of public compromise would ever compel Miss Whitford to accept this man's suit, and that would happen over Ashley's dead body.

"Say, Missh Whitford did mention you still have that vagrant you found on the property. Why is he shtill there? I wouldn't think you'd want him near the ladies."

Ashley felt Fielding stiffen beside him. He would have to warn Patience to hold her tongue. She would compromise their efforts!

Ashley waved his hand. "He will be gone shortly. It's only been a matter of transport, but I assure you, the ladies are well-protected from him."

It occurred to Ashley that if Rupert were the go-between, he might be provoked into revealing himself. If they could somehow involve him—or make him think he was—and give him access to Devil, it ought to be quickly apparent if there was a link.

Ashley glanced at Fielding, who seemed to be considering the same thing, and then nodded. He leaned forward and slapped Rupert on the back, acting as though he was just as inebriated. He lowered his voice and looked around. "I'll say, Rupert, we've been trying to get the man to talk a little and tell us where his friends are. We don't think he was vandalizing the properties alone."

"Why, why would you think that?"

Ashley shrugged. "Just a hunch my commander has."

"Oh?"

Ashley nodded. "Mayhap with your superior knowledge of the area, you could help us."

"Me?" he asked us, though no one had ever asked for his help before. It seemed to be a common theme with him.

"Why not? We aren't having any luck. Why don't you give him a go? Fresh eyes and all that." Ashley waved his hand back and forth.

"I suppose I could."

"Excellent!" Ashley slapped him on the back again then refilled his glass before raising his own. "A toast! To a new partnership."

"A new partnership," Rupert slurred as he barely managed to raise his glass.

One thing Ashley knew for certain, Patience was not going to like his next plan, and he almost felt guilty for asking it of her.

CHAPTER 11

I beg your pardon? You cannot be serious!" Patience was incredulous.

Major Stuart had the grace to look sheepish. He and Fielding had beat them back to the house since they had to return in the carriage. When she entered the house, he surprised her by asking to speak with her. Now they were closeted in the study.

She paced with fury.

"But I am. I need you to woo Rupert."

"I think I am going to be sick."

"You are always wanting to help, and now you can."

"You mean to tell me this is part of the mission?" The glare she cast at him would have frozen a fiery furnace. "Surely there is some other way to help."

"We have a hunch that his speculation might be related to the missing arms. We need to keep him close."

She stopped and put her hands on her hips. "Surely you cannot believe he could orchestrate any such thing."

"No, but he could certainly be the mastermind's pawn. For the location alone, he would prove useful."

"Why can you not befriend him?"

"I have done so, but his interest is you," he pointed out a bit too gleefully.

"My, how you must be laughing at me!"

"Not at all."

"And what happens when he compromises me?"

"I would never let that happen."

She raised her brows doubtfully. "You intend to shadow us everywhere? He is already like a parasite without any encouragement. Then, if Lady Fagge gets wind of any possible connection to the house of Westwood, she will facilitate the matter by any means possible." Patience resumed pacing as her fury gained momentum. "He does not listen to any repulsion, and I am certain any objections I make will be excused as maidenly modesty and that he would be happy to guide me."

She looked up to see Major Stuart's surprised face. "What is it?"

"I will swear on my life that I will not let him harm you."

"That's a mighty big promise, Major, but I will hold you to it."

"Then you agree to help?"

She held her hand out to shake on it like she'd seen gentlemen do before, but she wasn't quite prepared for the sensation she felt when he took her hand. Neither of them wore gloves and the skin-to-skin contact was intense. His hands were nothing like Rupert's—whereas Rupert's were chubby and clammy, Major Stuart's were warm, firm, and slightly callused. He was no idle gentleman. The sensations went beyond her hands. She felt his touch pulse throughout her entire body.

Instead of shaking her hand, he held it and began to play with it, rubbing his thumb over her knuckles and fingers. She could only stare at the motion, afraid to look into his eyes.

They stood thus for some time—it was probably only seconds but felt as though time had suspended. He cleared his throat and dropped her hand.

"I should inform you that he asked for my assistance in courting you in exchange for information on the scheme that made him rich."

"Now this makes more sense."

"Indeed. By allowing him to come here under the guise of courting you, we may draw him out. I will send him a note in the morning encouraging him to call."

"I will await my fate with bated breath." Only a slightly sarcastic tone laced her response.

"Good girl," he said as he chucked her under the chin as if she were a young child, then bid her goodnight.

Patience made her way to her chambers and went through her evening ablutions in complete dismay over the task before her. "Be careful what you wish for," she whispered to her reflection in the mirror as she brushed her hair out.

She should be grateful for any sort of adventure, and she knew they couldn't all be glamorous and exciting. But to allow Rupert to woo her? An involuntary shudder of disgust ran through her body. Major Stuart expected her to fail, which only made her more determined. He never would have allowed her to assist if he didn't think it would provide him more access to extract the information from Rupert himself. She would prove she could do it without him.

How could the man both annoy and attract her in the same breath?

And the attraction was strong. She'd made a complete and utter fool of herself earlier with her reaction to him. She'd been so transparent, but at least he did not seem disgusted by her, even if he had stepped away and left her quickly thereafter. When was her infatuation with him going to end? She thought that being around him more would surely cease the fantasy by nature of reality, but in fact, quite the opposite was true.

But ridding herself of her infatuation could only happen if she was separated from Stuart. The sooner he left the better.

What needed to happen was for her to draw Rupert out quickly and efficiently without further engaging his affections. Patience was capable of patience, was she not?

Then she could prove to Major Stuart and even Westwood that she was proficient in handling delicate situations. Moreover, when she later approached Westwood to aid her in her quest to be a spy, she would be able to cite her experience in this matter.

Climbing in bed, she quickly fell asleep after having reassured herself that Rupert was no more than an assignment.

In the morning, the prospect looked no more pleasant than it had the night before. She gathered Xander for a reassuring cuddle, then dressed and took him outside.

By the time they returned to the house, there was still no one in the breakfast room. How odd. She drank her coffee then filled her plate, sneaking kippers and bacon to Xander under the table. "It's not really sneaking them if no one is here to watch, is it?" she remarked.

Where could everyone be? Was everyone exceptionally lazy today? The dinner party had not been very fatiguing, except mentally. It certainly did not compare to an evening out in London when they would not have reached their beds until dawn.

She ate very slowly, but still there was no one—not even her sisters or the other gentlemen. Perhaps all of them had gone for a ride?

It would be odd of them not to inform her. She rose from the table and decided to check the barn. Grace and Joy were very likely there fawning over the kittens.

There certainly was no sleeping in the barn. It was teeming with activity and Patience found Freddy with her kittens. Patience could only get near to pet them if she left Xander outside the stall they were in, so she left him whining on the other side of the door. After snuggling one to her face, she could no longer stand Xander's whimpers so she put the kitten down and took the puppy back outside.

Immediately, Xander began running towards the stables.

"You are determined to get me into trouble, are you not?" she scolded as she took off after him. Thankfully, he did not run inside but stopped to sniff something of interest near one of the water troughs. That should be harmless enough.

She leaned against the wall while Xander circled and sniffed. Then her ears immediately perked up when she heard a familiar voice. Looking upward, there was a window open, and she smiled. In all honesty, she could say she had not been snooping this time. Moreover, she was hardly going to leave when the ripe fruit was dangling before her very eyes.

"Time is running out, Devil." Major Stuart's voice.

There was no apparent response. Surely, the prisoner must be reacting. If only she could see! She stretched up on her tiptoes and tried to pull herself up, but the window was just a few inches too high. She put her foot on the nearby water trough and boosted herself up. With a little grunt, she managed to get both of her forearms onto the sill and could see Major Stuart leaning over Devil, who was tied to a wooden chair. She could see the boots of someone else in the room, but no one else.

"You must know we cannot delay longer. Either the person delivering messages is going to realize you are gone, or you will not show up for your rendezvous. Surely there is more you can tell us without being too specific."

The man shuffled a bit in the chair he was tied to. "Not all is as it appears to be."

"Tell me something I was unaware of," Stuart drawled.

"I don't know the real toff, only the middleman. I don't even know his real name, but he is an actor if I've ever seen one."

Stuart looked up and caught her eyes before she could duck down again. Unfortunately, the quick movement caused her to lose her balance and her arms circled in the air and a squeal escaped her as she fell backwards, straight into the water trough.

Patience closed her eyes in exasperation, knowing what she must look like. She had to hurry away before anyone found her like this—not that she expected Stuart to run out to her rescue.

Opening her eyes, she looked up to find him standing over her with a raised brow and a knowing smirk. How did he get outside so quickly?

"Do not say a word," she growled. As if she were not already humiliated enough, to hear scolding words right now from him might be enough for her to pull him into the trough with her.

"May I at least help you up?" He held out a hand to her.

She stared at the hand as though it were a viperous snake, and she was just tempted to take it and pull him in.

"You could never manage it." His eyes twinkled at her as though he knew exactly what she was contemplating.

Realizing what she must look like with her pale gown soaking wet and stuck to her skin, she only wanted him to leave. "I think it best if you will just return to the stables. It would be hard enough to return to the house without putting on a show for the servants."

"Very well." For once, he behaved as a gentleman, turning his back and walking away.

She climbed from the trough, then attempted to wring the water from her gown before she took off running for the house.

APPARENTLY, Ashley was no gentleman. He watched Patience run back to the house, unable to look away. Part of him rationalized that he wanted to make sure no one accosted her, but the other part knew he was likely the biggest threat to her. He wanted her badly and he knew that was not what was best for Patience.

He had to clear his head so he could concentrate on resolving this matter and leaving. As he made to return inside the stables, he saw Rupert riding up. Never would he say he was glad to see the man, but perhaps it would give them a clue as to whether he and Devil knew each other. Thankfully, Baines was there and they could each watch one of them.

"Well met, Stuart!" Rupert called as he rode near and dismounted. One thing he could say for the man, at least he seemed to know his way about a horse, despite his garish outfit. Today he was in hues of pink and puce, with a bright green neckcloth.

"Coming a courting?" Ashley asked with a wave up and down at the man's attire.

"Indeed, I have." He beamed. He pulled a bouquet of pink roses from his saddlebag. "Do you think she'll like them? I do not know what her favourite flower is, but roses are universally well liked."

"Yes, they are. How can she not approve?"

Rupert smiled as one of the grooms took his horse.

"Do you think I could trouble you to assist me in the matter we spoke about? Miss Whitford may be a little while. She had a little mishap when walking the dog this morning and went in to change into a fresh gown." Ashley barely said that with a straight face as he recalled the incident fondly.

"If it will not delay my courting, then by all means," he said with a smile that sickened Ashley. He did not think the buffoon would harm Patience, but neither did he intend to give him the opportunity.

"Where is this man? The sooner he is away from the ladies, the better."

"We have arranged transport for today," Ashley assured him. "But if you think you can pry any information from him more the better." If nothing else, it would be amusing to see Rupert make the effort.

"Yes, of course."

Ashley led him through the stables to the master's office. Ashley opened the door and paused to signal Baines before Devil was able to get a glimpse of him.

Baines gave a slight nod of understanding and turned his eyes on the person behind Ashley while he kept his eyes fixed upon Devil.

"I brought someone new for you today, Devil. A guest if you will."

The prisoner grunted, unimpressed.

Ashley stepped aside to allow Rupert to enter. Devil narrowed his gaze when he saw the sight before him. Was it because of recognition or was it because of the outlandish attire?

Ashley could only pray they gave something away if there was anything to give.

It seemed Rupert was not going to speak. "Any recognition?" Ashley prompted.

"None at all, I am afraid." He lifted his chin and his eyes darted towards the prisoner. He was lying.

"I was hoping you might have seen him with someone in the village that might lead us to his associates."

"Why would you think I associate with his sort?"

Was he nervous, or was he just not used to being around criminals?

"Thank you for trying, my man. Perhaps Miss Whitford is prepared to receive you by now."

Rupert seemed to snap back to his normal affectious self.

"I will walk you out."

Rupert hurried through the stables. Ashley needed to determine why.

When they reached the door, Rupert took a deep breath. "I know the way from here."

"I suppose you do."

"I'll say, I wish you would remove that man from here. It's not seemly to have him around."

"I assure you, he will be gone today. My apologies if taking you in there offended your sensibilities. I only thought you might be able to help. We want to ensure he was not working with anyone else that might continue where he left off."

"I was obliged to do my duty, but unfortunately, I cannot help you, nor can I imagine anyone that I associate with having any dealings with his kind."

"You misunderstand, my friend, we only wish to see if you'd seen him around with anyone else."

Rupert shook his head. "I'm afraid not. I had best be on my way. I would not wish to keep Miss Whitford waiting."

Ashley gave him a mock salute and watched as Rupert scurried away towards the house, waiting until he entered the doors, wanting to ensure he did not side-track to the clearing. He turned and went back to see Baines and Devil.

"Well?" Ashley asked as he entered and leaned on the desk.

"That popinjay makes my skin crawl," Baines said.

Devil snorted.

"Anything useful?"

"He's lying."

"Agreed, but will our distinguished guest enlighten us as to how they know each other?"

"I've never seen that clown in my life," Devil spat.

He was being truthful. "You are certain he's not the toff that gives you messages?"

Devil shook his head. "We've only met in the dark. He's very careful, but I've heard his voice and it's not nasally and whiney."

"If he disguises it?"

Devil closed his eyes as if trying to imagine the sound. "I s'pose."

"He was delivering messages to you at the clearing at night?"

Devil nodded. "Then I'd signal the others."

"Since I am in a generous mood, I'll have some of Cook's dinner sent to you if you tell us what happened when the signal was three flashes."

He shrugged. "It meant we picked up the crates as what he told us to do."

"But how did he tell you which ones and where?" Baines asked.

"Some bloke named Hocks knew that bit. He meets us at the Company and tells us what to swap."

It was much as they suspected, but frustrating not to have more to go on.

"Does this Hocks work at the shipyard with the others?"

Devil shrugged.

Ashley sighed. It was clear he was not going to get anything more from Devil at the moment. He believed what he said about the toff, but how else could they find the man?

He and Baines returned back to the house, leaving Chauncy to guard Devil. It was time they all sat down together and exchanged what they knew. Hopefully, Renforth would have received word back from London on Layton.

They gathered in Westwood's study, the viscount himself present as well.

Ashley was beginning to feel like they were running in circles, but such was often common in an investigation until they found the one missing link.

"Let us go around the room and share what we found." The methodical approach Renforth employed was soothing and gave structure to the otherwise chaotic nature of looking for a needle in a haystack.

"Manners and Chum, begin." Renforth directed the two who had just returned for this purpose.

"We've been following the gang, but they seem to be wholly dependent upon what Devil tells them. They work at the shipyard by day then wait at the docks until dark for a signal."

"Baines?"

"I do not believe Devil has more to share. I think he's told us what he knows."

"Stuart?"

"I agree with Baines. It's hard to credit, but it's possible Rupert is the messenger, but impossible to credit that he could orchestrate such a campaign. He's come upon some scheme that has put him flush in the pocket. He's made a deal with me that if I assist his courtship with Miss Whitford, he will let me in on it."

"Why would Rupert bring a military officer in on a probably illegal scheme?" Renforth questioned.

"Rupert is an idiot and only focusing on Patience. He may not even realize what he is doing is illegal."

Renforth raised his brows and shook his head as though he could not fathom such idiocy. "Fielding?"

"I cannot believe Miss Whitford would agree to that, but I suppose it is worth a try. I have little else to add."

"And I have seen nothing else from keeping watch. While there is a nice view, my rump is heartily sick of sitting in a tree. I expect a report today from my contact about Layton's son, which I hope will be the key to unlocking this once and for all. It seems we have gleaned as much as we are going to from Devil. Even if Rupert is delivering the messages, he knows we are waiting to pounce."

"I think we need to set a trap. There is a little else for us to do here without any messages being delivered," Baines recommended.

"It will need to be very enticing," Ashley warned.

CHAPTER 12

$\mathcal{P}$atience did not know how much more of this she could take. Rupert seemed to have decided that she was his for the taking and had decided her space was his own. She'd thought he was bad enough before. Clearly, she was mistaken.

They were taking a walk through the park, and Patience made every effort to stay within sight of the house, but every bench they sat upon, every tree they neared, Rupert attempted to press his attentions on her.

Likely sensing her irritation, Xander had now taken a jealous dislike to the man and was trying to insert himself between them. What an excellent dog he was.

How much longer was she to suffer? Did the man not understand there were still social rules of etiquette to follow?

There was no understanding between them, but if Major Stuart had told Rupert she was more interested than she was, she would strangle him.

How was she to draw the man out when she could scarcely keep him at bay?

A heavy sigh escaped her and Rupert turned to look at her. "Is something the matter, my dear?"

It took great strength of will not to openly cringe at being called his dear. "I am restless, is all."

"Are you missing Society in London?"

"Perhaps I am, but I would not miss being with Faith for the birth."

"The time is very soon, is it not?" He looked strangely eager for that answer. Why would that be? Did he wish for her to go to London because he desired to himself?

"Dr. Harvey suspects it will be within the week. I know it will not be a moment too soon for my sister."

"And you wish to have children yourself?"

"I suppose." She tried to remain noncommittal. "It is not something I have thought on overly much. If and when I marry, that will be a decision to be made with my husband."

"Well," he said, making that awful gesture that Patience could only relate to puffing out his chest and preening like a rooster. "I fancy I will produce a healthy brood and you have all the promising signs of being an excellent breeder." He glanced at her hips that she was well aware were wider than her sisters'.

"You go too far, sir. We scarcely know each other." Even speaking of such things in London Society was taboo.

"Forgive my country manners. We speak plainly here and I meant it as the highest compliment."

Country manners, indeed.

"I have a small gift for you." He reached into his pocket and pulled out a small rectangular chest that was ornate in design. How had he fit that into his pocket? "It is a music box." He turned a lever on the back and opened it to play a song she thought was Beethoven.

Patience frowned. A lady could not accept a gift from a man she was not betrothed to. He placed it in her hand and she did not know how to react.

"Do you like it?" he asked eagerly.

"I cannot accept a gift from you, Rupert. We hardly know each other."

"I should like to know you very well. We will remedy that," he continued, unaware of the effort she was making not to shove the box in his face and run back to the house. Indeed, shoving all thoughts of actually marrying this buffoon and what it would intimate, she knew this was the perfect opening to ask him questions.

"As you say, sir. Why not begin with telling me who your friends are?"

He furrowed his brow in thought, then just as quickly released the frown. "Of course, you wish to know with what Society company we would be keeping. I can assure you once married, we would only keep the best of company."

That was hardly reassuring. She knew whoever she married in actuality would be welcomed by her family and therefore Society. "But with whom do you keep company now?" she prodded.

He waved a dismissive hand. "Mostly chums from my school days, but I hardly think them relevant."

"Westwood is quite close with his school chums as you call them," she argued, also wondering why no one was saving her. She told her sisters to rescue her if Rupert stayed longer than half an hour. She glanced longingly back towards the house. Xander, the traitor, had left her side to sniff something interesting in the woods.

Next time, she would insist on someone accompanying them. She did not trust Rupert to behave much longer.

"Shall we meander this way?" Back towards the house she meant. "You can tell me about your friends as we go. I'd love to know what you do with your spare time in London."

She called to Xander, who came bouncing back towards her. She never would have thought a dog could bounce, but that was precisely what he did. She scooped up his lead instead of taking Rupert's arm and began to hasten towards safety.

It did not stop him from hurrying after her and taking her arm.

"Your friends?" she prompted. Why was he so hesitant to speak? Perhaps he did not have friends?

"I cannot say I have many friends, though there are one or two. I do not foresee them settling down and mixing with any Society company we would keep when married."

"Anyone I would know? It would help to know you better."

"I suppose you might know Sir Layton's son, Edwin."

"I cannot recall having met the son. I believe I met the father once."

"He is very well-connected. You will have nothing to worry about, I assure you. There is also another friend named Oscar Beckett, but I cannot think he would have run in the same circles as you. He's terrified of the leg-shackle."

They had reached the rose garden and Patience saw the end in sight. She turned to bid him adieu, but when she did, he stepped forward and planted a wet, smacking kiss on her lips. The repulsion was like nothing else she had ever felt. "Unhand me, sir!" She pushed him away with as much maidenly modesty and outrage as she could muster along with the desire to wretch.

"Your modesty does you credit, but I assure you this is nothing between a betrothed couple."

"We are not betrothed!"

"Rupert Fagge!" the Dowager's voice trilled. "You will not behave like a cad in my garden! Explain yourself!"

Patience was a bit terrified of the Dowager in that moment, though she knew her to be an old dear. The relief of having Rupert's assault against her stopped combined with the fear of what she might expect finding them in such a position.

"Your ladyship!" He jumped back. "I meant no offence to Miss Whitford. I intend to make her my wife."

The Dowager's black brows lifted almost to the silvery curls that adorned her head. "Is that so? Have you received Westwood's permission? If so, I've heard nothing about it."

"I-I," he stuttered and stumbled.

"As I thought. I think it's time you returned home, Rupert. Once you've apologized to Miss Whitford."

"I meant no offence, Miss Whitford." He made her a bow and then scurried away.

They both watched him leave, then the Dowager turned to Patience. "What was the meaning of that? You should not have encouraged him in such a manner."

"Of course not, my lady. I thank you for your timely intervention."

"I do not think he would have pressed himself on you more than he did. However, he is clearly under some delusion that you will be his bride."

"A delusion I intend to rectify with due haste."

She nodded. "Then I will pretend I saw nothing. Especially if his encroaching mother arrives trying to say otherwise."

"You are our jewel amongst jewels, my lady. Do you wish to return to the house?"

"No. Thomas will retrieve me in a little while. I need some more fresh air after that unpleasant scene."

She could not agree more. Patience curtsied and turned about to find Major Stuart and make clear what she was and was not willing to do in the name of help. However, she paused, thinking it might be better to vent some steam before speaking with him.

Diverting to the east lawn where the games and targets were, she promptly positioned herself to throw her knife. A few good throws should relieve her of some of the angst that was built up inside.

She took the knife from its sheath, then grabbed the hilt, honing in on the target. Pull back, release. Thud. Dead centre. "That one was for Rupert."

After marching to the target to pull out the blade with satisfaction, she returned right back to her starting position. Position, pull back, release. Thud. "That one was for Stuart."

"Imagining my face as the target, I see?" he asked lazily as he leaned against a marble balustrade behind her.

"Notice I hit your face dead centre," she retorted without missing a beat, even though her heart was racing at his surprising her. Some fine guard dog Xander was, who was now licking Stuart's hands.

"I heard Rupert was a bit overly effusive in his admiration today."

Patience marched right up to Major Stuart and stood toe to toe with him. "And where were you? Promising someone else to protect them and failing?"

"I deserved that, I suppose. I never imagined you would leave the drawing room or walk on the grounds alone. Without a chaperone." *What were you thinking?* He refrained from saying that but implied it.

"So it is my fault. I see. There was no one available, but your grandmother saved me."

"Saved you?" He straightened up from his lazy stance. "Did he try to harm you?"

She made a huffing noise. "It depends on what you refer to as harm. My nerves will certainly suffer at every remembrance of his wet, slimy lips pressed against mine."

"He kissed you?"

"If you could call what he did such a thing." She shuddered with disgust and wiped at her mouth.

He cursed under his breath.

IT WAS a good thing Rupert had left, because Ashley would have murdered him for daring to accost Miss Whitford in such a manner. He'd wanted to take her in his arms and comfort her, but he'd not been prepared for the reaction. He would've erased that disgusting memory and replaced it with a much better one, if he did say so himself.

As they walked back to the house, there was laughter, and they both stopped to look for the source.

Patience inclined her head to the left and he followed around the hedge. They came upon the open lawn, where Grace, Joy, Lord Montford, and Mr. and Miss Cunningham were playing pall mall with one of his aunts.

"Would you two care to join us? We've only just begun and can start over," Aunt Rosemary offered graciously.

"Unfortunately, duty calls," Ashley answered.

Patience also waved away the offer with a mutter. "I have a desperate need to wash my mouth with soap."

Xander took off after one of the balls, and Mr. Cunningham scooped him up with much laughter. "I can hardly blame him when we played fetch with one of these at home."

"I will return him to the house so you may carry on with your game." Patience made to go for the pup.

"Oh, can he please stay with us for a while? I've scarcely seen him with all the attention to Freddy and her kittens." Joy was now scratching behind his ears.

"Of course," Patience said, though Ashley detected some hesitance in her voice.

They walked in silence. He sensed she was more bothered than she let on. "Forgive me for leaving you to Rupert alone. Do I need to call him out?"

She seemed to relax a fraction. "No, of course not. I want to help, truly, but I would be appreciative if he did not touch my person nor continue under the disillusion that we are betrothed."

"He said that?"

She nodded in the affirmative. "Hopefully, your grandmother disabused him of that notion. She blistered his ears when she came upon him trying to kiss me in the garden."

"I would imagine so," he agreed, unaccountably angry that Rupert had kissed her.

"Is there no other way?" she pleaded.

"Certainly he shall never be alone with you again. I will think upon other avenues to try to draw him out."

"Has nothing else developed?" she asked eagerly.

His initial impulse was to deny her. What place did a lady have in an investigation? But then he checked himself. He knew the Foreign Office did employ some ladies in that regard, and they were quite skilled. "I am not certain what there is to tell that you do not already know." He turned to look down at her and raised a knowing brow.

"Most of it was being in the right place at the right time." She did not try to defend herself.

"We do not think there is anything more to glean from Devil. It did look as though Rupert recognized him, but Devil swears he never saw the man's face, and that Rupert's voice is too high to be his contact."

"You cannot truly believe that idiot orchestrated anything but the arrangement of his neckcloth!"

"No. I agree with you, but we have no other leads besides his scheme. Renforth is looking into possible connections. Sir Layton's son might be the only link we have between who had the information about the munitions being on that ship and Greenwich."

"That still seems a stretch."

"It is. I am hoping Renforth's sources have sent word. I am heading now to check."

"I will not attempt to insert myself, Major, but as I now have a vested interest in avoiding Rupert if possible, would you please inform me what my next orders are to be?"

Ashley could not help but smile. Most ladies would have had a fit of the vapours at what she'd endured only minutes ago, but she was not ready to quit.

"I assure you, I will let you know." They parted ways once inside the house, and he took to the study to look for his colleagues.

Renforth and Westwood were present.

His commander removed his reading glasses and looked up from the papers he was perusing.

"Any news, sir?"

"Perhaps." His face did not look convincing. "I've received a report from my contact, but there is nothing here that would incriminate Layton's son or Mr. Fagge of anything more than sewing their wild oats. Women, drink, gambling—those could be attributed to more than half the gentlemen in London."

"But have they been associated doing those things together?"

"Surprisingly, yes. It seems Mr. Fagge does occasionally slip out from under his mama's overbearing thumb."

Westwood snorted.

"And Layton?"

Renforth shook his head. "While we have not been able to obtain records of his finances, he does play very deep."

Ashley paced as he thought. "It seems too coincidental for there not to be a connection. Layton is one of the few with access to the information, Layton's son and Rupert are friends, at least one of them has recently come into funds, and Layton's son must lose a great deal of money on the tables if he plays deep."

"I agree. We must keep looking. Manners sent word to his father about arranging the trap, but it would be much better if we knew who we were trapping ahead of time."

"Most assuredly."

Manners entered the room and held up a letter. "I've just heard from my father."

"There's another East India vessel already scheduled. It's the perfect set up, exactly like last time. Only the same people will know about it, excepting us, of course, and this shipment will not really be ammunition and arms, except for lining the top of the crate."

"If they are on to us, they might not take the bait," Ashley pointed out.

"Maybe not, but it is worth a try."

"In my experience, once people taste a little success, they become greedy," Westwood added.

"I am afraid whomever it is will simply hide behind Devil's gang—and potentially Rupert. How can we draw him out?" Renforth asked.

"If they know we've got Devil, they will have to get a message to the others. Therein lies the potential to hook the big game," Manners added.

"Let's hope your father makes the shipment sound too enticing to pass up." Renforth tapped his glasses against his temple. I'm keeping men watching Layton. Hopefully, they will discover something—if we are on the right track before it's too late."

"We have one week from tonight," Manners added.

"Devil needs to be moved." Ashley had almost forgotten that small detail.

Renforth scowled at him. "Whyever for?"

"When Rupert questioned me on why we were keeping him here, I had to reassure him. There was no good reason I could give other than to say he was leaving immediately. That we'd had some delays in transporting him."

Renforth looked at the ceiling, exasperated.

"We can make a show of him leaving, then sneak him back in."

"I suppose so. We still need to keep watch to see if someone else tries to signal. They must know we have been doing it, but they will need to message them somehow. As far as the others know, Devil is still operating as usual. If we arouse their suspicion, the whole operation is in jeopardy."

"If someone signals twice, we will know they received the message."

"Assuming they know Devil's system."

"There is always the risk they will abandon this gang altogether and use another."

"True, but the notice is short and the more people involved, the greater the risk."

"I haven't any better ideas and we have to try something."

"Well, the bait should be out there by now. Chum and I will keep an eye on the gang. Please just send word on what the plan is. I'll be off." Manners turned and left.

"Should some of us return to London to help there?" Ashley asked.

"If this fails, then that would be the next option. As we are almost certain Taywards is only being used for its vantage point. And possibly for storage or transfer."

"What about also making a show of the others leaving, so that the mastermind lets down his guard? Lady Westwood's time is almost upon us, and I'd like this resolved so she can give birth in peace."

"Then let us prepare to put on a show."

CHAPTER 13

*P*atience waited for news, but what news came was not what she expected.

"Patience!" Joy rushed into the room. "Come, it's time!"

"The baby?"

"Yes!" Then she turned and ran back up the stairs, but stopped at the landing and turned around as though she had just remembered her original purpose in coming down in the first place. "Can you tell Westwood?"

"Of course." Patience shook her head. It was clear that Joy expected Patience to take care of everything. First, she found the butler. "Armstrong, please send for Dr. Harvey. Lady Westwood's labour pains have begun. And please ensure we are not at home to any visitors the rest of the day—no matter how insistent they are." At least she could have a brief reprieve from any Fagges the rest of the day.

"Very good, Miss Whitford."

Then she knocked on the door to the study, where Westwood had been for some time discussing matters with the soldiers.

Major Stuart opened the door.

"Forgive the intrusion."

He raised a brow at those words.

"But it appears Faith has begun her labour pains. I have already sent for the doctor."

Instantly, her ever-calm brother-in-law looked frantic. Without a word, he took off in search of his wife.

Patience fully expected the doctor would come and pronounce that it would be days before the babe was delivered, but it was always best to at least hear that reassurance, and make certain there were no complications.

Next, she found the housekeeper and asked Mrs. Armstrong to send up the necessary supplies.

Frankly, Patience was relieved to have something to divert her worries over Rupert. If he was already becoming so amorous without a betrothal, what would he try next?

Patience climbed the stairs to check on her sister, and she could hear the moans of pain before she reached her door.

Knocking lightly, she let herself in. Faith was walking around, holding her back. Grace, Joy, and Vivienne all sat there trying to distract Faith, while Westwood was hovering.

Patience looked on with dismay. If it were her, she would want her privacy, but perhaps Faith did not wish to be alone.

Her sister saw her then half-smiled, half-grimaced as a contraction overtook her, causing her to lean over the back of a chair, gripping it with white knuckles. She beckoned Patience over as soon as the pain subsided.

"Would you like me to make everyone to leave?" Patience asked.

Faith shook her head. "No. It helps distract me. I fear this may go on forever. Would you mind sending off a letter to Hope?"

"Of course not."

"Thank you. I am certain I will need you more later."

"Is there anything I can send up for your comfort? I've asked Mrs. Armstrong to bring towels and boiling water."

"I cannot think of a thing at this moment, but there are many here I can send if I need something. Westwood might need some distraction, however," she whispered.

Patience kissed Faith on the forehead before leaving, somewhat grateful to be sent away for now. Perhaps she was lacking something maternal, and she would, of course, be there for Faith when needed, but spending the entire time in there would drive her mad.

What did it say about her that she'd rather be solving the mystery surrounding the missing arms? Birth was messy and painful and she did not mind delaying the reality of it as long as possible.

She went to the ladies' sitting room and penned a missive to their sister, Hope, who had been the first of the sisters to have a child. Patience had little doubt Hope would come as quickly as possible, for they had delayed their trip to the Continent with the Duke until Faith gave birth.

There was a knock and she looked up to see Major Stuart with his head around the door. "May I come in?"

"Yes, of course."

"How is Faith doing?"

"Holding up as well as can be expected. There is a long way to go yet. I was given a reprieve for now." She indicated the letter. "Your brother, on the other hand, might need a sedative before long."

Stuart laughed. "I will look after him when Faith sends him away, which she most assuredly will."

Patience folded up her letter and sealed it. She'd have a footman take this to Rotham instead of sending it by post.

"May I help you with that?" he asked.

"I was just going to take it to Armstrong. Was there any news about the situation?"

"Very little, I'm afraid. We are to pretend that we are removing Devil, hoping that will give our man a false sense of security. Manners was able to have his father arrange another shipment within the next week. We are hoping to narrow down who is either profiting from the information or who is leaking it to someone else—even if unwittingly."

"Will you continue to signal?"

"Yes, as well as have the rest of the gang followed."

"But won't the man have to send his own signal if he needs to indicate there is a shipment to take?"

"Indeed, and that is how we hope to catch him. If they are aware we are flashing one signal each night, they might position themselves to send the extra flash or two."

"Clever. You think they will be bold enough to come onto the estate?"

"When they see all of us supposedly leaving today, I think they will."

"So you will hide, then? It could work."

"It could also be a dead end. They may have decided to contact the gang another way and abandon this altogether, but Manners and Cholmely are following them."

"I assume the shipment will also be followed from London."

"Indeed. Along with the one we suspect to be the culprit."

She pondered. "There's little else you can do if Devil does not give you any further information."

"In some aspects, I think he has told us all he knows, but then I think perhaps I have not asked the right questions. He is more willing to speak with us than at first, on account of wanting to protect his son, Billy. Once we threatened Billy and offered transportation, he has been more compliant."

"And Cook's food?" She had heard of the requests to bribe the prisoner with delicacies.

"Treacle sponge."

"I would sell my soul for some of that if I was starving," she agreed while standing to take the letter to the butler.

It was rare to have this moment of camaraderie with him. Was it due to guilt over Rupert? Whatever the reason, it felt wonderful to be included—to feel that her opinions mattered. When he behaved that way, it was hard to remember why he annoyed her so much. It was not a deterrent for her childish infatuation in the least.

A loud groan of pain echoed through the house and they exchanged mutual grimaces.

"I have a feeling it is going to be a very long day and night for Faith. Why do I think it will be harder on Dominic, somehow?"

"At least he will think it was harder on him. Men!" Patience muttered with exasperation.

"I am off to arrange for Devil's transportation. I will be back to see to Dominic later."

They walked together to the marbled entrance hall where they found Armstrong. Major Stuart was leaving just as a trap pulled up the front drive with Dr. Harvey inside.

Patience waited until he approached the door. "Good afternoon, Doctor. I will take you to my sister."

"How is her ladyship faring?" he asked as they ascended the stairs.

"The contractions seem to be causing her discomfort, but she is very resilient."

They reached the door and she knocked lightly again, then opened it as she could hear the chatter from those in the room.

Westwood exhaled with visible relief at the sight of the doctor, while her sisters and Vivienne stood to leave so Faith could be examined.

If Dr. Harvey thought it was strange that there seemed to be calling hours in Lady Westwood's chambers, he did not mention it.

As she closed the door behind them, she heard the doctor ask, "How far apart have your pains been, my lady?"

"Why don't we send for tea?" Patience suggested, steering the ladies towards the drawing room where she knew the dowagers and the aunts would be.

The tea tray had already been delivered, and Mr. Cunningham and Lord Montford were sitting there entertaining the ladies. Xander jumped up and came to greet Patience.

"There you are!" She kneeled to pet him while his whole body shook with excitement as though he'd not seen her in weeks.

"I apologize, Miss Whitford. I did not mean to monopolize him, but I did not find you when we returned to the house."

She waved his apology away.

"How is dear Faith?" Aunt Flora asked.

"The doctor is with her now."

"Her pains sound too close together for just beginning labour," the Dowager remarked.

"Oh, she did not just begin," Joy informed them. "Faith said the pains started last evening before bed."

All heads swung towards Joy. "I beg your pardon? The younger of the two Dowager Lady Westwood's asked. "Perhaps I should go and attend her now." She hurriedly rose and left the room.

"It seems we might have a baby soon, after all," the elder dowager remarked.

"Dash it all, I'll lose the wager," Aunt Rosemary bemoaned.

Patience supposed she should go and assist as well.

ASHLEY COULD NOT SAY why he had sought Patience out. It was one of the first conversations they'd had where they seemed to be in harmony. One of the things he liked most about her was her unpredictability. While she exasperated him at every chance, she also intrigued him more than was healthy. It was impossible to stop thinking about her.

Ashley was glad to escape the house. He wanted to be as far away from childbirth as possible. If he were being honest, he would be as bad as Westwood or worse if it was his wife going through those pains and he could do nothing to help. Worse, being the cause of it. So many women and babies did not survive, and he knew his brother must be suffering from crippling fear that he might lose his beloved.

Ashley found the others in the stables, preparing their show. He would look in upon Dominic later.

It had been agreed upon ahead of time that Ashley would remain since it was his brother's house and Lady Westwood was giving birth. It would be more unusual were he to leave at a time like this.

A plain, hired conveyance was waiting near the stables, and all of the men had gathered in the yard. Renforth pulled them aside.

A few of them would ride along surrounding the carriage for

protection as they would a normal prisoner. Westwood had some horses to be taken to London to their new homes.

He would ride with them as far as the village. The carriage would go all of the way to London's Newgate Prison, just in case they were followed. It was an elaborate ruse, but they could not be too careful.

"There is a chance there could be trouble, so be prepared. Remember that everything you do, treat it as though you're being watched. Any servant, anyone in the woods, do not trust that your actions or words are not being shared elsewhere." Renforth prepared them as he used to do before battle.

Those things were deeply ingrained in Ashley and in all of them, but it was a good reminder to tell Patience. He'd shared details of their operation with her for some unknown reason, and she did not have the training that he and the others did.

He knew why he'd involved her—he wanted to share with her—be with her—even though it was putting her in danger.

"Should I follow all the way to London?" Ashley asked, riding his own horse.

"So long as you are back in place to signal tonight," Renforth replied.

Ashley inclined his head and they all mounted up and followed the carriage.

When they turned down the drive, two riders were approaching. It did not take long for Ashley to recognize the round, pudgy form of Rupert, along with Sir Horace. He cursed under his breath. "What the devil is he doing back here?" He looked to Fielding, who shook his head. "I need to head them off. I will catch up to you."

Ashley pulled up and spoke with a civility he was far from feeling. "Good afternoon. What brings you back to Taywards today?"

"I thought to assist you with the prisoner," Rupert answered.

Sir Horace snorted.

"Good of you, but as you can see, we soldiers have it well in hand."

Rupert could hardly argue with that, but his face evidenced visible disappointment. The carriage was surrounded by armed men. He appeared to be looking inside, not too subtly. Ashley wanted him to be the culprit, but for one, it was too obvious, and for two, he had not the wits to be secretive.

"I am glad to see you heeded my advice about removing him."

Ashley continued, hoping to divert the visitors from the house. "And not a moment too soon. Lady Westwood is with the doctor right now."

"Lady Fagge is just following us to pay a call on them." Indeed, a carriage was waiting for the prisoner convoy to leave the drive so it could enter.

"Perhaps you can head them off and inform them that now would not be the best time for a visit." Ashley did not bother with niceties. He feared they would be lost on them.

Sir Horace's face indicated he would rather not inform his wife of anything of the sort. "I suppose not," he conceded, as he began turning his horse.

They pulled to the end of the drive where Lady Fagge and her three daughters were stopped. Sir Horace hailed the driver. "Lady Westwood is indisposed and it is therefore not a good time to visit. We will be home later."

Thankfully, Ashley could not hear what Lady Fagge said. He tipped his hat to the carriage in case they were looking, but dared not get close enough to engage in conversation.

"I bid you a good day," he said, hoping to escape.

"Wait! We are going to follow," Rupert called.

Ashley gritted his teeth, but he could hardly deny them. "Have you a fancy to see Newgate?" he teased, but wondered what he was up to. "I must catch up to the others." If Sir Horace and Rupert wished to follow, they could do as they will. He had not the rank nor authority to gainsay them, but his commander did.

He caught up with the others just past the village. He could not gallop through it, so the Fagge men kept pace with him. What a devilish awkward situation this was and the look of irritation on Renforth's face when he saw his companions should have been a warning. Neither Fagge had any jurisdiction over the situation and they could certainly risk everything.

Renforth pulled up. "May I ask your destination?" he asked Sir Horace.

"We thought to follow along for extra security," Rupert answered pompously.

"While I appreciate the thought, I must ask that you either turn back or proceed ahead of our convoy. I cannot be liable for your safety nor jeopardize the prisoner."

Sir Horace looked taken back. Rupert sputtered.

Just then, four masked men shot out of the woods straight towards the carriage. Someone must have given them away!

"We are all armed and will shoot!" Renforth warned as all guns were raised, cocked, and aimed.

Ashley did not see any peaceful way out of this, but he knew his commander would not shoot first.

"Let 'em go, and we will leave in peace."

Ashley recognized the voice from the night at the pub. It was Devil's gang. Even with Chum and Manners following them, they would not have been able to prevent this or even send warning in time had they not left to participate in this ruse.

"I am afraid I cannot do that," Renforth said. "He will have a fair trial."

"Bollocks!" the man spat loudly. "I'm afraid you leave me no choice." The eldest man cocked his pistol and took aim at Baines, who was guarding the door of the carriage. Fielding shot the gun out of his hand, then they all dove for cover as was their training. But who shot whom during what became a blur as the following eruption was akin to the heat of battle? Pistols discharged in a staccato of sound, the acrid smell of gunpowder as foul as the smoke that clouded the air.

When shots were expended, the gang fled back into the woods, no longer able to claim any advantage with empty barrels.

"Are they gone?" Ashley called.

"For now," Renforth answered. Everyone began to emerge from their places to take stock of the damage.

Baines stood and wiped the dirt from his front where he'd taken cover on the ground. It was a miracle the horses hadn't bolted in the melee.

Chum and Manners had taken off after the gang, which was a good sign that they were unharmed.

Fielding and Renforth were checking the prisoner and inside the carriage, so Ashley turned to see Sir Horace standing over Rupert's prone form. He had fallen from his horse, and a large pool of blood covered his back.

Ashley slid off his horse and felt for Rupert's pulse, but his lifeless eyes staring back at him told the story. Rupert had been shot dead. But how and by whom?

Rupert had been beside him the whole time. Had he turned around? Ashley could not think that he had. The others came over to see once they were certain the prisoner and driver were unharmed.

"Sir Horace, I am terribly sorry. Did you see what happened?"

Sir Horace stood there, immobile.

Renforth shook his head. They would get nothing useful from him for now.

"I would send for the magistrate, but he is currently attending his wife in childbed."

Sir Horace continued to stand over the body in disbelief, as if too numb to cry and shocked into inaction. A farmer in a cart was passing by and stopped to help. Another horse and rider rode towards them, looking frantic. It was Greening.

"I heard the gunfire. What has happened?"

Ashley was surprised the entire village was not yet upon them after the gun battle that had just happened.

Renforth pulled Ashley aside. "Are you able to manage this? I think we should proceed with our original plan before the gang has time to regroup. I think at least one of them was winged."

"I will see to having Rupert removed to the icehouse. Taywards is the only one hereabouts. Westwood will unfortunately have to make a decision about the inquest. He may call someone else in if necessary." Thankfully, they were close enough to the village that he could get help quickly there if this farmer would oblige, and Greening would see to Sir Horace.

"We should return just after dark as planned."

"I will be there." Ashley turned to take charge of the mess.

CHAPTER 14

*B*y the time Patience and the Dowager made it to Faith's side, the doctor was already preparing Faith to push, and her maid and the housekeeper were assisting. A nervous Westwood was rubbing Faith's back and wiping her brow. There was little for either of them to do, but Faith reached out a hand to Patience, so she held it while her sister displayed amazing strength. If her hand suffered permanent damage, well, Patience would not complain.

She marvelled at the process of childbirth, but she did not necessarily wish to go through it herself anytime soon.

"Most fathers wish to wait downstairs for the remainder, my lord," Dr. Harvey said, though Patience thought it was for Westwood's benefit more than any other reason. He was looking decidedly green, but Faith clung to him like a lifeline, so he shook his head and remained.

The pains Faith endured seemed as though she would not survive them, but then they would stop just in time. Then the doctor commanded her to push, and with just a few difficult pushes, a baby was wailing. Patience had never seen anything like it. She knew Faith was not out of danger, but the baby seemed healthy.

"Congratulations, my lord, my lady, you have a son with a strapping set of lungs," Dr. Harvey announced.

The look Faith and Dominic shared with each other as they put their heads together with exhaustion and relief made Patience feel like the worst sort of intruder. It also made her long for what they had and made her more determined not to settle for less. There were much worse fates than being a spinster aunt to a beautiful baby boy. Even though he wasn't so beautiful at the moment, she revised as the doctor unveiled the red, wrinkly mess to his doting parents.

He handed the baby off to the maid, who took the child away to clean him. Patience decided she was no longer needed and escaped with mixed emotions about the miracle she had just witnessed. "I will just go and let the others know," she said in case anyone was paying attention.

Maybe one day that would be for her, but she was not in a hurry. She still wanted adventure and could not help but wonder how Stuart and the soldiers were doing with their ruse. It would still be several hours before they would return beneath the cover of darkness.

Patience returned to the drawing room to ease everyone's suspense. Perhaps they'd heard the baby's cries, but she could at least reassure them that mother and baby were well.

Two lively games of whist were underway, but all heads turned to look at her expectantly. "It's a boy. He looks to be healthy with excellent lungs. I am sure Westwood will bring him down shortly."

The Dowager smiled with proud satisfaction.

"At least I won this wager," Aunt Rosemary breathed.

"Faith is always telling me I shouldn't wager," Joy remarked.

"Yes, yes, that is true for young ladies. As I am old and have nothing better to do, and no one cares, Flora and I have to have our fun where we can."

Joy seemed to accept and appreciate the notion, though Patience would not put it past her to join in with the aunts.

"Have Armstrong bring champagne," the Dowager commanded.

"Oh, I love a reason for an afternoon tipple."

Joy giggled at that remark. Patience glanced at Aunt Rosemary in disbelief.

Xander rose from his nap and stretched, then began to nip at her heels to go out. Patience realized she could also do with a bit of fresh air as she was feeling decidedly out of sorts for some reason. "Would you like to go outside?"

The pup leaned back as if ready to pounce and wagged his tail. "Very good, let's go, then."

She heard the others begin to resume their game as she led Xander from the room.

They walked through the park near the house, but Patience desperately wanted to go further. Was there still danger with the prisoner being gone? She did not relish the company of having a footman following her.

Perhaps she would stay within shouting distance, but decided it was all right to venture a little further than the immediate gardens and park. It seemed eerily quiet, knowing the men had gone.

There was little to do to dispel the unsettling feelings within her besides exercise and being in nature. A long, hard ride would have been preferable, but also not practical with Faith's having just given birth, and the danger lying in wait like a spider that you knew was in the room but cannot find to kill.

Was it because of the danger surrounding the prisoner and the missing arms? Or was it from having just witnessed the miracle of life?

Perhaps it was time to go to London and see to her future. If no one else wished to go, she could always go stay with Hope for a spell. It was unlikely this feeling would go away easily, and she was inclined to take control of her life instead of letting life happen to her.

She stopped on the bridge and watched the water rush beneath her feet. She had not meant to walk this far, but was not surprised that her feet had led her there during her wanderings. It was the place she'd always thought best. However, the day was growing late with the sun low in the western sky, so she turned to walk back to the house. Hopefully, the men would make it back without issue.

Her boots crunched on the pebbled path as Xander began to bark and ran on ahead. Patience picked up her pace to see what had excited him—probably Peter, his favourite stable hand.

Except it wasn't Peter. She screamed and stared in shock.

"Patience, it's not my blood!" Major Stuart exclaimed.

ASHLEY HAD NOT CONSIDERED his appearance, but as he looked down, he could see why Patience had reacted as she did. Rupert's blood was all over him from having moved the body to the cart and then just now to the icehouse.

Ashley was in desperate need of a bath and to inform Westwood as magistrate, but he would need to console Patience a little.

"What has happened?" She continued to look him over as though she did not believe he was unharmed. It was rather touching.

"We were set upon by Devil's gang just on the other side of the village."

Patience gasped in response. "They were tipped off. And they began shooting?"

"Yes. When we refused to let the prisoner go."

"Who was harmed if that is not your blood?"

"I suspect some of them were winged, as most of us rarely miss our targets, but this blood is from Rupert."

"Rupert?"

"He died instantly." He was not surprised at her disbelief. Ashley was there and could scarcely believe it himself.

"What was he doing there?"

That was certainly not the reaction he anticipated, but that was one of the things he appreciated most about her.

"As we were leaving the estate, Sir Horace and Rupert came upon us. They pronounced they were coming to assist us with the prisoner."

"Why would they do that? There were six of you." She furrowed her brow, leaving a crease there that he longed to smooth away, but he did not touch her with his soiled hands.

"An excellent question and one that is bothering me most about this entire situation. They were quite insistent upon following me, and when Renforth told them they needed to leave—that he could not be responsible for them—that was when the gang set upon us. It seemed too premeditated, if that makes sense."

"You think Rupert was set up?"

"I think he was deliberately shot, so possibly, yes."

He could see her considering the possibility.

"If the point of the ambush was to dispose of Rupert, then we were correct in our suppositions that he was only the middleman."

"And had outlived his usefulness?" he supplied. "Also, it must mean they have other plans for the future or they do not yet know of the trap," he said quietly, mindful of listening ears.

"How do you figure that?" she asked.

"If he knew of another shipment, would he have risked his gang?"

It was likely Rupert was the one who had given away their movements that day and had been directed to follow along. When Sir Horace came out of his stupor, he would have to be questioned closely to see if Rupert had revealed anything. He still had not spoken in his state of shock.

If he knew nothing of the scheme or who Rupert was working with, then Rupert's rooms would have to be searched both here and in London. It should be done anyway, and the sooner the better. Much though he hated to disturb Westwood, it was necessary. Speaking of Westwood...

"How is Faith's labour progressing?" he asked. It would have been the first question from his mouth had Patience not needed reassuring, though she was out on a walk, so things could not be too dire.

"Oh! She's already given birth."

"So soon?" Even he knew that first births tended to be a lengthy process.

"Indeed. Apparently, she had been having pains the entire night and had not told anyone. How very like Faith not to wish to bother people and bear the burden alone."

"I assume the babe is healthy?"

"All is well. The boy and Faith were well when I stepped out."

"Did you say a boy?"

"I did. He had no name yet when I left them."

"Thank the heavens." The last thing he ever wanted to be was the heir.

"Forgive me, but I must bathe and then speak to my brother about this matter. There is little time to waste."

She nodded her agreement and then fell in beside him as they walked to the house.

"Have the plans changed for this evening?" she asked.

"I cannot say what might have happened in London, but I've heard no word otherwise from Renforth."

They parted at the staircase and Ashley immediately rang for a bath. It would not be the luxurious soaking he desired, but a quick clean and change.

Soon after, he found his brother who was sitting in a rocking chair, doting upon the new baby with Faith sleeping nearby. He crept quietly over to greet his nephew.

"Congratulations, Brother. I cannot yet claim he is the most handsome lad I've ever seen, but I'm certain he soon will be."

"Would you like to hold him?"

"That will have to wait until later. Much though I hate to disturb you, there is an urgent matter that must be dealt with."

Westwood raised his brows, but rose with his son in his arms and placed him in the bassinet near the bed by his mother.

They exited the room quietly and went down the stairs to the study.

"You are not even supposed to be here, so I suppose I should have realized something was amiss sooner." He slid into his favourite worn leather chair.

"I think your mind has been rightly somewhere else this day."

"Indeed. And my relief that Faith and Benjamin are healthy has consumed my thoughts."

"You named him after Father." Ashley smiled as he went to the side table and poured them both a healthy measure of brandy. He handed Dominic a glass and then toasted. "To Faith and Benjamin."

Dominic raised his glass and then drank. "Now, tell me what the urgent matter is."

Ashley repeated much the story he had told Patience. "We were set upon just on the other side of the village by Devil's gang. Gunfire erupted when Renforth refused to release Devil. Fielding shot the gun out of the leader's hand as he cocked and began to pull the trigger. That's when all hell broke loose."

He took a drink.

"When all of the chambers were emptied, and the smoke had cleared, the gang fled quickly, but then we discovered Rupert was dead."

Westwood looked up sharply. "Why was Rupert there?"

"He and Sir Horace found us on our way down the drive and refused to leave. Renforth had just warned them off when the gang came out of the woods, masked, on horseback, like highwaymen."

"And how is Sir Horace?"

"Shocked to the bone. He did not speak a word. Farmer Jones happened by with his cart and helped me bring the body back to the icehouse. Greening took Fagge home."

His brother ran an exhausted hand over his face. "That was certainly an unexpected turn of events. Do you believe it was one of the gang's stray bullets that hit him?"

"Actually, no. Whoever shot him did it on purpose."

"How can you be certain?"

"Because Rupert was beside me and he was shot in the back. He was silenced."

"It appears so." Dominic leaned his head back against his chair. "This is certainly not what I wish to be doing right now. Would you write the report with all of the details exactly as you remember them, including a sketch of where everyone was at the time?"

"Certainly."

"Dr. Harvey said he would stop by this evening to check on Faith and the baby, so I will ask him to take a look at the body when he arrives. It would have been much better had Rupert been caught in the crossfire."

"I imagine whoever shot him believes that will be the assumption. In fact, it might be better to play on that instead of announcing our suspicions."

"Do you think it will make them more careless?"

"We can only hope, but if we declare a verdict of murder, then they will know we are seeking them."

"There are no guarantees with the inquest," Westwood warned. "I can delay a little, but this needs to be resolved quickly."

"Understood. We best pray our trap works. It just became much more serious. The leader was willing to murder to keep his identity hidden. And at least we know that it's someone who associated with Rupert."

"That only leaves us two suspects then. I am very grateful for Rupert's lack of acquaintance. See to having them followed if Renforth has not already done so. This needs to end before anyone else is killed. Let me know if the men make it back safely tonight and if there are any further developments." Westwood drained his glass and stood.

"Yes, Brother."

"Now, I think I'll go hold my son some more."

Ashley shook his head. If you had told him a year ago his brother would be like this, he never would have believed it.

Now, he needed to prepare for the return of his troop. He had not really discussed with Westwood where to put Devil next, but he had an idea.

CHAPTER 15

*I*t occurred to Patience, after she calmed down from the sight of Ashley covered in blood, that he might need help that night. Westwood was preoccupied with Faith and the baby, and now that Rupert had been killed, the threat was considerably higher.

Someone needed to be there to help him. What if someone had given away the plan and they were ambushed tonight just as they had been that morning? She could not prevent that, but she could at least be on the lookout. He would not want her help, of course. She also considered that Mr. Cunningham and Lord Montford could be of service and she hoped he would see reason.

Everyone was gathered in the drawing room to go in to dinner, and Major Stuart was there, but he was dressed informally in unrelieved black. He must be preparing to leave, she assumed.

He acknowledged her with a nod and she went directly to speak with him. "Are you to go out to meet them alone, then?"

"I am. Does this surprise you?" His brows drew together.

"I think after this morning's events, that perhaps proceeding with more help might be wise."

"After this morning, I think the more covert is the best way forward."

She shook her head. "You should have more eyes, more cover."

His brows straightened, then rose. "Are you suggesting yourself?"

"Assuming you would object, I would suggest Cunningham and Montford. But I can be quiet when called for and can wield a knife with deadly accuracy."

"In the dark?"

"I've never attempted throwing in the dark as you well know."

"Your suggestion is not without merit." His tone surprised her.

"Why, thank you."

"However, it would be putting yourself and others at risk when it is not their duty. As this morning was a prime example."

"This morning, Sir Horace and Rupert were acting of their own accord against your wishes. Anything we did would be at your direction only—and only to serve as a lookout or as back up only in the most extreme necessity." Patience could see that he was considering, which gave her hope.

"I am trying to think how best to employ all of you for the best advantage. First, I should speak with Cunningham and Montford to see if they are willing." He called to both of the gentlemen, beckoning them over to his side.

"Gentlemen, you may have heard about this morning's unfortunate events."

"Horrific!" Mr. Cunningham acknowledged.

"As Westwood is indisposed, I wondered if I might prevail upon you two to assist me this evening. Mainly to serve as lookouts for trouble should our plans for the return of our troop have been compromised as this morning's was. I do not believe there is any threat, but it is best to be prepared."

"Yes, of course. What do you need from us?" Montford asked.

"Let us dine quickly, and then we must be gone to be in position well before dark."

Patience thrummed with excitement, knowing a typical lady would be offended by her eagerness to participate in such a thing. She was hardly able to eat any of her food, then rushed upstairs to change into dark clothing, including the pair of breeches she'd used before.

There was too much at stake to be risking her safety with propriety when no one would see her in the dark anyway. When she met with the others in the study for their departure, the men were checking their pistols and loading them.

Over dinner, they had planned their positioning, steering clear of the lookout tree in the clearing in case someone else was making use of it. Patience did not think the person would be so bold, but one could never be too careful.

"Remember your signals?" Ashley asked.

"Mine is a bird call," Freddy answered.

"Mine is a whistle," Montford replied.

"Mine is a loud cough," Patience answered, wishing she had somehow garnered a talent for more exotic noises as a child, but it could not be helped.

"All right. We exit from different doorways from the house so we are not all seen leaving together. I will not leave my post until it is dark. Remember, your safety is foremost. Do not risk yourselves under any circumstances." He looked directly at her as he said it.

Patience stuffed her hair up under a cap, then left and strolled to the stables. Major Stuart thought it best for her to leave from there because she looked more like a young groom than the rest of them. She wandered down the path and over the bridge then diverted towards her spot behind a tree, just shy of the dock.

It was still probably an hour until full darkness. Hopefully, there was to be a little bit of moon, because it would be scary being there alone, even though she knew the others to be nearby.

As she stood there alone, the enormity of the situation and what they were dealing with sunk in. It was hard to believe that Rupert was dead—murdered. Before, it had felt like a game of wits to be solved.

As darkness fell and shades of blue turned to dark purples, every sound intensified. Every leaf that rustled, every pine cone that fell, every chirp from a bird, and every chitter from an animal made her tighten her hand around the hilt of her knife.

Patience tried to think of pleasant things besides being there alone in the woods with a killer possibly lurking nearby, ready to slit her throat. So when a deep voice whispered into her ear, she jumped, barely swallowing the scream threatening to escape her lips. An unladylike curse might have been uttered.

"What are you doing sneaking up on me like that?" she scolded him, as much as anyone could trying to do so in a whisper. "You are fortunate there is not a knife in your chest."

"You were supposed to be looking out for me," he retorted.

"Once it was dark." That he was right didn't make her less annoyed at her deficiency because he was standing so close he was touching her. His nearness was scrambling her wits. His breath tickled her ear, and if she turned her head just a little, their lips would meet. He was doing it on purpose, but she would not let him distract her. Her gaze intensified on the water just beyond the dock. A few vessels had already passed, but none of them had slowed down or come near.

"Do you know what type of vessel they were to arrive in?" she asked, hoping she did not sound as breathless as she felt.

"I assume a river barge. Something big enough to look unobtrusive and something small enough to sneak into the dock quietly."

"Must you stand so close?"

"Oh, I think I must. Otherwise, how are we to talk?"

"The object was to be quiet and listen. It's difficult enough to hear over the water."

"As evidenced by my sneaking up on you."

"So good of you to remind me of my mistake."

He knew he was torturing her, and he was enjoying every moment of it. Perhaps two could play the game. She leaned back a little and nuzzled closer. His sharp intake of breath told her everything she needed to know. She smiled with satisfaction. He could hardly chastise her for giving him a dish of his own medicine.

"You are playing with fire, Patience," he breathed into her ear, sending a delicious shiver up her spine. Before she thought more about it, she turned her head slightly and their lips met.

If this was fire, then she was fully prepared to let it consume her, burn her. His lips felt nothing like Rupert's had, and she was very willing to replace that awful memory with this one.

He pulled away and she grasped his head and brought it back to her lips. She wasn't ready for this to end. She felt him smile against her lips, the oaf.

"Had a taste of me, and now you are ravenous?"

She harrumphed.

"Much as I'd like this to continue, there is a boat approaching." How had he been able to keep his wits about him?

Patience was grateful for the darkness, because her cheeks were burning with embarrassment. Some lookout she was.

As the boat pulled into the dock, the crew was anything but quiet.

"What the devil?" he muttered, and she felt him pull his gun from its holster and began moving towards the dock.

Patience took that to mean that this was not his men arriving. Remaining where she was, she put her hand on the hilt of her knife, just in case this was some sort of trick.

"Carew? Well met!" Mr. Cunningham's voice greeted rather loudly.

Stuart hissed his annoyance and muttered something she could not discern, though it was obvious he was displeased with the turn of events. Would it risk his men?

"This is not the normal welcoming party," Carew drawled. "Were you expecting someone else?"

"You could say that, but no matter. How can we help?"

"If someone could send for the grooms. They are used to helping me unload. I've only brought four this time."

Montford and Cunningham offered to go, while Patience remained where she was, unsure of what to do. Did Carew's arrival mean that the others could not land?

Stuart seemed to be discussing something with Carew quietly. Perhaps he was conveying the situation to him. The next thing she knew, he was back at her side.

"I will escort you back to the house. As you can see, there are plenty of people here."

"You stay and help. I can see my own way back. I saw myself here, after all."

"It was not yet dark." He wanted to argue more, but it was best if he remained.

"Will your men still be able to land?" she whispered.

"I believe they may be able to still come in well-hidden by the other boat. Carew's arrival is an excellent distraction."

Patience made her way back to the house, keeping her hand on the hilt of her knife. At least Grace would be happy by this unexpected arrival.

THE MEN HAD INDEED BEEN able to sneak in behind the arrival of Carew's boat and crew. They jumped in and helped with the horses and looked like they were part of the crew that had come from Ireland.

As they moved Devil to the gamekeeper's cottage, he cursed his own recklessness for having given in to temptation. He needed to apologize to Patience because nothing could ever come of it. She might think it was fun now, but would soon grow weary of it. Of him. But that would have to come later.

Once inside the cottage, Baines and Fielding looked around. It was not a large place with only a bedroom and a living space with a small kitchen, but it was a better choice than the dovecote.

"I thought you two could stay here with Devil." Who they had just sat down in the wooden chair. He angled his head to the table. "There is some dinner Cook made for you."

"We've certainly stayed in much less desirable places than this," Baines remarked as he headed towards the food.

He served some food on a plate and set it before Devil then untied his hands.

"Much obliged."

Baines inclined his head as though uncomfortable with thanks from a prisoner. It appeared they had garnered some grudging respect for each other throughout this ordeal.

Fielding also made himself a plate and they dug into Cook's delicious mash and chops.

"Did the rest of the trip go as planned?" Ashley asked as he took the jug of ale Cook had packed and filled up pewter tankards for each of them.

"Much better than the beginning," Fielding answered. "How were things here? It felt wrong to leave you to clean up the mess."

Ashley could not deny it had been less than ideal. "Needs must when the devil drives, as they say. If Farmer Jones had not happened by, it would have been much more difficult. With Sir Horace shocked into a statue, and Westwood indisposed with Faith giving birth, it was a strange day to be sure."

"Has the babe been born, then?"

He nodded in the affirmative. "She had already given birth by the time I returned with the body. A healthy baby boy. I am off the hook!"

"Hear, hear!" They raised their mugs and drank to Lady Westwood.

"One development that deepens the mystery is that Rupert was shot in the back."

Baines let out a low whistle. He and Fielding certainly understood how it complicated matters. "Westwood has agreed to delay the inquest as long as possible so we may try to root out who is behind this." Ashley turned towards Devil, who was unusually subdued and looked deep in thought. "Any thoughts on what the plan will be now that the gang knows you are a prisoner? I imagine they may not be waiting for signals from you."

"I've been wondering meself."

"Where will they go at night if not waiting for you?"

Devil squirmed restlessly in his seat, looking reluctant to answer.

"We will not harm Billy. You have our word," Baines promised.

"Did any of you 'appen to see 'im? Is 'e alright?"

Ashley shook his head. "Everything happened so quickly, but I only counted four men. I can ask our men for an accounting."

Devil nodded. "I've been thinking the whole day that maybe the toff would try to kill all of us. If he knows I'm captured, he won't want to risk using us again."

"But there are also risks involved in finding someone new and in a very short time," Ashley pointed out.

"True. Shorty and Smith work at the docks—that's how we got in the first time. But with the coin he offered, it's more than a year's wages for the company."

No one could keep his morals when it came down to them having a roof over his head and food in his belly. It was hard not to be sympathetic. Ashley knew what he was saying was true. A drive through one of the rookeries was enough testament to the fact that most of London lived in abject poverty.

"We can only hope his mightiness will decide to take the risk on your gang again, Devil. If there is anything at all that you recall about the man you were in contact with that might help us narrow down who he is, now is the time to tell us. If he killed Rupert off for knowing too much, then chances are he may try to execute your entire gang when he is through with you." He knew they'd questioned him a hundred times and for hours on end, but Ashley could not give up. They were desperate.

Devil closed his eyes and let out a slow breath through his nose.

"You said he spoke in a deep voice and he would not let you see his face."

"We always met in the shadows."

"Where did you meet?"

"Sometimes he would sneak up on me in the clearing—always behind me, mind you. He was very particular that I never turn around. Or at first, we would meet at a warehouse by the docks."

It was the same thing he had been saying all along.

"Is there anything else at all? Did he wear a scent?"

"Aye, but I couldn't name it. One of them fancy smells only Lunnoners wear. It was strong as though 'e was trying to mask the smell of tobacco on 'im."

"What about his hands? Did he ever pass anything to you?"

Devil squinted his eyes. Then Ashley saw a change pass over his face. "You remembered something."

"'E wore a ring. One of them what you call a signet. It 'ad a big dark stone in it. I could not tell the colour, but it looked black in the dark."

Ashley exchange glances with Fielding and Baines. Both gave little shakes of their heads. At least half, if not more, of the gentlemen in England wore signet rings. There was no immediate connection to anyone they could think of. But it was certainly a lead.

"Our time searching might be better spent in London," Fielding said.

"None of us belongs to that set. Perhaps Renforth knows which club Rupert frequented."

"I'm not certain much more will happen here anyway. At least until we spring the trap."

CHAPTER 16

*P*eter was walking Xander whilst Patience was drinking her cup of coffee alone the next morning. She was reliving the kiss she'd shared with Ashley when Armstrong announced Lord and Lady Rotham.

"Armstrong, if his lordship is awake, can you let him know that Lord and Lady Rotham have arrived?"

"I have already done so, miss." He bowed and left, no doubt to set the servants to work.

Patience barely had time to glance at the clock before Hope and Rotham walked in. She stood up to embrace her sister.

"Welcome. Did you travel all night?"

Rotham scoffed. "Might as well have."

"Where is Sylvester?"

"He was still asleep, so our nurse took him to the nursery. How is Faith?"

"Doing well when I looked in on her and Benjamin last night."

"I am so pleased it is a boy so he and Sylvester can be best of friends," Hope said with a fond, tired smile. Motherhood looked well on her.

"Is no one else about?" Rotham asked as they took seats at the table and the footmen began to bring in food.

"We had a rather late night. Carew arrived with some horses after dark." Patience did not want to be the one to mention that Stuart and the soldiers were here investigating a dangerous crime. She would let someone else broach that topic. Rothman tended to be a bit temperamental when it came to his wife and child's safety.

"So everyone is here then?" Hope asked.

"It seems so."

She smiled. "I have missed all of you. We were considering removing to London for part of the Season to be closer, then leaving for the Continent after Christmas."

"May I go with you?"

"Of course, if you are not needed here."

Patience waved her hand in the air. "There are more than enough hands to hold the baby should they be required."

Rotham smirked at her remark.

"I never was much of a country girl," she conceded.

Apparently, Armstrong had awakened the entire household. Westwood, Stuart, Montford, the Cunningham siblings, and her sisters, with the exception of Faith, all came into the room within minutes of each other.

There was a lively reunion as the sisters embraced, the men shook hands, and they immediately divided with the gentlemen on one end of the table and the ladies on the other. It was a much different breakfast than Patience had experienced in some time.

They remained where they were chatting long after they finished eating. It was hard for Patience not to steal glances towards the end of the table, but she desperately wanted to speak with Stuart and find out what else had happened last night. What else had she missed? If there had been shots fired, she thought she would have heard them this close.

None of the other soldiers were there, and she knew they were hidden somewhere on the estate, but she didn't know where that would be.

The nursemaid entered with a little bundle. "Her ladyship thought you might want to show the little master off." She handed the baby to his proud father. But Westwood was quickly relieved of his son by his doting Aunt Hope.

"Shall we remove to the drawing room where we can be more comfortable?" she asked.

Everyone took turns with the sleeping baby. Even Patience held him for a while, noting he did look much better today, sleeping like a cherubic angel.

Then the two aunts came down earlier than usual, so either they had heard the commotion or someone alerted them. With two babies to dote upon, all of the ladies appeared to be in heaven. Why did Patience feel the need to escape? When it was her own child, she would feel differently, would she not?

Perhaps she could use Xander as an excuse to escape. Usually, Peter would have returned him by now. She stood and walked over to the window and frowned when she saw a carriage rolling up the drive. Who could that be? It was certainly too early for calling on anyone. As it drew near, she recognized the black brougham, and while it was not Rupert, his family was just as bad. Especially now. Why would they be calling before noon?

Armstrong soon walked in to speak with Westwood. "A very distraught Lady Fagge and Sir Horace are here, my lord. Under the circumstances, I was not certain what to do. I placed them in the red drawing room."

"What circumstances? No one calls at this hour," Rotham asked, making no pretence about listening.

"There was an unfortunate event yesterday involving their son. As magistrate, I'm afraid I must deal with it. They have likely come to claim their son. Please excuse me."

"I will join you," Major Stuart said, and Patience bristled that she could not follow and listen.

After they left the room, Rotham turned towards those at that end of the room. "Would anyone care to enlighten me?"

Cunningham and Montford looked at each other. "We do not

know many of the details. Ash and some of the soldiers were moving a prisoner to London yesterday when they were set upon by a gang. Sir Horace's son, Rupert, was shot and killed."

"You have Sir Horace Fagge's son in your icehouse?" Rotham asked, clearly none too pleased about what was happening here. "A prisoner. Here."

"I don't understand it myself," Cunningham admitted, which surprised none of his friends.

"But the prisoner is gone now. The danger is past," Montford reassured Rotham, and Patience realized perhaps the others did not know they had all returned. That it was a ruse. She would hardly be the one to inform them. No one expected her to know anything.

Lady Fagge began wailing loud enough that conversation amongst them was impossible.

"Oh, dear. Agatha never did cry gracefully," Aunt Rosemary said with a grimace.

"That is not crying, it is an assault on the ears," Rotham retorted.

The babies began to stir at the noise, so Hope and Grace ushered them back upstairs.

The others looked as though they'd rather be anywhere but there and made their escapes as well. Patience decided she was glad she was not in the room with Lady Fagge after all, but waited to see if anything came of the visit.

The woman wept for twenty more minutes. It was another ten minutes before she finally heard the door open and their being shown to the door.

Once assured that they were gone, Patience hurried out into the entrance hall, full of curiosity.

"That is the worst part of being magistrate," Westwood said, looking done for. "I will let you update Renforth. I am going to check on Faith."

Once the others were gone, Patience sensed that Ashley was afraid to be alone with her. If he was regretting their kiss, she would not let it bother her. Lady Halbury had always told them kisses meant nothing to men other than a way to lure women into sin. Well, she could see why his kisses would tempt, but she would not lose her head over it.

She narrowed her gaze and he must have sensed he was about to get a dressing down. "Come walk with me."

"Where are we going?"

"I must report to the colonel. Fetch Xander and we can pretend we are walking him."

Technically, they would be walking him, but she would not split hairs.

"What happened?" she asked once they were out of doors and far enough away from the house.

"Besides Lady Fagge erupting into histrionics?"

"She did just lose her son," Patience felt the need to point out.

"I would have understood yesterday, but why first thing this morning?" He waved the question away as if there was no good answer. There really wasn't.

"She demanded to have the body released to her, and Dom explained why it must remain here until the inquest. So naturally, she began demanding the inquest to be held tomorrow." They found Xander with Peter near the barn, and the pup bounced over to her and began to walk with them.

"Did Sir Horace say anything?"

"Very little. He still seemed shocked, like his tongue had been frozen in place."

"Some people deal with grief that way. Grace did not speak for weeks after our parents died. Were you able to question them at all?"

He shook his head. "You really are not a typical female."

"Would you like me to be?" Disbelief laced her words.

"Absolutely not."

"Now that's sorted, were you able to discover anything?"

"I asked Sir Horace if he noticed anyone else besides the gang during the shooting, but he barely shook his head no. Then Westwood asked where Rupert's rooms are and if he had any particular friends."

"I could've told you that. He has only two. Layton and Beckett."

"Did you not feel the need to impart this information to me?"

"I suppose I could have last night, but he only told me yesterday morning. It did not seem as important after that."

"Fair enough. Did he mention any particular club he favours in Town?"

She squinted in the distance, trying to recall. "I cannot think that he mentioned a club."

"Searching his rooms and finding that out will be in my next order of business."

"You will be removing to London, then?"

"It appears that way. I will see what the colonel says."

She smiled. "I may well see you there then."

He stopped immediately and turned to face her. "Do not be ridiculous. You cannot follow me to London and go searching gentlemen's clubs and apartments!"

"I am not following you. I had already made plans to return there with Hope."

He looked as though he wished to argue with her, but then his gaze turned darker. What did that mean?

"I must go, Patience. Remain vigilant."

RENFORTH AGREED that a trip to London was in order, but he wanted Manners to go with him instead of Fielding. There were times that Fielding's background hindered him, and exclusive gentlemen's clubs was one of them.

He went to inform Westwood where he was going, but found the others in the study.

Carew had joined them, and was regaling them with a story about his trip over from Ireland.

Ashley went to the desk and wrote a quick note to his brother, choosing to do that rather than disturb his brother's time with Faith and the baby.

"What is this about a prisoner, Stuart?" Rotham demanded.

Ashley did not particularly want to rehash the entire scenario, but then again, Rotham or even Carew might have insight.

He sunk down into the chair behind the desk and explained about the stolen arms. "So, if either of you know anything about Rupert or his friends Layton and Beckett or any other avenues we can explore, I'd be much obliged. I feel like I'm heading to London looking for a needle in a haystack."

"If I were looking, I would begin at Inferno."

All brows raised and glanced at Carew. He raised his shoulder in a careless Gaelic manner, even though he was Irish. "I might have seen him there from time to time."

Carew was the biggest rogue of Westwood's friends, but Ashley did not think that behaviour was from anything more than boredom. Whatever the reason, Ashley could use the help. The shipment was scheduled for two days hence and they needed the brains behind the operation, not the hired hands.

"I am beginning to see a pattern here. Devil, 666 symbols, inferno, gaming hells…"

"The three of them play deep. Fagge may have looked like a fool, but he had a keen mind for cards. I played him once or twice and he always gave me a run for it."

This didn't surprise Ashley overly much. A time or two, he wondered if Rupert had been playing a part to some extent. He didn't think all of it was feigned, but it was easier to manipulate people if they had no expectations of you.

"Perhaps I should take you with me tonight."

"I could be persuaded," Carew drawled. "You need to go with a member, and as it happens, I still belong though I haven't been there in months."

"How soon could you be ready? Time is of the essence."

"Let me change into riding gear and pack a bag."

"I'll send for the horses."

After he'd given the message to Armstrong, he returned to the study to wait for Carew.

"You know, Stuart, I've been thinking about what you said. Besides money, who would have the most to gain by stealing arms?" Rotham asked.

"My first inclination is always going to be the French. Although we have been at relative peace for a while."

"Precisely. I just remembered who happens to have a French mother."

Ashley looked blankly.

"Beckett. Rupert's other bosom beau."

Rotham meant that literally. Beckett was a well-known pink of the *ton*, similar to Rupert but stylish.

"At least it bears looking into. Even if we are not currently at war with the French, there is still enough hatred for the sympathizers to want to strip our army and its allies of the ability to fight. Moreover, his father is a pompous Whig."

"An unforgivable sin."

"We will likely be in London soon, but should you need help of any sort, send for me," Rotham offered. "Westwood has his mind on other things, and I'd be glad to fill in for him where I may."

"I appreciate that." Ashley shook his hand before stepping outside to join Carew. They stopped off to collect Manners, then rode hard and fast, which suited Ashley's mood. It gave him time to try to sort things out in his mind. There was little doubt with Rupert being killed that they were close enough for the murderer to be uncomfortable. Now they just had to hone in and find proof.

"Let us stop off to speak with my father," Manners said as they reached the outskirts of Mayfair before they would turn to their home.

"Lead the way," Ashley agreed. Anything that would help, he welcomed.

"Good afternoon, Major, sirs," the butler greeted Manners as they entered.

"Is my father in?"

"He's in his study."

"Very good. I know the way."

"I will have some sandwiches sent in for you."

Manners indicated for Ashley and Carew to follow as they climbed a set of curving marble steps and entered a room lined with oak panels and leather filled bookshelves.

"This is an unexpected surprise," Lord Upton said, taking off his glasses and rising from behind his desk to come around and greet his son and friends. "Please have a seat. I know Havers will bring something in shortly. Now, tell me what brings you here."

"We've come to see if we can discover some information about Layton and Beckett. Rupert Fagge was shot in the back yesterday when the gang set out upon our prisoner's caravan to Newgate."

"So it was deliberate."

"Yes, my lord. There is no way from where Rupert was that it could have been otherwise," Ashley explained. "He was almost directly beside me."

"And no one saw anything?"

"I was on the opposite side of the carriage," Manners said. "Stuart would've had the best vantage point, but it was quite a chaotic gunfight until everyone ran out of balls. The smoke was thick and he would have been an easy mark."

Lord Upton was thoughtful for a moment. "It means you are too close to the culprit for his comfort. At least it seems you are on the right path. What do you hope to find here?"

"More motive, more evidence."

"Carew here has seen Fagge with his friends at Inferno. We intend to do a bit of investigating there tonight and hope we uncover more." With the recent close of Watier's exclusive gaming club, men were finding other outlets for their habit.

"Rupert Fagge at Inferno?" From the look on his face, it was clear that his lordship did not approve of the place. "I suppose it can't be helped. It is a dangerous place. Wise of you to take Carew here along. They would pluck the two of you bare within the hour."

"Your confidence in our abilities is astonishing, Father."

"It is not your abilities that concern me, but the lack of scruples of these men. Tell them, Carew."

"'Tis true. It is not if they cheat, but how they evade detection. It's a game of wits, you could say."

"One that often leads to ruinous consequences, which is likely where the motive for stealing and murder lies," Upton said on a heavy sigh as if he answered his own question as to the validity of their going. "Report to me here when you are done."

"Yes, Father."

"Now, eat and avail yourself of whatever you need for the evening. Chambers will be prepared for you."

Once they'd had full stomachs, they were shown to their own chambers to wash and dress for their evening out. The plan was to go to a few clubs for the latest gossip before ending the evening at the gaming hell.

They did not bother with White's or Brooks's. Neither Layton nor Beckett would have been the hunting ground for the young pinks as Rupert was.

"I do not know if I have the stomach for Boodle's," Carew drawled. "I might sit this one out." He inclined his head to an Irish pub across the street.

"We will find you after."

As it happened, the two they sought were there, both names listed on the registry, and Ashley and Manners quickly bowed out, not wanting to be discovered. They returned to Carew, who'd just received his first pint. They sat and ordered one for themselves and then made sure they could see the door to the club.

"They were inside," Manners said by way of explanation.

Carew nodded, not needing or requiring explanation. "I suspect it will be another hour or so before they head over."

"At least the ale is good here," Ashley remarked.

"Do you really expect it is one of these two you're looking into?"

"We have to make the connection to Fagge. We have little else to go on besides Layton being the son of one of the five men with access to the classified information."

"Then are you not putting yourselves at risk by being seen tonight?"

"Would it be that obvious for us to be seen?" Ashley asked.

"Inferno is not that big of a place. I am more likely to discover something without you there. I think whoever shot Mr. Fagge knows exactly who you are."

Ashley exchanged glances with Manners, who inclined his head. "It is a fair point and my brother trusts you implicitly."

"What, exactly, is it you want me to discover?"

"Well, Rupert had mentioned a scheme that made him rich. Perhaps exploring that angle might be of benefit."

Carew nodded. "If I have an opening. The best way is to make them indebted to me. I stayed away because it was all too easy to fleece these young, wild bucks from their family fortunes. But tonight, I can do it without any guilt."

"If nothing else, more information about Layton and Beckett."

He finished off his pint and stood. "I will see what I can do. I think it best if I'm there first."

They watched him sneak away into the night, unused to being the ones left waiting.

"I hope this is the right decision."

"What other choice do we have besides risking our necks?"

"Let us hope he knows what he's doing."

CHAPTER 17

$\mathcal{I}$t was always difficult being left behind, but Patience was well aware she could not jaunt off to London on her own and visit a gentlemen's club. A dangerous, depraved one at that. It did not stop her from wondering what they were doing, and if they were any closer to finding out who the leader of the thieves was. By all accounts, it was someone very powerful and well-connected, else this elite unit would not have been called in.

It was hard not to be excited and worried at the same time. However, before, Patience had not been concerned that one of them would be executed for standing in this person's way. She knew she would not rest easy until they were returned safely. How long would that be?

Patience stared at the canopy and realized it was late in the morning. It had been hours before she had finally fallen asleep, having tossed and turned worrying about whether Major Stuart and Manners had met with a bad end at that awful club.

"Xander!" She shot up out of bed and realized he wasn't there. She must have slept through someone else letting him out, bless them. Quickly, she dressed without calling for a maid and hurried downstairs. Everyone else was breakfasting by the sounds of laughter coming from the dining room.

Xander was not there, not that she expected him to be. Likely, Peter had walked him and kept him out in the yard so she could sleep.

"Good morning," she called as she went to the table and was promptly served her usual cup of coffee with cream and sugar.

"It is not like you to sleep so late, Patience," Grace remarked with concern.

"I did not sleep well," she mumbled. Everyone appeared to be down except for Rotham and Hope and Westwood and Faith.

"Worried about the gentlemen?" her sister asked knowingly.

Of course, Grace would be worried, too.

"Hopefully, we will hear something soon." She reached over and squeezed Grace's hand with more reassurance than she felt.

"Who wants to go for a ride this morning?" Mr. Cunningham asked. "One last, long ride before we leave for London the day after."

Patience looked at Joy, whose mulish expression told her what she thought of them leaving. Mr. Cunningham had become her bosom beau, and though they often fought like siblings, she was never as happy as when he was around.

"I think a ride would be good for all of us to keep us occupied," Montford stated. Patience was surprised anyone else might be as concerned as she.

"Perhaps a ride would be a good diversion." Miss Cunningham agreed.

Patience was the first downstairs after changing into riding gear, so she went to look for Xander to say good morning. However, when she found him, she could not have been more surprised. He was in the stall with Freddy and her kittens, snuggled up amongst them as if he were one of the family. She stood there, mouth gaping. Xander looked up at her and thumped his tail proudly, but did not move from his spot where one of the kittens was nuzzled against him.

"Well, I'll be," she whispered. Perhaps he would not be hers to keep, after all. It's saddened her a little, but Xander had been a gift from Mr.

Cunningham to Joy, after all. Maybe she could have a pup from the next litter. She reached down and scratched his ears then let him be.

When she left the barn, everyone had gathered at the stables, and the grooms were leading out the horses.

"Are you certain you have to leave?" Grace was asking Miss Cunningham.

"Monty and Freddy think it's best to leave the new parents to themselves for a while. Why do you all not come to London with us?"

"I do not think the Dowager would wish to leave the baby."

"Then I am certain you could stay with us," Vivienne offered. "I know my mother would not mind. It is not so grand as Westwood House, but we have room, nonetheless."

"I will speak to Joy and Patience about it."

Patience had heard. "I was already planning on joining Hope there. I'm certain she would not mind all of us going."

Joy had heard and whipped her head around and was listening intently. She did not look pleased, but by what, Patience couldn't say. She would speak to her later, but she knew Joy vastly preferred the country.

Joy quickly mounted and took off, which was a bad habit she had when she was not happy or defiant. It was what had led to her accident the previous summer.

Mr. Cunningham practically leapt onto his own mount and was giving chase. Patience could only smile at his protectiveness.

No one else in the party seemed overly bothered and let the two go before mounting at their own leisure and riding off in the same direction.

As Montford and Vivienne paired off with Grace and began chatting, Patience followed along behind, which perfectly suited her mood. She wanted to help figure out this mystery, and chatting idly would not leave her time to think.

So what were they missing? Something was nagging at her that she could not put a finger on. Were all of the situations the men investigated like this?

It was as though they had reached a dead end, literally with Rupert now being killed. Hopefully, the men would find some clue in London before anyone else was hurt.

As they approached a hedge, she returned her attention to the jump, which her horse handled beautifully. However, something spooked Midnight at the last moment and while she cleared the fence, she shied on the way down, throwing Patience to the side.

As she lay on her back, the wind knocked out of her, she tested all of her limbs, and everything was in working order. Slowly, she regained her breath, while watching the clouds move across the sky. Midnight nudged at her in apology, and Patience was relieved to see the horse was unharmed.

How long would it be until the others realized she was not with them? She would catch up in a few minutes once her body stopped smarting.

A rustling in the hedge reminded her that Midnight had spooked and she turned to see a figure running away. That spurred her to her feet and she found the strength to pull herself up and look around for who she'd seen. She ran towards the hedge, finding a small opening she could crawl beneath. Looking around, it seemed as though he had headed into the woods. She took off running, but quickly lost any sight or trace of him. She cursed her frustration before heading back to where Midnight was lazily grazing beyond the hedge.

Boosting herself into the saddle ungracefully, she hurried to catch up with the others. A proper adventuress would have given chase to see who'd been watching her, but with a murderer out there, she did not care to be the next victim.

After the ride, they changed and met in the drawing room where the dowagers and the aunts were about to take tea. Patience was still shaking from her incident, but did not tell the others what had happened yet.

Faith and Westwood entered the room, and all of the gentlemen promptly stood.

"Are you certain you should be down, my dear?" the younger dowager asked.

"Oh, yes. If I stay abed any longer, I shall go mad."

Faith had never been one to lay about, and Patience did not think she would be capable either.

"Do you think we should call on the Fagges today?" the Dowager asked Westwood.

"In fact, I was planning to go now. Out of both condolence and as magistrate. I need to question Sir Horace if he has composed himself enough to talk now."

"I was afraid you would say that."

"You need not go."

"Well, one of us should go with you, and Faith should not be making calls yet," his mother explained.

"I can go," Patience offered.

The surprise on the Dowager's face was quickly changed into relief. As much as Patience did not wish to go, she felt she might learn something to help solve the mystery.

"Are you certain, my dear? I know I should probably go, but I never could abide Agatha Fagge, and she will be more unbearable than usual if yesterday's display is anything to measure by."

"If she is not prostrate in bed, she will be castaway on the chaise with her smelling salts being wafted beneath her nose," Aunt Flora added.

"There is no need to be cruel. She did lose her son," the elder dowager scolded.

"If the truth is cruel..." Aunt Flora held up her hands.

"I will call for the curricle," Westwood said to Patience as he took a ginger biscuit and popped it in his mouth.

"I am as ready as I will ever be."

They were soon on their way, and Patience decided to tell West-wood what had happened earlier.

"Dominic," she began. "When we were out riding earlier, something spooked my horse."

"Did you see what it was?" he asked with appropriate concern. "You are unharmed?"

"We are both unharmed, thankfully. It only knocked the wind out of me for a moment. As for what spooked Midnight, when I regained my wits, I heard a rustling in the hedge and saw someone running away."

He quickly turned towards her, blessedly experienced enough with the reins not to let it affect the horses. "Did you get a good glimpse?"

"Unfortunately, no. I only saw them from behind and through a hedge, at that. The only thing I could say is it was not a large person."

"A child? Or a woman perhaps?"

"I suppose either could be the case. I'm sorry I did not see better."

"You were stunned from being thrown, Patience." She could hear the worry in his voice. They had thought the threat was gone, at least temporarily. It must mean that the ruse had not worked.

"Do you think it means they are on to us?"

"Perhaps, but it definitely means we need to remain vigilant."

"I DO NOT THINK I can sit here and wait," Manners said after only ten minutes.

Ashley blew out a breath of frustration. Neither of them excelled at waiting. "But do we risk catching our man if it is one of them?"

"Possibly, but it also might goad them into making a mistake. Many clever criminals like toying with their prey."

"Then I think we should toy back. If we hurry, we can catch him."

Neither of them needed convincing. They tossed some coins on the table, placed their hats on their heads, and hurried out into the night towards Inferno.

Neither of them had ever been there, but most everyone had heard of it. Masked in a location of respectability, the gaming hell was just off St. James's Street.

They barely caught up to Carew as he reached the door. His look of surprise quickly turned to a scowl of displeasure.

"Ye don' trust me?" His Irish brogue broke through his normally perfect Etonian English.

"It is more that we cannot be idle. We mean to toy with the boys. If one of them is our man and they know who we are, then they will either be so arrogant that they might give us a clue, or be so nervous by our presence that they crack."

"Or assassinate you as they did windbag Fagge. I can see I will not talk you out of it regardless. Let's go."

From the outside, it appeared as any other residence along the street. A small panel in the door slid open as they approached, and Carew held up an engraved gold coin with their insignia to show as proof to the doorman. If he could be called something so mundane. Even through the panel, the beefy hand that took the coin and the slight bit of face that surveyed them looked like a giant ogre from a storybook.

"Who's with you?" he growled.

"Two of my associates. I vouch for them."

They heard a grunt of disapproval, but the bolt slid back and the door opened to admit them.

"Anyone here worth my time?" Carew asked the man, likely to diffuse his interest from Ashley and Manners.

"Not many worth your ilk here, my lord. The night is young yet."

Carew really had perfected the art of appearing unaffected. They went on through down to the cellar of the house where a large room was arranged with multiple gaming tables and booths surrounding them for watching and drinking. It was not as luxurious a setting as White's or Brooks's, despite the usual dark panel walls and leather chairs. It appeared to be there solely for the gambling.

A couple of tables had games of cards proceeding, but there was not much of interest.

"We are early yet. Do either of you play? It would help if we looked to be amusing ourselves."

A buxom waitress sauntered over towards them, wearing a short skirt and tiny bodice which left little to the imagination.

"What can I offer you fellas?" the dark-haired seductress asked with a practiced smile as she perched on Carew's lap and put one arm around his shoulder. "It's been too long, my lord. What brings you back at last?"

"Boredom." He shrugged a shoulder carelessly. "Is there anyone new that can offer me a challenge?"

She looked thoughtful for a moment and shook her head. "No one of your skill, but there are some new faces that you might enjoy toying with."

"In other words, you would not mind if I handed it to them?"

"Precisely, my lord."

She brought them drinks and they settled in to a game of piquet. It was an hour before the club began to fill. Soon, the room was crowded, filled with smoke, the shuffle of cards, and the smell of strong spirits. It was not particularly jovial or friendly in nature, as if small talk were not allowed, and they moved straight to serious gaming. The stakes began high as they overheard the betting at the table next to them. It gave Ashley the chills. This was where addicts won or lost entire estates in one flip of a card.

"Your quarry has arrived," Carew muttered without looking up.

"How will it work, then?" Manners asked.

"I suspect a new game will form soon."

That was, in fact, what occurred. With the arrival of Layton and Beckett, one of them spotted Carew and approached. "My lord, your reputation precedes you. I wonder if we could interest you in a game."

Carew was a born actor, as he finished his hand before respond-ing. Then he coolly laid his cards down before giving them a hooded once over. "Have we met?"

"Layton and Beckett at your service," Edwin Layton said with a small bow and an indicative nod at his friend. They looked younger than Ashley had expected, though of age with Rupert. However, there was a gleam in their eyes that spoke to their lack of innocence.

"Will it be worth my while?" Carew drawled.

"Begin at a hundred quid a point."

Carew pretended as if that were barely worth the bother, but conceded. "I suppose one game will tell," he said and waved the newcomers to join him.

Ashley had to bite back a grin. Carew was good. Very, very good. He exchanged glances with Manners, who appeared to be thinking the same thing. Ashley and Manners moved back from the table, as if they were not with Carew, but took their seats where they could observe.

"Shall we add a fourth?" Carew looked about the room to assess if there were any others worth his time. "Last time, there was a fellow who gave me a decent challenge." He narrowed his gaze as if trying to conjure up the name. "Dressed like a Macaroni...named...Hag? No Bag?"

"You must mean Rupert Fagge. He is in the country."

Ashley wondered if they knew of his murder. If so, they were extremely cool customers.

Layton glanced at Ashley and Manners without any recognition as he scanned the room for a fourth player. He did not know if that meant anything or not.

"There is Lord Singleton just come in. His play will be worth your while. We play with him often."

As if their word meant anything to Carew. He looked sideways as if considering. "I think I may have heard of him."

"He was always to be found at Watier's previously."

Carew gave a shrug of indifference. "Call him over then."

Manners gave Ashley a little nudge and whispered. "Isn't that Chum's brother?"

It was, in fact. Ashley didn't know him well. He was the heir to the earl, but did not look much like his brother at all. His profligate ways were taking their toll on his appearance with bloodshot eyes and dark circles, red cheeks, and a telling paunch.

Layton went over and began talking close to Singleton. It was clear they were well-acquainted. Chum's father and brother had quite the reputations, but did he often associate with this younger set? He supposed people weren't too discriminating as long as someone would give them a good game. It would be worth mentioning to Chum.

Apparently, he was convinced. He came to the table and was introduced to Carew. Singleton was sizing them up. He glanced over at Ashley and Manners and gave a nod of recognition. "How's my broth-

ELIZABETH JOHNS

er?" he drawled in a manner that spoke little care what the answer was.

"He was well last I saw him," Manners replied.

Singleton had already turned towards the game, and pulled out a cigar and clipped it. But instead of lighting it, chewed on it. Ashley felt for Chum, who was constantly humiliated by his father and brother. Ashley had never been more grateful for his own brother.

Ashley knew a little bit about cards, but was uninterested in the game itself. He watched as cards were shuffled and dealt, and bets were placed. Unfortunately, there was a little talk. He was beginning to lose hope that they would discover anything at all from this other than a motive for needing money. But they needed something much more substantial to go on and time was running out. As Ashley's mind drifted away from the game, Singleton placed a card slowly down to roars of surprise and congratulations. He must've won the hand.

Ashley looked at Carew, who had a gleam in his eyes that he was beginning to recognize as calculating. He'd let Singleton win on purpose. "That was a nice warm-up. Best two out of three?"

"A gentleman always allows a man to recoup." He signalled the barmaid and called for another round of drinks.

A fresh deck of cards was brought out and Beckett began to shuffle. Layton took snuff agitatedly, as if to shore up his nerves for the next round.

Now was the time for talk if ever there would be.

"Why have I never played you before, my lord?" Singleton thankfully asked.

"I favour the hells over the respectable jaunts," he droned.

"I confess to grief over the loss of Watier's." A well-known club that had recently closed, where the stakes had been outrageous under the guise of a gentlemen's club. It had been Brummell's weakness. Layton and Beckett took a pinch of snuff with a possessed look in their eyes that made Ashley feel decidedly unclean.

"What about your estate?" someone called from the back of the group that had gathered to watch.

168

Singleton waved a hand as if losing an estate mattered not, though he chewed harder on his cigar. "I will come about. I always do."

Said every better gambler and profligate heir, Ashley thought cynically. Chum would be incensed if he heard his brother speaking so.

Apparently, Carew agreed because he handed it to him the next two games. Ashley didn't know whether he cheated or not, but he was not sad to see the three men squirm in their seats and sweat as they realized they would lose.

When Carew tossed the winning card down, gathered their vowels, and made them a bow, they all looked as if they were about to be led to the gallows.

Ashley and Manners left shortly after Carew, feeling no closer to finding their man.

CHAPTER 18

*P*atience was hard-pressed not to giggle when they were shown into the drawing room. It was exactly as Aunt Rosemary had described, with Lady Fagge prostrate upon the chaise longue, with one daughter wafting smelling salts beneath her nose, and another plying a fan in her face. Her own hand was dabbing at the corners of her eyes with a lacy handkerchief.

But the woman's son was dead, and even though Patience had not liked the man, she was sorry for what had happened to him. Sir Horace stood at their entrance, but did not speak. He looked as though he'd aged decades since she'd seen him a few days before.

"How kind of you to call, my lord. Forgive me for not rising, but I barely made it downstairs today," Lady Fagge said, then proceeded into a frenzy of heavy breathing and dabbing her eyes.

"I quite understand. Lady Westwood sends her condolences."

"That's very kind of her to think of us at a time like this. I trust she delivered?"

Westwood was obviously smitten by the look on his face, but he tried to mask it. "She did, and they are both well, my lady. Is there anything we may do for you?"

"No one can bring my son back, my lord." She began to wail, and the discomfort level in the room was unbearable. Sir Horace stood and waved for them to follow. Patience could have hugged the man because she had not really come to see Lady Fagge anyway.

"Lady Fagge is not herself," he said by way of explanation once they had reached safety.

"Of course, and we are sorry to cause her distress. May I have a word with you?"

Sir Horace looked acutely uncomfortable at the prospect, but he could hardly refuse. Whether Westwood was asking as a friend or the magistrate.

He nodded, and led them into a small study.

Patience went along because where else was she to go?

"I am sorry to also distress you as well, but there are some questions I must ask before the inquest so I can rule properly. I know you wish to have the funeral soon, so this must be resolved."

Sir Horace gave a reluctant nod.

"It seems your son was shot in the back. After speaking with the others involved, and where Rupert was positioned, they do not believe he was shot by accident."

Patience was watching the man's reactions closely. If it was possible for someone to look as pale as a ghost, then he did in that moment.

"How could they know that?" he muttered.

"He never turned around, and he was next to my brother," Westwood said gently.

Sir Horace just sat there and looked down.

"We have reason to believe Rupert might have been involved in some sort of scheme that got him killed. He confessed to Patience here at your dinner the other evening that he had recently come into a windfall. He even intimated to my brother that he would let him in on it in exchange for helping him advance his courtship with her."

Patience could see the man was about to break. His chin was quivering and his head began to shake back and forth as if denying it would make it go away.

"You think it was somehow related to the gang of thieves?" he asked.

"Possibly. Were you aware of what he was in on?"

"No, my lord, but he had been acting strange the last few months. All secretive and sure of himself and dressing like some popinjay with affectations to make your stomach sour. I knew he couldn't afford that lifestyle on the allowance I gave him."

"Did he confide anything at all to you that made you suspicious he was into something?"

"At first, it was just his puffed-up consequence. Then he was sneaking off at night. He'd never done that when he was home before. As man of the house, I don't sleep well and I hear what is going on."

"Did you ever follow to see where he went?"

The look on the man's face gave him away. "A time or two he went down to the local tavern. I suppose that's natural for any man, but he'd have to sneak away as his mother would never let him hear the end of it if he was carrying on with one of the barmaids." He hesitated. "Another couple of times he sneaked over to your land. I did not follow him any further than that. I'm sorry, my lord."

Patience could attest to that, but she had never been out at night alone and ran into him then.

"I never thought he could be involved."

"Do you know who he was associating with?"

Sir Horace shook his head. "All I know of was his two school chums, Layton and Beckett. Bad business the two of them, if you ask me. They used him as their punching bag and as a puppet to do their dirty work at school. Rupert was thrilled to be included and didn't see that they laughed at him. Beckett and Layton have the dash to pull it off. Rupert did not."

"When did you suspect that he was into something underhanded?"

"Not until that morning. He insisted on accompanying the prisoner's caravan. I could not talk him out of it. He was in a panic to do so, and let slip that if he didn't, something very bad would happen. I never thought he might be involved in smuggling."

Stuart had mentioned that he had told Sir Horace a brief account of the situation, but not all of the details. He knew that some goods had been stolen.

"Sir Horace, can you think of anywhere on your property that might be used to store the missing goods?"

"Aye, there are any number of places, but there is nothing there now. I looked. I think if they were there, then they are long gone."

"Did you shoot Rupert?" Patience asked.

Sir Horace looked pensive. "I couldn't let him shame the family. You must see that."

Westwood looked at her with disbelief.

"I didn't mean to kill him."

He lost his composure, and Westwood handed the man his handkerchief and they waited while he gathered himself.

"If you insist on making it public, at least give me a few moments alone first."

Westwood sighed loudly. "I do not know that it is necessary to make it public. Do not do anything rash while I think this over. We still need to discover who was directing Rupert in this scheme."

"Thank you, my lord. I don't know what's worse, though. I'll have to live every day knowing I killed my son. Can you at least spare Lady Fagge from knowing?"

"Unless it becomes necessary to the overall investigation. I believe knowing that your son is gone by your hand is enough punishment. Unfortunately, I will need to have a quick look through his things. If you show me where they are, we will be as discreet as possible."

Sir Horace did not argue, probably too relieved to be spared his life. He directed them up a staircase to the end of the hallway.

"We will show ourselves out when we are done," Westwood said and gave the man a sympathetic squeeze on the arm before Sir Horace hung his head and left them there.

Once they were back in the curricle on their way home, Westwood drove in silence until they reached the main road. They had found nothing of consequence in Rupert's room.

"How did you know, Patience? You seem to have a keen mind for this. I'd appreciate your thoughts."

"I think it is unfortunate that Rupert is dead. He would have been the key to unlocking this. He was not good at subterfuge and liked to boast. I think if Sir Horace had not killed him, then someone would have. He had become a liability."

"Why do you think he was desperate to accompany the prisoner that day?"

"That is an oddity. One would think he'd be relieved that Devil was gone. Perhaps he wanted to make certain. Or the attack by the gang was ordered, but went very wrong."

"I hope Major Stuart and Major Manners are having more luck than us since our biggest lead is dead."

"There has to be a connection with Layton and Beckett. I'm certain of it, but will we be able to catch them?"

"Let us hope they take the bait. Is Layton's father aware of the trap?"

"To my knowledge, only Lord Upton is aware. Let us hope the bait winds up in the right hands."

A cart pulled over to let them pass, and Westwood waved his thanks.

"I confess. I never expected something of this magnitude when I first brought Ashley into it. Who could have guessed there would be an arms smuggling ring somehow connected to our small village?"

Indeed. They were approaching the gates of Taywards and Patience thought she saw something in the hedge again. Perhaps it was her imagination since her horse had spooked earlier, but she placed a hand on Westwood's arm to alert him and angled her head.

He nodded acknowledgment and drew back on the reins to bring the horses to a walk. "What did you see?" he asked quietly.

"Someone is in the hedge."

"Do you think it's the same person?"

"It would be a great coincidence to have two people lurking in the hedge on your land in one day."

Westwood pulled the conveyance to a stop. "Who's there?"

They were met with silence, but Patience thought she detected a dark outline crouch down behind the foliage.

"Show yourself. We mean you no harm."

"Do you need help?" Patience called out.

There was a bit of rustling before a face emerged through the leaves.

He looked to be around fourteen years of age. Not a boy, not yet a man. This could have been who spooked Midnight.

"Do you need help?" she asked again.

"I'm looking for the soldier man. The one with the light 'air." The boy's voice shook with fear.

"He is my brother," Westwood said cautiously. "He is currently in London. Can I help you?"

The boy looked as though he were about to bolt. He was rightfully nervous, his eyes darting back and forth.

"What is your name?"

He hesitated a moment as if it were a trick question.

"Billy."

"Are you Devil's son?" Westwood asked.

"Yes, sir."

"Did you sneak away from the gang?"

He nodded as though he were terrified he'd be found and killed at any moment. "I 'eard 'em say my pa would be transported, and I was going to beg to go with 'im."

Westwood pretended to think about it for a moment before answering. "I believe that could be arranged, Billy. But I need your help."

"Anyfing. Anyfing at all." His face was so full of eager desperation, Patience could but wonder what he'd been through in his young life.

"Hop on the back and we will talk in a safe place."

Billy eagerly jumped up to the tiger's position and Westwood drove through the gates to the stables. If Patience had imagined how this adventure would go, that was one scenario she would not have imagined. Now there was one mystery solved. But unfortunately, only more questions remained.

~

"You were certain there was no recognition from Layton or Beckett?" Lord Upton asked once they had returned to report.

"Not at all. I would swear the only one who knew us was Single-ton. How that family produced Chum, I will never know." Manners shook his head.

"What is your next step?"

Ashley explained the plans. "We will search Fagge's rooms today, then we will return to Taywards and review the information we have. Westwood was to question Sir Horace and search Rupert's rooms there."

"I feel like the gang leader must know something more he is not telling us."

"Likely. Baines, Fielding, and I have tried everything. I keep thinking perhaps we have not asked the right question, but nothing else has come to mind. He wore an expensive scent that overlaid the smell of tobacco. He never saw the man except for his hands. He wore a signet ring, but that hardly signifies as he could not identify it."

Upton scoffed and held up his own hand which bore the crest of his own marquessate.

"Indeed, even Singleton wore one last night. If it were not for Chum, I would love to pin this on him."

"We still need to know what they did with the cargo, and how the gang was approached. I would centre my efforts on that. Devil is the key to pinning our man down. The details of the shipment were posted and will be discussed at our committee meeting this morning. The bait is out there, so you'd best watch the game closely for contact."

"I'll return to my post as soon as we are finished this morning," Manners said.

"If you'd like me to return to Taywards now to pass something on, I can," Carew offered.

"That would be a great help. I will write quick notes if you could see them in the hands of Westwood and the colonel."

That done, Ashley and Manners saw Carew off, then headed to

Rupert's chambers at a respectable rooming house for gentlemen. It was not the calibre of The Albany, but still situated near Pall Mall.

It did not take much convincing for the landlord to open Rupert's door for them.

"We are here on behalf of Mr. Fagge's family. He has met with an unfortunate accident, and we have been asked to collect his belongings." In addition, a little charm and a little mention of the service he would be doing for His Majesty, and they were inside.

Manners let out a low whistle at the scene of destruction before them. "Someone beat us here."

Ashley doubted there would be anything left to find, but a search had to be conducted nonetheless. Thankfully, Carew had taken the messages on or they would be unaccountably rushed. By the time they had sorted and packed Rupert's belongings into a trunk, two hours had passed.

"I've looked through every pocket," Manners said. "We would be doing the world a favour were we to burn this." He indicated the trunk of brightly coloured clothing.

"I've been through all of his bills. There is nothing beyond the outrageous cost of those ridiculous garments."

"I detected no loose boards in the floor for hiding things. Whoever was searching would have looked there. If I were Rupert, where would I hide something?" Manners asked.

"Was he smart enough to retain any evidence? Carew swears he was a keen card player. He must not have been as big a fool as he behaved."

"What of keys? Perhaps a deposit box at the bank?" Manners continued to question before they left London.

They sat on the sofa contemplating. The room was now bare.

"It is hard to think there is nothing at all here to help, though it all could be in the country. Was there not a case we had where a lady hid something in her shoe?"

"I do not recall such a one, but I did look in his shoes, ghastly things. I never could abide a man in pumps. With his physique, it's a wonder he could walk in them."

Ashley was already rummaging through the recently packed trunk.

There were four pairs of shoes, heeled pumps with brightly jewelled buckles. Ashley turned them over and worked at the sole of the heel. He tossed a pair to Manners, who did the same.

One slipped off more easily than the others and a small key slipped out. "Voilà."

"Excellent, now to what does it belong?"

"I do not think we will discover that quickly. Let us return to Greenwich and perhaps Westwood can discover from Sir Horace where Rupert banked."

They left instructions with the landlord for where to have Rupert's belongings delivered, then rode hard and fast back to the village. They found Chum twiddling his thumbs at the tavern near the East India docks. His face brightened when he saw them. "I'm waiting for our fellows to gather here after work. You should try the pies. They are the best I've ever tasted."

"I do not need convincing. I am a famished." Ashley held up his hand and ordered pies and ale for himself and Manners did the same.

"Anything new?" Ashley asked, letting Chum talk while he chewed.

"One of the men was winged pretty good when Fielding shot the gun out of his hand. Unfortunately, that had to happen or one of our own men would be dead."

"Was he the only one?"

"The only one I noticed. His arm is in a sling. He's lucky he did not lose it. Yet, at least. The boy ran away, apparently. He hasn't been seen since the hold up."

"Do you think he ran away?"

"I couldn't say for certain," Chum answered thoughtfully. "Where would he go?"

"Maybe he chased after his father?"

"It's possible. We will keep a lookout," Manners said. "I think we should follow them from the docks today. The shipment information has been disseminated and if anyone is going to try to contact them, it will be soon."

"Excellent. I am ready to catch this weasel. Did you find anything in London?" Chum asked.

"Very little. I cannot think Layton and Beckett at the helm on this. Neither did they seem to recognize us, nor did they seem to have anything on their consciences."

"Some people are consummate actors."

"The only thing on their mind was the cards. It gives me the creeps to watch a man possessed over the turn of a card or toss of the dice."

"By the by, we ran into Singleton. We sought out Layton and Beckett at Inferno, and Carew played cards against him. He made up the fourth at their table."

Chum seemed unsurprised by this knowledge. "Did he cheat his way to winning?"

"Carew bested him. If there was cheating, it was smoother than I could detect." Not that Ashley had been looking too closely.

"I wonder what he had to lose since he already lost his unintended estate." Chum's tone was laced with well-placed bitterness.

"We found a key hidden in one of Rupert's shoes. We have no idea what it belongs to other than possibly a bank box. Something to have Westwood ask about."

Ashley drained the rest of his ale and stood. "I will be off to Taywards then. If anything changes, we will send word."

Ashley found Caesar and made his way back to Taywards, trying to consider everything they had learned. It felt like they were vultures circling in the air waiting for their prey to show themselves. Unfortunately, time was running out, and if this trap did not work, he was afraid they might lose this one for good.

CHAPTER 19

*B*illy looked around wide-eyed as they pulled into the yard
before the stables, as if he had never seen the like.

"This way, lad," Westwood said.

Patience directed Peter to go in and fetch some biscuits and milk
from Cook and bring them back to the stables. She then followed
Westwood. He led Billy to the room where they had held his father
only a day before. Had it only been one day?

"Have a seat and tell us why you've come." Westwood leaned
against the desk and pointed to a chair, and the boy sat nervously, his
gaze darting back and forth between them. "I over'eard 'em talkin'
about 'ow my pa might get transported. I wanted to offer meself up to
go with 'im."

"Does the gang know you've left, Billy?"

He looked down at his hands. "I suspect they know by now."

"I can arrange for you to be with your father, but you must help
me first."

Peter entered, carrying a tray with a jug of milk, sandwiches, and
fresh jam tarts. He set it down on the table and gave Patience a wary
look. "Thank you, Peter."

She put some sandwiches and tarts on a plate and set them before Billy, then filled him a glass of milk. "Go on. I am guessing you have not eaten today."

"No, miss. I was tryin' to get to Da before they rode out, but 'e was too well guarded." He practically inhaled the sandwiches.

Westwood waited until Billy finished and drank down the milk.

"Billy, were you ever with your dad when he received messages?"

The look of guilt on his face was telling. "Only once when I wasn't 'posed to be there. I followed 'im and 'id."

"Where was this?"

"At The Golden Goose. It's where everyone gathers after work of the evenin'."

"Did you ever see the man that gives orders?"

"I didn't see 'is face. 'E was a right fancy toff. 'E wore one of them tall 'ats and carried a stick with a shiny snake on top and smoked a cigar."

"Was he tall or short? Fat or thin?"

"Mebbe neither. Middle, I'd say. Liked his drink, though. 'E patted 'is stomach."

"Could you tell how old he was?" Patience asked.

"Old, mebbe bout 'is age. But not as old as Da."

Patience was hard-pressed not to laugh aloud. Old, indeed.

"You seem to have a keen eye, Billy." Patience detected sarcasm is Westwood's voice.

Billy shrugged a shoulder. "People never think I know nuffink."

"Is there anything else you saw that might help us identify the man? It could be very important."

"Like what?"

"The colour of his hair? Did he leave in a carriage or by horse? Did you see what colour the stone was in his ring?"

"No, miss." He shook his head, disappointed as if he were failing them.

"You've done well. If you think of anything else, just tell someone that you need to speak with me. Even if it seems small, it might help."

"Did I 'elp you some?" he asked eagerly.

Xander began to bark and she could hear Peter trying to hush him outside the door.

"He must have realized I've returned." She cast an apologetic glance at Westwood.

"Is that your dog, miss?"

Patience looked to Westwood, who gave his assent. She walked over and opened the door, and Xander ran in and circled her excitedly. Once he had calmed down, she showed Billy how to hold out his hands and let Xander sniff before he petted him.

Westwood stood from the desk. "I need to find a place for you tonight, Billy. I am going to speak to Chauncy, perhaps he can stay with Peter and the others," he said to Patience. That seemed like a good plan. The boy certainly did not seem like a threat, especially as she heard him giggle when Xander licked him, and she hoped Westwood would not feel compelled to lock him up. He had come there of his own free will. How did a man with Devil's reputation wind up with a son like this?

"Do you often work for your father, Billy?" Patience could not help but ask.

He shook his head. "Everyfin' changed when me mum died last year. Pa 'as always worked near the docks, and sometimes there would be jobs 'e'd take me along on when they needed more 'ands to move cargo if it were small enough." He looked down with shame, as though it was an immortal failure not to be big and strong yet.

Patience remained quiet, hoping he would continue to chat.

"A few months ago, 'E got this big offer and said we were goin' to be rich and move from Lunnon. It was too far, so 'e brought me along with 'im."

"What kind of jobs did you do?"

"Sometimes I moved cargo, but mostly I was a lookout." He was petting Xander, who had now decided the boy was friendly enough that he could roll over on his back. Billy knelt down and continued petting the shameless pup. "This job were different."

"What did you do with the cargo once you had it?"

"Sometimes it were loaded straight onto a cart, and sometimes onto a boat."

Patience nodded, but that was not the information she needed. Where else would they load it? She had to think of a way to ask the question differently. "Did you ever see or hear what happened to the cargo after you moved it?"

"Not really. 'Cept with the last one, it 'ad to be 'eld till the coast were clear, they said."

"Is it still being held somewhere?"

"I couldn't say. We stuffed it in some fancy ship."

Patience could barely contain her excitement at finally discovering something, even if the likelihood that the ship with the stolen arms was long gone.

"Do you know anything about what you've been waiting for this time?"

"Only that it were the big job. The one wot would make us rich."

She could see he was growing tired of all the questions. She would have to try again later.

Peter returned and looked with a bit of trepidation at the boy. "Miss, his lordship has asked me to look out for Billy. Maybe have him help me with my chores."

Patience looked at Billy, who looked as though he could not believe his good fortune. He looked at her for approval.

"I think that is a fine idea. You will be safe with Peter. We will let you know if we have any further questions."

As Patience left the stables, Xander on her heels, Major Stuart rode up on Caesar. Both males were magnificent specimens, but the two of them together in motion was something otherworldly to witness. She waited for him to come to her as she wondered at her reaction to the man.

He tipped his hat to her and smiled.

"Major Stuart." She curtsied. "Returning alone?"

"Did Carew not arrive earlier with messages?" He looked concerned.

"He may have. Westwood and I called on Sir Horace, and we had a surprise visitor that I have been in the stables with until now."

"Oh?" He slid down from his mount.

"Devil's son, Billy. We found him near the gates as we were returning. It seems he ran away and wanted to beg Westwood's mercy to let him be with his father."

"What an interesting turn. Chum just told me that he was not with the gang."

"We have been questioning him over Cook's sandwiches and jam tarts. He was very eager to be helpful, but the only thing of note that we learned was our man carries a walking stick with a shiny snake on top and that he smokes cigars."

"Where is he now?"

"Shadowing Peter. Westwood thought it best to keep him with one of the younger boys."

"We need to make certain he does not discover his father is still here on the estate. For now, I think it is to our advantage in case we need him as a bargaining chip."

A groom must have realized Stuart had arrived and came out to take Caesar. "I will see him brushed down and given a bucket of oats, sir."

Stuart nodded his thanks to the groom. "Where is Westwood? I would like to confer with him and Renforth," he said as they began to walk.

"He must have gone back to the house."

Apparently, Renforth was keeping to himself in the Dower House, she discovered once they found Westwood. Surprisingly, Patience was invited to come and share her observations since she'd spent more time talking with Billy after Westwood had left to make arrangements for him.

Fielding also came from where they were keeping Devil in the gamekeeper's cottage, while Baines remained with Devil. If Renforth and Fielding were surprised to see her, they did not say as much as they stood when she entered with Westwood and Stuart.

Quickly, Stuart relayed what they had discovered in London,

followed by Westwood's observations with Sir Horace being responsible for Rupert's death, then finally Patience was invited to convey how they had found Billy and what he had told them.

"That's quite a bit for the past four and twenty hours," Renforth remarked. "Not that I am complaining, mind you."

"It is," Stuart agreed, "but I think what we need to centre our efforts on is who they are working for. We need to use Billy to make Devil talk. Billy is the only thing he seems to care about."

"Agreed. We need to make sure Billy does not find out his pa is here," Westwood added.

"I think he's been on the estate. Midnight was spooked when I was out riding and I'm certain it was him I saw." Patience noticed Stuart's glare at that news. She ignored it.

"He didn't ride out to attack the caravan. There were only four riders."

"Very well. Let's give Devil one more chance so we are going in with as much ammunition as possible. Fielding, I'd like you to go to the docks and see what you can discover about the fancy ships moored there. Perhaps the goods have been hiding in plain sight the whole time."

"What I'd like to know is what shipment they were waiting for. They could not have known about the one we instigated," Stuart said.

"We could clarify with Upton, but I imagine it has been touted as one and the same. We may never know the answer to that. After you finish questioning Devil and Fielding returns, I want to reconvene to finalize our plans for tomorrow."

ASHLEY WAS NOT surprised that Patience was upset with him for not letting her go along to question Devil. Even though the risk was small that Devil would ever be within reach of her, he would not put her in such danger. He'd rather risk her wrath. Not that he minded her wrath one bit. She was fierce and beautiful, like a warrior queen when she was in a taking.

Part of him would be sad to see this mission complete. He had grown rather accustomed to being around the little termagant every day.

He entered the cottage with a nod to Baines, who certainly looked like he was quite done with this assignment. Ashley took one of the wooden chairs at the table and spun it around, sitting backwards on it to face Devil, who also looked worse for the wear after almost a week of very little food and sleep.

"I've got news," he began.

"Finally." Baines stood and stretched and took a turn about the room.

"It seems your son Billy has turned himself in."

Devil sat up straight at attention. "Where is he?"

"It just so happens that he threw himself on his lordship's mercy. He ran away from the gang and asked to be sent to be with you."

A string of curses that would put a sailor to the blush erupted from Devil.

"I think it's rather touching." Ashley taunted a bit.

Devil spat at his feet.

"He's been talking rather a lot, which is unexpectedly helpful considering tomorrow is the big day." Ashley inspected his fingernails. "He was very willing to open his budget so eager he is to be with you."

"He doesn't know anything."

"Apparently, he knows more than you give him credit for. He snuck out to see you meeting with our man at The Golden Goose one evening."

Angry, Devil was a sight to behold. The veins on his face and neck were bulging and the hue of his face was somewhere between red and purple.

"If you'd like to see your son again, I suggest you tell us the rest of what you know."

"I've done told you everything."

"I'm beginning to think not. Billy mentioned you offloaded the goods onto a fancy ship. You never mentioned that, and I am quite, quite certain we asked that."

"What of it?

"I want to know where and the name of the ship."

"'Ow is that important if it's long gone by now?"

"You're telling me you weren't to load the next shipment onto it as well?"

He shrugged his shoulders. "We ain't been told what to do with it yet. 'Tis need to know with this fella."

"The name and location," Baines demanded.

"It was just across the way at the Greenwich docks. It was *Le Coquette* or something Frenchie like that."

"But you do not know where it went after that?"

"I assumed it went wherever he wanted it to go. I ain't no sea captain."

Ashley glanced at Baines. It appeared Devil was telling the truth. It all came down to asking the right questions, which they had not. Another question they had not yet asked. "Do you know where the goods were to go?"

He shifted uncomfortably in his seat. "Aye, that I do know, least with the next shipment. We were to take it and the goods to America. Me and Billy, we're going to make a new life there."

Ashley paused for a few moments to contemplate that knowledge and how best to use it.

"I'll tell you what, Devil. If we can catch this man, I'll try to make that happen. It matters not to me whether you go to Botany Bay or the untamed colonies."

"Why would you do that?"

"It just so happens your Billy has charmed one of my partners."

Wouldn't Patience Whitford cackle with glee if she'd heard him call her that? He dared not look over at Baines, lest he be fully transparent.

"Is there anything—anything at all you can think of that would help us catch this man?" Baines asked.

Devil hesitated. "Iffen you'll let me go long enough, I can try to send a message to 'im."

"I beg your pardon?" Baines growled. "I've been asking you day and night if you knew how to contact him."

"You never offered America to me," Devil shot back.

Ashley would have laughed if they weren't so close to moving in for the kill.

"How can we trust you won't tip him off?"

"I don't s'ppose you can, but all I do is let someone at The Golden Goose know and he magically appears later that night."

"He must know you've been taken prisoner. He may smell it for the trap that it is."

"'E might, but I reckon it's the best chance ye've got."

"Very well. I will run the plan by my commander. We will need a plausible story of how you managed to escape. But we will hold Billy here until you've kept up your end of the bargain."

Devil gave a reluctant nod of agreement. It was his only chance for freedom and he knew it. At least there was a glimpse of soul left in the man.

After leaving the stables, feeling as if they were finally getting somewhere, Ashley sought out Patience. He found her in the garden, tossing a stick with Xander.

Pausing just beyond Patience's vision, he stole a few minutes of watching her unbidden in order to try to sort his thoughts.

His heart clenched as he watched her and could not help but wonder at the possibilities. Certainly, she was unlike any female he had ever known, and none of which had tempted him to consider the thoughts he was having now. Life would never be dull with Patience Whitford, and he could not imagine a future without her. For one, her spirit of adventure seemed to match his. Would she be content with the life he could offer? It would be comfortable, but not grand.

He could envision discussing his work with her in the evenings, seeking her opinion even. Would she be content with that level of involvement? He was not sure, but as he watched her laugh as she tried to wrestle the stick from the dog, he wanted to see that smile every day. When had she changed his mind? He shook his head. He had no notion if she was aware of his feelings. Though that kiss…

Xander finally dropped the stick and sensed his presence. He bounded towards Ashley, ending his moments of guilty pleasure.

He raised his hand in greeting and her wide smile encouraged him.

"May I join you?" he asked.

"Of course."

He offered his arm and they began to walk like they were in Hyde Park, London on promenade.

"Were you able to obtain any further information from Devil?" she asked, bringing his thoughts back to the task at hand, breaking the spell of his mind's dangerous wanderings.

"Indeed. He was much more forthcoming, knowing we have Billy. He admitted they had unloaded the goods onto a private yacht named *Le Coquette*, but seemed to believe the goods had already sailed away. He and the gang have been waiting for the next job, which would be to transfer the goods to a ship that would take them to America. He planned to start a new life with Billy there."

He heard her swift intake of breath and knew what she was thinking before she said it.

"I've already thought the same thing, Patience. If he agrees to help us, then I will petition on his behalf. I can see little difference between sending him there versus Botany Bay."

Patience stopped and turned to look up at him, and the look in her eyes encouraged him. "You are a good man, Ashley Stuart."

"You doubted it?" He was not feeling precisely good in that moment with where his thoughts were leading. They had wandered far from the house, and he saw no reason at all why he should not take advantage of the most excellent circumstances. He brushed a finger down her cheek, giving her plenty of time to object. Instead, she wound her arms around his neck and pulled his face to hers.

And the rest of his thoughts were lost in the moment. The taste and feel of her were intoxicating in a new way. This did not feel like a temporary drug to relieve a craving, but something necessary for his existence. How did she always seem to take control of the situation?

Her lips were soft, but the kiss was not. She was as eager as he, and he pulled her closer, wanting all of her, needing her. This would not be enough. They would need to have a discussion, but now was not the time. He forced himself to pull away whilst he could maintain any semblance of control. This time, he could see her face, and the look in her eyes and the blush on her cheeks told him that she was just as affected as he. "We need to return to the house," he said softly.

She opened her mouth to speak, but he hushed her with a gentle finger over her lips. "Later."

CHAPTER 20

*P*atience was frustrated by being put off without any acknowledgment of what was between them. There was most definitely a mutual attraction, but part of her also understood that Ashley was preoccupied with his duties. She knew she had helped some with the investigation, but she wanted to do more. She knew the likelihood of them allowing her to go to the docks was next to nil. If she were to make any more contributions, it had to be soon.

Peter had come to fetch Xander early, which had awakened her, so she rang for a cup of coffee and luxuriated in bed. As she sipped her cup of coffee, she tried to put all of the pieces she knew into a logical order.

If Rupert had been the middleman, then it had to be someone within his circle. One did not run crime rings with a mere acquaintance. Even for a criminal, there had to be some level of trust involved.

She sipped some coffee and let the taste and warmth roll over her, and wondered if that was necessarily true. What if the person had some sort of hold over him? Blackmail of sorts. Was that too far-fetched? It must happen in real life, though she'd only read of such things in stories. But it was very easy to imagine a situation where one could lord something over another to get what they wanted.

Ashley had described Carew playing cards with Layton, Beckett, and Singleton, who happened to be Cholmely's brother. He mentioned it seemed as though the three were well-acquainted through gaming at least. When they enquired about Rupert, he had not detected any indications they knew of his death. Now that they knew Sir Horace had discovered his son's involvement and had shot Rupert to cover his family's shame, it was possible the others might not have known. Which begged the question, was Rupert delivering messages or solely a lookout? It was hard to imagine the mastermind doing that work himself, and potentially being caught. If only Rupert had left some sort of diary. She scoffed as she looked at the small music box he had gifted her. Perhaps she should return that to Lady Fagge. Maybe she would do so after the funeral.

So what next? Two of the men were watching the gang to see if they were contacted. Fielding had been set to watch the boat. Devil was to be allowed out to direct the operation, but what if nothing happened?

To Patience, the key here would be the contact. If it was the man himself meeting with Devil at the tavern, that was where they needed to catch him. Would that be enough proof? If it was someone very important indeed, would it be his word against Devil's? There had to be evidence of some form, but what?

The morning was growing late, and she could think of nothing else to aid in the solution. Unless Billy could think of something else to help them identify the man, or Rupert had left some sort of journal, she was out of ideas.

It appeared that she had missed breakfast, but it was no matter. The coffee would sustain her for some time. She went to look for Xander and suspected she might also find Billy.

Her supposition was correct. Xander was with both Peter and Billy in the barn, putting down fresh hay. As soon as Xander saw her, he bounded over to greet her.

"Morning, miss," Peter greeted. "I hope you don't mind I kept him with us. He seemed happy enough."

"Not at all. I came to see how Billy was settling in."

"I'm all right, miss. I like this work better than the other."

Interesting notion, and encouraging, Patience thought. "I am glad you are comfortable here."

"I even learned a couple of me letters this mornin'."

"Indeed?"

"His lordship has someone teach all of us for a bit each week," Peter informed her.

Patience smiled. Westwood was something of a reformer and thought it more helpful than hurtful to have his servants given a perfunctory education at a minimum.

"I learned 'ow to write me name."

She was not certain Billy would be there long enough to learn more, but everyone should be able to read and write their own name.

"I got to thinkin', miss. That walkin' stick I said the gent carried?"

"Yes," she said encouragingly.

"It might 'ave 'ad a letter on it. Now wot I seen them, I can't be sure."

Fair enough. "Perhaps you could describe it to my sister and she could try to draw it?" Grace was rather skilled in that way.

"I suppose we could try."

Patience left to find Grace and encountered both Westwood and Stuart talking at the entrance to the study.

"Good morning, Patience. I did not see you at breakfast. Is everything all right?" Westwood asked.

Patience was frankly surprised he'd noticed with the new baby around.

"Everything is well," she assured him. "I've just been checking on Billy and he seems to be settling in well. He learned some letters this morning and was delighted to be able to spell his name." She smiled at her brother-in-law. "Quite a lovely thing for you to do."

He waved away the praise.

"Of note, Billy did mention that the walking stick might have been a letter instead of a snake. I am going to see if he can describe it better to Grace to draw."

"Excellent idea," Stuart agreed. "I do have a favour to ask." He pulled a small key out of his pocket.

"I was wondering if you would mind calling on the Fagges to see if they recognize this key."

She angled her head to take a closer look, and he held it out to her.

"We found it hidden inside of a shoe in Rupert's rooms in London."

"It's a peculiar size," she remarked. "It is too small for a door."

"If you could see to that, I would be forever grateful. It's possible it is nothing more than to a box at the bank, but I hate not to try to discover its purpose. We must prepare to get Devil to the tavern and position ourselves before contact is made." He gave her hand an affectionate squeeze, then kissed the back of it while looking into her eyes with some kind of unspoken message. She could not precisely say what that message was, but the look warmed her to her toes.

Of course, the men would leave to scout the tavern, and she was left behind again.

She found her sisters in Faith's sitting room admiring the two babies.

"There you are, Patience! I have hardly seen you these past few days," Faith remarked.

"I have been trying not to bother you," she muttered as she accepted baby Benjamin from his loving mother.

"And you have also been assisting Ashley, I hear."

She could feel her cheeks warm, curse them. "A little. There is not much I can do, unfortunately. He has asked me to call upon Sir Horace and Lady Fagge to see if they know what a key might belong to. Can I ask one of you to accompany me?"

All of the sisters exchanged looks. Hope was the only one with little awareness of what a visit to that household might mean. "I suppose I could go. Faith certainly should rest."

"You are the best of sisters, Hope. I would have pulled Grace along, but I need her to do me a favour."

THE GIFT OF PATIENCE

Grace looked up from where she was playing peekaboo with Sylvester. "What can I do?"

"I need your drawing skills. I want someone to describe an image to you and see if you can draw it."

"That sounds intriguing," Joy said.

"I have never attempted such a thing," Grace said with obvious hesitation.

"It is worth a try. If you do not succeed, then we are no worse off."

"I suppose." It was clear she did not agree. "Who is it?"

That was a whole other explanation Patience had to describe.

"Now I am doubly intrigued," Joy said, rising to her feet from the floor, where she'd also been entertaining Sylvester. "I will accompany you, Grace. I want to see this gang member."

"His *father* is the gang member we've been holding prisoner. Billy is actually quite sweet," she told them as they left to fetch Grace's drawing pad.

"I suppose we might as well get the call over with," Patience said with a long-suffering sigh.

Hope left instructions for returning Sylvester to the nursemaid for his nap, then agreed to meet Patience downstairs in a quarter of an hour.

Patience returned to her own room to make sure she was presentable for a call, then saw the small music box Rupert had given her. She might as well return it to perhaps reduce the amount of calls she'd have to make there.

The carriage was called, and when they were on their way, Patience pulled out the box.

"What is that?" Hope asked.

"A music box that Rupert gave me. I was going to return it."

"May I see it?"

Patience handed it to Hope, who began to examine it. "The craftsmanship on this is exquisite." She turned the lever to start the music, but it fell out.

"That is odd. I thought those were part of the mechanism and could not be removed. I do hope I didn't break it."

Patience knew nothing of music boxes whatsoever.

Hope attempted to replace the lever. "It is like trying to fit a key into a difficult lock."

"What did you say?" Patience asked as an idea took hold. "May I try?" She pulled out the key and compared it to the lever. They looked identical. She slid it inside the hole and turned. A click popped a small drawer underneath open.

They both gasped with excitement. A slender book was inside, but she couldn't make heads or tails of the writing.

"Is it some sort of code?" Hope asked, looking over her shoulder.

"Perhaps." Patience rapped on the ceiling of the carriage. "Turn us back around, John. We need to return home."

"As you wish, miss."

Why would Rupert have given this to her if it was what she hoped it was? She wouldn't curse her good luck. She only hoped they weren't too late to catch Major Stuart.

ALL OF THE men set out for the gamekeeper's cottage, horses in tow. They were to finish formulating their plan and then head to their respective positions either inside or surrounding the tavern. Devil would first send word with his contact that he wanted to speak with the gent, then seek out his gang so they were aware of his escape.

"When will I be free?" Devil asked.

"Soon enough," Baines remarked. "I want to make sure you don't get any wild ideas."

"Why would I do that? Ye've got my Billy and I gave ye my word."

None of them questioned when a man gave his word. There was apparently still some honour amongst thieves.

"Can you ride?" Renforth asked.

"I can stay on, but that's about it."

"That's is good enough. I've one for you that will follow where the others lead."

He rolled out a small hand-drawn map. "Now, here's a basic layout of The Golden Goose and surrounding streets. Where do you usually meet our friend?"

Devil took a moment to study the map, then pointed to an area between a warehouse and the docks. "Here. It's well-hidden after dark."

"Cunningham, Montford, and Rotham, I would like you to watch the front. Here, here, and here." Ashley knew they'd been placed there as the least risky positions, but at this point, they needed all eyes and ears. He pointed to the three sides of the tavern.

"Baines and Cholmely will watch inside, and Fielding and Manners will guard the yacht."

"Stuart and I will watch Devil." That man made an ungentlemanly sound.

"And me?" Westwood asked.

"I'd like you to keep watch at the clearing and send us a signal if you see anything from your vantage point."

"Any particular signal?" he asked.

"Any signal at all will mean you saw something and put us on alert. Fielding and Manners will know to watch for it."

Westwood nodded his understanding. "Carew is also available if needed."

It seemed like as good a plan as they could make without having proof beyond the sound of a voice, a fancy scent, and possibly a snake-shaped walking stick.

"And you remember your part, Devil? Renforth asked.

"I am to tell the gang there's been word of another shipment. I 'eard tell when I was being dragged to Newgate. I'll send word to our man to see if 'e's 'eard of it or if 'e wants in on it."

Renforth nodded. "There is the possibility he may have already heard or that he will not show, fearing a trap. I've alerted the customs authority to seize them once everything is aboard the ship. Everyone's weapons checked and ready?"

"Yes, sir."

"We will leave our horses at the pier, ride across, then disperse from there on foot."

They made their way outside to where the horses were saddled and waiting for them. A sombre mein shown on all of their faces, the seriousness of their task not lost on them. Sometimes people were hurt in these operations, and sometimes one of them didn't come back.

Ashley and Westwood helped Devil into the saddle, then ensured he knew the basic commands.

"Luna here will follow anywhere Triton goes. She won't give you any problems."

It did not take them very long to reach their destination. They dismounted and left their horses at The Anchor, then took a ferryman took them across to The Golden Goose just south of the East India docks.

Devil went inside the tavern, and Ashley and Renforth followed inside to witness the reunion with his gang to make certain the man upheld his word.

Once they positioned themselves with a good vantage point inside the pub, Devil went to speak with the publican, then picked a table apart from them. He gave a little signal that he successfully sent the message, then kept to himself and waited.

It was over an hour before the others entered. To say there was a bit of a dust-up was putting it mildly.

"What the devil?" the man who had been injured by Fielding's shot exclaimed as the barmaid put down pints for them all.

"Am I seein' a ghost?" the one Ashley assumed to be Shorty asked.

Smith reached over and pinched Devil and got punched in the arm for his pains.

"Just makin' sure you're real," he defended as he rubbed his sore arm.

"It's me. Now quit your caterwaulin' and sit down."

"'Ow did you get away? I don't believe fer a minute they let ye out with their good wishes."

"Where is Billy?" Devil demanded, avoiding the question. Ashley had to admit he was playing his part convincingly.

None of them looked like they wanted to explain that they had lost his son. If Ashley had not seen the softer side of Devil, he would not have believed it existed.

"We don't rightly know. 'E didn't ride out with us when we came after you that day. We 'aven't seen 'im since."

"'Ave you checked back at Wapping?" Devil growled.

"Nay. If 'e went there, they will look after 'im. We've been waiting for this last job. There ain't much 'ere for us."

"Aye. The sooner the better and I can get to Billy." He leaned in to speak quietly. "I over'eard it's to be delivered tonight. We got to work quick. I just need to be certain the details ain't changed. I sent word."

"Might as well eat while we wait," Shorty suggested.

"I could do with a nice pie an' a pint," Devil agreed and signalled the barmaid.

"I bet ye ain't been fed right in prison."

"Ye could say that."

The barmaid came over and took their orders.

"Got your arm, did they, Floyd?"

"Shorty 'ad to dig the bullet out. Still can't use me arm. Been 'avin' to move cargo with one."

"At least you still 'ave it."

"Aye. Got a bit of infection now."

"It were nice of you to try to rescue me."

The barmaid delivered more pints of ale for each of them, which they quickly drained and called for another.

"We were tipped off by Daniels there." Ashley took that to be the publican.

"Ye were?"

Smith nodded. "Didn't ask 'ow 'e knew."

Ashley and Renforth exchanged glances. Their pies were delivered with more ale. At the rate they were going, Ashley hoped their man didn't delay long in arriving.

"Guess ye didn't need our 'elp any'ow," Floyd grumbled.

Devil grunted.

"Ye think 'e'll show?"

"Not worth doing the job if 'e don't."

That sobered them up a bit.

"Everything's arranged?"

"Aye. Carts are ready."

They continued to listen as the gang shared what they had been doing while Devil had been gone. After another hour had passed, Renforth slipped out to get in place. Ashley would follow in a few minutes. He drained his own ale and left some coins on the table. As he was slipping out, he saw the publican walk over and incline his head to Devil. It seemed their man had arrived at last.

CHAPTER 21

"Drat!" Patience muttered as she tried to catch her breath. She had returned to the house to find the men had gone to the gamekeeper's cottage, but she met Westwood returning from there.

"Has something happened?" he asked her.

"Of sorts. I have information I need to give them. Are they gone?"

"They left ten minutes past on horseback. You will never catch them now."

"Drat, drat, drat."

"Climb on and tell me what you found on the way back." He held out a hand to assist her, and she mounted the horse behind him. Never mind that her skirts were hiked up to her knees. This was urgent.

As they rode back to the stables, she told him about the encrypted journal.

"Let's have a look at it quickly before we go rushing off to the docks headlong into danger. It could be entirely unrelated, and we might put their safety in jeopardy."

"You have experience with this sort of thing?"

"A little. Ash and I used to send letters back and forth that way when he was serving on the Continent."

"That's more experience than I have." Which was none.

They did not bother going to the stables. They rode directly to the house and handed the horse off.

"We might need Maximus again," Westwood informed the groom.

"Yes, my lord. He will be ready."

Patience and Westwood hurried into his study, where he pulled out some sheets of paper. "You can assist me by writing out patterns for me. Use one sheet for the letters and another when deciphering the message."

"You have done this a fair bit," she remarked.

"As long as it is not overly complex, we should be able to manage in time. My only concern is delivering it to them. I am to be in position and signal from here."

Patience wanted to offer to go, but knew he'd proclaim it too dangerous. While Westwood sorted through the code, her mind was awhirl with how she could manage to deliver the message herself if the code turned out to be something worthwhile.

It was about an hour before he recognized the pattern. "I do think I have it now."

She wrote down everything as he instructed and the various numbers and a list of four pairs of letters became apparent. "They could be initials."

"It's the numbers I can't make sense of." He stood and looked over her shoulder at what she had written.

"It's almost like a code within a code. Surely Rupert was not that clever."

"Since they gambled together, could those numbers simply be sums of money? Perhaps earnings or debts? Or even amounts made in their scheme?"

"Indeed, it could be that, but is it enough to implicate anyone in anything? We need something to tie them to the shipments."

"Do you recognize any other initials?"

"No, but Ashley or one of the others probably would. I don't think we have enough information worth the risk of riding this out to them tonight."

"Unfortunately not," she agreed.

"If you want to continue trying to make sense of it, be my guest." He showed her his pattern, then left to make preparations for sitting watch.

Patience knew there had to be something there, but her eyes were beginning to cross from looking at letters and numbers so long. They had only as yet deciphered two pages, and there were probably a dozen or so more left.

She rose from the chair, stretched, then went to see if Grace had managed to draw anything useful.

"There you are," Grace remarked when Patience found her in their sitting room. "I've made an attempt, but I have no idea if it will be helpful." She handed Patience her drawing pad with the page opened.

It was an excellent drawing, and one that was well enough it could be sold in a shop window.

The picture was the full scene—a man in the shadows of a wooden roof overhang with a top hat pulled low, only the lower half of his face protruding from beneath the shadows, a cigar hanging from his lips. He wore a long caped driving coat, and both hands crossed atop a walking stick that did indeed look like a snake's head, the tail forming into an 's' shape. A large signet ring with a dark oval centre sat on his pinkie finger.

"It is quite good," Patience remarked. "Perhaps one of the men will recognize him."

"Billy says it is a perfect likeness," Joy added. Grace would never have said as much.

"I need to take this."

Of course, Grace agreed. Patience gently removed the drawing and thanked her sister before returning to the study. As she returned to her work on the journal, something began to nag at her.

There were dates next to each notation and various numbers listed next to the pair of letters. If those numbers indicated money, then there was a lifetime's fortune listed next to each of the initials. Why wasn't there any listed for Rupert?

Patience flipped through each of the other pages, and there were a few blank ones before the notations seemed to begin backwards from the other side of the small journal. There were no initials listed there, only dates and numbers. Could those be Rupert's own profits or debts?

If this was money he'd won or lost from the other men, then it might be some sort of evidence. Perhaps Carew might recognize the pattern as he'd been a gamester. If it was even related to that.

Argh! She wanted to pull her hair in frustration. Why could Rupert not have left something more substantial?

Much though she wanted to figure it all out on her own, time was of the essence. Carew was somewhere on the estate, most likely with his horses.

As she trudged towards the stables, never in a thousand years would Patience have guessed how much work went into solving these mysteries. As soon as she found one piece of information, it raised several other questions. It felt like a maze with no centre or escape.

Carew was in the paddock with some colts, dressed in his shirt sleeves, buckskin breeches, and old Hessians. He was glistening with sweat and looked like a stable hand. Patience could certainly understand her sister's attraction. She only hoped Grace would not have her heart broken. Carew seemed as untamed and elusive as the colts he was now working with.

When he saw her approaching, he stopped and walked towards the fence. "Is it time?"

Patience cocked her head. "Time for what?"

"I thought you were sent to fetch me. Westwood asked me to assist him this evening."

"That, I cannot speak to. I was hoping you could help me with something else."

The light was beginning to fade, but she pulled out the journal and could just make out the letters and numbers.

"Do you have any idea what these mean?" She opened the small leather-bound book to show him.

"Where did you get this, lass?"

"It's Rupert Fagge's diary. I found it concealed in a music box. He gave it to me as a gift the morning he died. Westwood has been helping me decipher it." She then held up the decoded pages.

"A gift, you say?" Carew flipped through the pages and let out a low whistle.

"I am not sure he ever meant me to find it. What is it?" she begged.

"It appears to be a ledger of sorts. I've seen bookies use these columns. That's a great deal of money changing hands."

"Are those initials?" She pointed to the letters.

"Aye. And you can guess who some of those are."

"Edwin Layton and Oscar Beckett," she said.

"Unless I miss my guess, this one is Alastair Cholmely, Lord Singleton."

"Captain Cholmely's brother?"

He nodded. She turned the book over and opened it from the back.

"Are these Rupert's numbers, then?"

"That would be my guess," he agreed.

"Thank you for your help. I am not certain it will help them know who is smuggling arms."

"It could certainly be motive for why someone would do it. That's a lot of money to owe someone if that's what it means."

"It's difficult to credit Rupert with that sort of cunning. If you are right, then there are any number of men it could be. Now we've added two more to the list."

"Three of them lost a great sum to me that night and kept on wagering." He turned to signal to the grooms to take the colts, then he took his waistcoat and jacket from a nearby post and climbed over the fence. They began to walk back to the house, and Xander shot out of the barn towards her. Peter and Billy ran out after him, but stopped when they saw her. They made quick bows.

"You may keep him for now," she said, bending down to scratch behind the pup's ears. "I am tending to some business and I know he enjoys your company."

"Thank you, miss," Billy said excitedly.

Another thought occurred to her as they returned to the house. She pulled Grace's drawing from her pocket. "Do you recognize this gentleman at all? Perhaps he was at Inferno that night?"

Carew narrowed his gaze and studied the drawing. "Aye, I believe he was."

ASHLEY CURSED himself as he tried to slip out into the darkness. He should have come out sooner and now he was at a disadvantage, knowing Renforth and their man were in the shadows. He went loudly past where Renforth was and Devil's meeting place, then a few steps beyond where he was supposed to be doubling back quietly to his lookout post.

Devil was already exiting the back door by that time and Ashley could feel his pulse race with the thrum of anticipation. The mix of being on the hunt blended with danger as they moved in for the kill was what they lived for.

Devil stepped into the shadows and Ashley could see why it was the chosen place, and he doubted they would hear much of anything of their conversation. It was too risky to move closer. However, their man would not be able to leave without passing by Ashley or Renforth unless he went into the pub. Hopefully, they would get a good look. But he would be followed until the shipment was on the boat.

When the first words reached his ears, Ashley was grateful for the acoustic gods.

"It's been some time, Devil. Where have you been?" The scent of cigar smoke wafted in the breeze towards him. It wasn't pleasant mixed with the Thames at low tide.

"I 'ad a spot of trouble but now I'm back."

"I see that. And you have some news for me?"

"Aye. Shorty and Smith 'eard as there's to be another shipment like the last. Is it ours like ye promised before?"

"What kind of trouble were you in? I heard you'd been captured."

Ashley cursed under his breath. It could be much more difficult to fool this man than the gang. Devil had been instructed to stay as close to the truth as possible, because they did not know what the man knew.

"Let's just say I had a little visit with a prison."

"And you managed to escape?" Disbelief laced the man's raspy voice.

"My gang 'eld up the caravan on the way to Newgate. It was a bit of a mess and one man was shot."

"Now you're a fugitive."

"Something like that. I need this job to get away."

"When is this shipment?"

"Tonight."

The gent cursed rather loudly. "You are certain? My contacts have not mentioned the shipment going out tonight."

"Shorty saw them being brought in secret like last time. Mebbe your sources missed 'em themselves. I suppose if they are wrong, then we wait longer. No 'arm in looking."

There was a long pause and for a while, Ashley thought he was going to refuse. Until the goods were actually stolen, they could not act upon anything.

"Very well. Once the goods are on board, you and the boy can sail with it. The captain will have your payment."

"We will see it done." Devil slipped back into the tavern, and soon exited again with the gang.

Ashley thought their man would follow, but he did not leave the shadows.

Baines and Cholmely would be following along behind shortly. Did he suspect they were being followed?

Ashley should not have worried.

A large group of very drunk men poured from the door, Baines and Chum included in that number. Had he not been looking for them, he would never have known it was them.

Still, their man waited to leave. What was his hesitation? Did he sense their presence?

Hopefully, he did not intend to wait there until the job was completed. Was he too smart to be caught? Would he then simply claim his yacht had been commandeered unbeknownst to him?

It seemed he was waiting to finish his cigar. Ashley saw a few puffs of smoke over the minutes they waited, then the man finally emerged. He went straight to where a horse was tied up and mounted before riding like the devil was on his heels.

Renforth was soon beside him. "We did not account for that."

"He rode towards London."

"Perhaps he went for reinforcements. I will hire a hack and go after him."

"I will go with you."

Renforth shook his head. "I know I always say to work in pairs, but I am only watching, not acting. You wait with the others at the yacht. I have a feeling our man will return before the night is over."

"We can only hope."

Ashley found his way down to where Le Coquette was moored. As he walked, there was a nagging feeling that he should have recognized their gentleman traitor. There was something distinctly familiar about him that Ashley could not quite nail down. When he reached the pier where the private yachts were docked, the place was eerie in its lack of humanity—the only sounds coming from the creaking ships and splash of the Thames against the shore.

It certainly did not look like a ship awaiting a long voyage to America. Was that why the gent had ridden hell-for-leather towards London? He needed to arrange for a crew? It had all seemed very odd, though he had been surprised by the news. Yet had he not told Devil the captain would be waiting with payment?

Ashley was not certain where Fielding and Manners were hiding, but he could make an educated guess from his own experiences with spying and covert locations.

Manners saw him and made a welcoming sound. He was just beneath a tarp on the next ship over. Ashley climbed aboard and joined him, both lying flat on their bellies.

"Where is Fielding?"

"In the shed on the other side of the ship. Is all going according to plan?"

"Yes, and no. Devil reunited with his gang, and made contact with the gentleman, but he took off in a hurry towards London instead of coming here."

"What do you think it means?"

"He was taken aback, not only by Devil's escape, but he also had no notion of the shipment drop tonight. I can only surmise he had to leave to make arrangements for a crew."

"If that is the case, the goods will not be leaving tonight."

"Unlikely," Ashley agreed. "Devil will not be pleased if they arrive to find the ship deserted. They can hardly load it themselves."

"Though they can hardly sit here with a wagonload of cargo, can they? But we need the excise man to wait until we have our man. I pray they wait for Renforth's command."

"I wonder what Renforth has discovered. He was following our man back to London." Ashley could but wonder.

"Who can say if he even caught up with the man in a hired hack?"

"We won't know until he arrives. I will go and speak with Fielding now. I have no idea how long it will take for the gang to steal the cargo and deliver it here."

"Excellent. What's another hour or two of waiting?" Manners drawled.

Ashley climbed out from under the tarp and kept to the shadows, just in case, as he made his way towards a small wooden shed on the pier. Fielding saw him coming and opened and closed the door quickly behind him. Ashley filled him in on everything he had just told Manners as they settled in to wait. Occasional ships would pass through the deeper waters of the river, but this far out of London there was not much river traffic at low tide.

"Vessel approaching," Fielding alerted him as his thoughts had begun to drift off.

"Is it the gang?" Ashley asked as Fielding used a spyglass to look through the small window.

"I'm not certain what I am seeing. It's appears to be a ferryman and several large sacks of something. Perhaps some sort of cargo."

"We will keep alert."

The barge pulled alongside of the pier and the ferryman secured his boat with a rope. They could hear the man speaking quietly with someone, but could not see the recipient.

"Dare we enquire?"

"He does not appear to be related to the shipment we're awaiting."

Ashley cracked the door open. "May I help you?" he asked, startling the ferryman.

"Psst. Ashley."

Dear God in heaven. He looked up at the night sky. If that was Patience Whitford, he was going to wring her neck right then and there.

"Ashley!"

"As I live and breathe, Patience. Can you not use the sense that the good Lord gave you? You should not be here, and certainly not alone!"

"I'm not alone." She lifted the large canvas that covered her and the other lumps to reveal several familiar faces: Carew, Montford, Cunningham, and Rotham, who looked less than pleased to be in his current state. "Do not blame them. We found them outside the tavern and needed to find you."

"I take it none of you can gainsay a slip of a woman?"

"Have you tried to say nay to the lass? Besides, I think she's found your man for you," Carew drawled.

"What do you mean?"

"I mean, she discovered Rupert's diary, which appears he was holding thousands of pounds worth of debt over four men, and then she had her sister draw a picture of the man Billy had seen from the boy's descriptions, and it just so happens that it's Lord Singleton." He realized what he'd said and looked apologetic. "Sorry, lass. I did not mean to steal your thunder."

"It is quite all right. You were defending me quite brilliantly."

Meanwhile, Ashley felt as though he'd been punched in the gut. Chum's brother was a traitor.

CHAPTER 22

$\mathcal{I}$ thank you for telling me, but you must get out of here. We do not know when the gang will arrive with the goods. There is no crew here for them, and I suspect they will be angry when they find there is no one to receive them. Perhaps you could row across to Taywards."

Ashley pointed out which of the piers belonged to his brother, and the ferryman gave his acknowledgment. "If you wait there, we might have need of you. You will be paid handsomely for your time."

"It's yer coin, guv. I'm 'appy to oblige."

The five stowaways covered themselves up again as the man released the ropes and began to push away from the pier. Ashley was hard-pressed not to laugh at the sight, but it was a very serious matter, and Chum had no idea what was about to occur. Ashley wished he could warn him.

The boat had not made it far at all when the sound of horse-drawn wagons approached. There was still no sign of a crew—or of Singleton. He listened as the wagons pulled to a stop and soft-stepped boots approached the yacht. Devil did not have to look very hard to realize no one was there.

He cursed under his breath, but Ashley heard it. He wished he

THE GIFT OF PATIENCE

could reveal himself and tell Devil to leave, that Singleton was likely setting him up to take the fall, but doing so would jeopardize everything.

One of the other men came forward. "What do we do? I don't trust we'll be paid if we just leave the goods on 'is boat."

"No. We have to take them elsewhere."

"What about the dock across the way where you been keepin' lookout? We could wait and see from there."

"Do you happen to have a barge in your back pocket?" Devil asked impatiently.

"I'll find one," Shorty said, then hurried away.

Now they were in a pickle. Ashley highly doubted that the others across the way would see them coming and move away in time. Why had nothing in this investigation gone according to plan? Hopefully, Renforth was having better fortune discovering where Singleton had gone and what his plans were. At the moment, Ashley was completely dependent on a gang leader to make quick decisions. He only hoped the hold they had over Devil was enough.

Somehow, Shorty managed to find a barge with a ferryman. Ashley did not how that had happened. Quickly and quietly they loaded the crates onto the barge.

"Take the wagons back to the warehouse, then return here and await my signal. I will wait across the way with the cargo."

"Aye, aye, sir," Shorty said mockingly, then disappeared.

That was quick thinking. Only then did Ashley dare open the door a very small bit to try to speak to Devil who, on the alert, turned at the sound of the door creaking.

"Take the barge across to the Taywards dock, but beware, there is another one there. You may tell them what is happening."

"Do you think the gent will come?"

"I cannot say. He took off towards London, and my commander followed."

Devil cursed, echoing Ashley's sentiments exactly.

"Beware. The excise men may be about."

"Aye, and my men will be back soon."

Where were Chum and Manners? They must be nearby. Had Chum yet realized this was his brother's yacht?

"I feel like I need to find Chum and tell him first." Ashley tried looking out the small window, but saw no hint of their hiding places.

"You have no idea where he is. It was one thing to whisper to Devil, but you do not know who's about. What if Singleton is lying in wait?"

"Where the devil is he, and where is Renforth?"

"At this point, there's nothing we can do but wait. Normally, you're not so impatient, Ash. Might it have something to do with the blue-eyed beauty waiting just across the water?"

Ashley gritted his teeth.

"She's your perfect match, you know. I hope you won't let her go over some misguided sense of honour all of us seem to have. We all feel unworthy having seen and done the things we have—besides being second sons as though it makes us unworthy somehow."

"You are dashed philosophical tonight, Fielding."

"Observant," he corrected. "This job leaves a great deal of time for overthinking everything. But watching the two of you together makes me somehow wish for even a chance with such a one."

"Such a one," Ashley muttered. Such little words for such a handful.

There was no more time for his friend to continue with the most uncomfortable conversation. Ashley knew he'd be a fool to let Patience go. If she'd even have him. She was hardly what could be called a traditional miss. Perhaps she was toying with him and had no intention of anything more than flirtation. It was a sobering, sickening thought.

Fielding put the spyglass back to his eye. "A small skiff in the distance."

"How many people?"

"Only one, I believe. Could be someone coming in for the night." Fielding handed him the glass, and he took a look. The person was not rowing hard, but being carried along with the current. When they came close, they began to turn towards the docks. There was little to decipher about the person, whomever they may be. A cloak with a hood shrouded them. They paddled closer and closer, and Ashley's hand went to the revolver at his waist.

"A crewman perhaps?"

"An odd way to travel, I would think, before a long voyage."

They slid right into where the barge had been before, put away the oars, and hooked a rope around one of the posts on the pier. As they climbed from the small skiff onto the pier and passed right before them, they could not see their face. The person climbed on board *Le Coquette*, then immediately went below deck.

Would Devil return to investigate? Ashley was almost certain, if he looked, he would see the barge approaching again.

With so much at stake, there was devilish little going on, even though the tension was thick in the air as though a storm was about to erupt. He wanted action and he wanted Patience tucked away safely in her bed.

As predicted, the barge with the cargo approached, but could not dock due to the skiff. The ferryman angled as close as he could, then Devil jumped to the pier and followed the other man down below deck.

Emerging again alone a few minutes later, Devil then somehow signalled to his gang who crawled out from nowhere like worms from the depths of the earth. They worked efficiently and put the crates down into the hull within minutes. It was frightful how quickly they offloaded the stolen goods then escaped into the night. No wonder the gang was sought-after.

Just as Devil himself emerged, Chum walked up. "This is my brother's ship," he said in disbelief to Devil. "Is he down on board?"

It was plain to see Devil did not wish to answer. He angled his head towards the boat without speaking.

"Oh, no," Ashley whispered. "Why would he do this?"

The timing could not have been worse. The excise men arrived at the same time and surrounded the ship.

"Are you the owner of the ship?" a uniformed officer in a tricorn hat demanded.

"It belongs to my family," Chum answered. "But there must be some mistake."

"I've orders to search the ship." He placed the warrant against Chum's chest and then proceeded to board the ship as the furrow between Chum's brow grew deep as realization crossed his face. He looked up towards where he knew his colleagues must be, then climbed aboard the ship himself.

"This is not going to end well," Fielding predicted.

"Shall we try to help?"

"That's not in our script. We lead the authorities to do the messy part."

"Neither is Chum jumping into the middle of apprehending the culprit," Ashley argued.

A string of curses assailed Ashley's ears. Fielding very much liked to operate by the rules, but this was a grey area. It involved one of their own.

"You may stay here and see if you're needed." Ashley was not waiting to find out. He slipped from the shed, and could already hear shouting and the sounds of a probable scuffle taking place. He hurried to the gangway and feared he was too late. Singleton was holding a knife to his brother's throat while two excise officers pointed guns at both of them.

"Get off my ship or I will hurt him," Singleton threatened.

"My lord, we have the right to search your ship."

"Take it up with my father. If you return with him and have his consent, then I will stand down."

You will be across the Channel by then, Ashley predicted to himself.

"Do as he says," Chum ordered.

Ashley crouched down behind a wooden box, trying to decide if he could manage to get behind Singleton. There was no doubt he was guilty, and when a guilty person's back was against the wall, figuratively speaking, they were unpredictable and could do anything—including sacrificing their brother. It was no secret there was no love lost between the two, but Chum didn't deserve the shame this would bring to his family.

THE GIFT OF PATIENCE

Singleton had to realize there was no way out for him. Even if he managed to thwart the search for now, there were several people who had seen the cargo being loaded onto his ship. They could not take the chance that he would escape. Ashley crawled to the next barrier he could hide behind on the ship. He'd never been nautical and barely knew one end of a ship from the other, but he also knew his men would protect him from where they were.

Singleton and Chum continued to argue with the excise man. Renforth had not shown himself for some reason. Had Singleton managed to evade him? It had not been long enough for him to have fully gone to Mayfair and back.

The excise man's gaze flickered towards Ashley creeping near, but the gleam in the man's eyes said he saw his opportunity for glory and taking down an entitled lord, and he was not going to let it go. "All of us saw cargo being loaded onto the ship. It's our right under the authority of the Crown to search anything that comes into port in this country." He took a step forward. "Now, let him go and move out of the way so I may perform my duty!"

"You don't want to do this, Brother!"

"You led them straight to me, you fool! Do you think this won't affect you?"

"I did nothing wrong except be born into the wrong family," Chum said with disgust.

"Not all of us can be models of propriety, Brother."

"Move or I will use force!" The officer was growing impatient, but it was clear Singleton had no intention of yielding.

Chum had to know one of his brethren would be there to protect him, because he shoved Singleton's arm forward while diving for the deck. Singleton threw his knife at the officer, then went for something in his coat pocket to head off the other officer. Ashley was already aiming his revolver, waiting for a clear shot, but Singleton managed to put himself behind Devil, who had stayed back through all of this. Did none of his men have a clear shot?

Singleton turned and took aim at him. Before he could fire, a knife flew into Singleton's back, his eyes wide with shock as he slumped to the ground.

Ashley closed in. He dared not remove his aim from the man as long as he lived. But when he reached him, there was no life left in the gaze. Chum sat against the wall, the blank stare of battle fatigue on his features. It would be some time before he regained his wits, and that might be for the best right then.

The others started to come out from their hiding positions, but none of them would have thrown a knife like that. He looked around and spotted the barge next to the yacht and groaned. Would that woman ever learn not to meddle?

~

"She insisted we move closer to help. How was I to know she would climb onto the next ship and throw a knife?" Rotham protested.

"Not only that, but with more bloody precision than any of our snipers!" Renforth exclaimed half-impressed, half-furious.

No one elaborated since Chum was still nearby and could possibly hear, though by the look on his face, he was somewhere else altogether.

"Manners, you and I will take Chum back to London and inform Lord Ormond. Fielding, you and Baines deal with the bodies and the excise men, and Stuart, if you and the others can take care of the matter of the gang. Have them unload the yacht and return the cargo to the East India docks, then we will see about negotiating their punishment."

Patience didn't care what they said as she sat nearby on the barge wrapped in the canvas tarp. The horror of what she'd done still setting in, both angry and terrified at the same time. The scene kept playing out over and over in her mind.

It had had to be done—it was him or Ashley. There had been no choice. She had waited and waited for someone else to take the shot, but the wily snake had shielded himself very well. When there had been an opening, she'd had to take it.

It was some time before anyone thought to wonder where she was. The other barge had been commandeered to take the bodies back to London, then there was a time where all of the men unloaded cargo and put it back on the wagons.

"Patience."

She did not wish to talk, for then she might cry and that would be unbearable.

"Patience, talk to me."

She shook her head a little. She just wanted to leave and be alone with her misery.

Ashley's fingers slid beneath her chin forcing her face to his. "You will be the death of me, Patience Whitford."

"I believe, in fact, it was quite the opposite."

He smiled with devastating effect. "There's my girl."

"I want to go home."

"I know." He took her into his arms with a gentle kiss to her head. Somehow, her subconscious allowed all self-control to let loose along with bodily control. Her teeth started to chatter and she cursed. Warm arms came around her body as it began to shake and she couldn't stop the cascade that fell from her eyes, hating the weakness and seeming dependence on another.

Ashley simply held her until the well had run dry. "The first time is the hardest. Not that killing a person ever becomes easy."

"What will happen to me?"

He sighed, then seemed to settle in for a lengthy talk.

"You mean will you be punished?"

A nod of acknowledgement was all she could muster.

"I suppose it's time to explain things to you."

Patience remained quiet, lest he change his mind.

"You may have noticed that my troop does not exactly perform normal duties."

She nodded.

"The duties we performed during the war did not precisely fit in with that of the Household Guards. When delicate matters arose, especially with Renforth's connections, we were asked to look into some sensitive matters, then one thing led to another. We have been doing it ever since. Our specialty is making situations disappear."

"Such as this one. Who do you officially work for?"

"That is a fine question and one I'm not sure I can or could answer."

She squeezed his hand and let him continue.

"This matter will go away with minimum fuss. When arms were stolen from the government, it quickly became apparent that information had been leaked from high channels."

"So Cholmely's brother will not be publicly branded a traitor?"

"Only if there's no other way to prevent it. It would be an embarrassment for our government as well as Lord Ormond and Chum. There is still the matter of discovering where Singleton obtained the information, but I have little doubt it will prove that Layton and Beckett were involved. They were likely desperate to find a way to pay Rupert's scheme, as it were."

"And what of Rupert's death?"

"It will be death by misadventure attributed to the attack by highwaymen."

"And my part will be swept under the rug."

"It will not be mentioned. While your actions were most admirable and heroic, Singleton's death will also be attributed to unfortunate events in no way linked to the stolen arms."

"That is harder for me to understand."

"Since he's already dead, the innocent involved would suffer more. Think of Chum. His family's title would most likely be stripped and they would lose all of their lands and estates."

"Oh, I see." A wave of emotion hit her again and she held back tears. "I thought I would lose you," she said softly. "I could bear almost anything but that."

"It will take a lot more than that to get rid of me, Patience. If you think you can put up with me, that is."

Was he saying what she thought he was? She looked up into his eyes, the deep blue watching her, vulnerable.

Before she could assimilate an answer, he pulled back the tarp, and directed the ferryman to take them back across the river. Slowly. Then he pulled the tarp back over them and adjusted her comfortably back into his arms. She wished they could stay like that forever, ridiculous though it may seem.

Instead of words, he showed her with a tender, yet passionate kiss that sent little arrows of sweetness deep into her heart and took hold. In his arms, his touch and lingering kiss almost drove her troubles from her mind.

Breathless with passion, it was hard to make sense of her reality while wrapped in Ashley's arms, hidden from the world beneath the canvas tarp, riding across the river.

"I never thought to marry, Patience. But I can't seem to stop thinking about you when you're not with me. It seems you are essential to my happiness."

"Even though I drive you crazy?"

"Especially because of that. I do not think any other sort of female would do for me. Ours will not be a traditional marriage, but you seem to understand and perhaps relish that fact."

A faint smile made its way to her lips.

"You are a gift, Patience."

"I will remind you of that often when I vex you," she teased, though it was she who felt as though she was the one who'd received the most precious gift. With him, every day would be a new adventure, and everything else would be all right.

EPILOGUE

$\mathcal{A}$s Patience was no traditional miss, neither would her wedding be. As a matter of fact, she'd been so taken with their encounter and proposal on the barge that they decided to marry on a yacht.

There would be no grand wedding at St. George's Hanover Square for her. A small private ceremony was just the thing. Too bad her family did not agree. Were it not for the size restrictions of the yacht, Patience was quite certain there would have been hundreds of people, regardless of her wishes.

Carew's yacht was still available, and there were still nigh thirty people, not including the crew.

There were five sisters, after all, plus the dowagers, the aunts, the new husbands, babies, and all of their closest friends in the troop... and yes, even Xander, Freddy and her kittens had to be brought along. It was smaller than a St. George's affair, but certainly not calm and quiet on board. Thankfully, the weather was mild for a late fall day. If the cold had set in, it would have not been a pleasant affair.

Thankfully, it was a short sail for the day from the Taywards dock out into the North Sea then back.

Somehow, the Dowager had persuaded her cousin, the archbishop, to perform the ceremony. Whilst she appreciated the sentiment and originality of such a wedding, she could not abide a common law ship's captain performing her grandson's wedding ceremony.

Miraculously, their vows were said amidst Xander lunging at the seagulls and the rocking ship. Due to the archbishop's seasickness, it was blessedly short.

The dowager viscountesses still somehow arranged a full wedding breakfast fit for a queen.

"I think it is time we began with a toast," Westwood began as the footmen handed out champagne. "To my baby brother, I am happy to see you've been well and truly caught. Welcome to the bonds of marriage, where a shackle never felt so good."

"Hear, hear!" everyone shouted to laughter.

Renforth stood to follow with his own toast. "I suppose if anyone was to break apart our little troop, you could not have found a better lady."

"Let us not look at it as breaking apart, but adding to," Patience suggested to more laughter and more echoes of, "hear, hear."

As everyone settled to a place to eat their food and converse, Patience and Ashley stood at the bow of the ship together in the first moments of privacy they'd had together in days. Ashley stood behind her and put his arms around her with his chin settling on her shoulder. The wind blew against their faces with the occasional spray of water as the ship cut through the sea.

"You are certain Devil and Billy will be alright?"

"I saw them on to the ship myself with enough funds for them to start over in Virginia."

She sighed happily.

"Are you pleased with your wedding?" he asked.

"It was perfect. The only negative—if one could even call it that—is there will be no escaping early."

Ashley chuckled in her ear, the deep sound reverberating through her.

"I will have you to myself soon."

"Not soon enough."

"Are you certain you do not wish to take a wedding trip?"

"There will be time enough later for that. Perhaps after Christmas, when the weather turns in London, we can go somewhere warm."

They were to take Westwood's bachelor house in Berkeley Square, London, as he no longer had need of it, and Patience and Ashley hardly wanted to live in his rooms where the rest of the troop did.

"As you wish."

"I like the sound of that," she teased.

"Baggage," he muttered as he turned her head to punish her impertinence with a passionate kiss.

By the time the ship docked at Taywards, it was afternoon and Patience was eager to be off to London. There were carriages, carts, and horses waiting to help everyone back to the house. The servants quickly cleared away all traces of the wedding breakfast as Carew had decided to return to Ireland and would sail with that evening's tide.

Montford and the Cunninghams were also making their way to London, and Patience assumed her sisters would leave when Hope and Rotham did. Frankly, all of her attention was on her husband, on the wedding, and packing her belongings. Therefore, three hours later, when it was time to pull away and no one had seen Grace, they began to grow concerned.

"When was the last time anyone saw her?" Westwood asked the group as they stood around, ready to load into carriages.

"She was not feeling well during the breakfast this morning, so I sent her to a cabin to lie down," Faith explained.

"She must've fallen asleep," Patience said with dawning realization.

All of the sisters exchanged panicked glances. Grace could sleep through the second coming.

"Oh, no!" Faith's hand flew to her mouth. "We must return to the docks to see if we can catch them before they sail."

"Ashley and I will go. The rest of you can go on to London if you wish before dark," Westwood said.

Patience could sense the hesitance, but Rotham took charge. "Even if she is on that ship, there is little for any of us to do. Carew will bring her back."

THE GIFT OF PATIENCE

Patience did not wait to see what the others decided. She was not about to be left behind. She ran to the stables and helped saddle another horse before they all took off towards the docks.

As they dismounted from their mounts, tied them to a post and ran out on the pier, they all stopped, their breaths heaving. There was no ship there.

"We're too late," Patience stated the obvious as Westwood uttered a curse.

"Do we follow after them?" Ashley asked.

"No," Patience answered. "What's done is done."

"Carew will bring her back unharmed," Westwood said with conviction.

But none of them asked the question that was heavy on all of their minds. What would happen to her reputation? There was no secret that Grace was enamoured with the Irish earl, but he'd shown her no more attention than mere solicitousness. Not the type of connection anyone would want for their sister. Especially not now that three of them had found true love.

They stood there staring at the water, as if they could beckon Carew's yacht back by sheer willpower.

"The tide is strong, and who knows how long it will be till he even realizes she is a stowaway?"

"She did not do it on purpose." Of that, Patience was certain. Grace was not bold enough nor confident enough in her feminine wiles to ever do such a thing.

"I trust him implicitly," Westwood said with a hand on her shoulder.

Patience nodded. It was of little comfort to know Grace's fate was out of their hands.

AFTERWORD

Author's note: British spellings and grammar have been used in an effort to reflect what would have been done in the time period in which the novels are set. While I realize all words may not be exact, I hope you can appreciate the differences and effort made to be historically accurate while attempting to retain readability for the modern audience.

Thank you for reading *The Gift of Patience*. I hope you enjoyed it. If you did, please help other readers find this book:

1. This ebook is lendable, so send it to a friend who you think might like it so she or he can discover me, too.

2. Help other people find this book by writing a review.

3. Sign up for my new releases at www.Elizabethjohnsauthor.com, so you can find out about the next book as soon as it's available.

4. Come like my Facebook page www.facebook.com/Eliza bethjohnsauthor or follow on Instagram @Ejohnsauthor or feel free to write me at elizabethjohnsauthor@gmail.com

ALSO BY ELIZABETH JOHNS

ACKNOWLEDGMENTS

There are many, many people who have contributed to making my books possible.

My family, who deals with the idiosyncrasies of a writer's life that do not fit into a 9 to 5 work day.

Dad, who reads every single version before and after anyone else—that alone qualifies him for sainthood.

Anj, who takes my visions and interpret them, making them into works of art people open in the first place.

To those friends who care about my stories enough to help me shape them before everyone else sees them.

Scott who helps me say what I mean to!

And to the readers who make all of this possible.

I am forever grateful to you all.

Made in the USA
Coppell, TX
01 September 2024

36587120R00142